To John,

I enjoyed this. And I'm looking forward to some good reading. Let's do this again.

11/14/98

Brown Sky

BROWN SKY

A Novel
by
David Covin

PATH PRESS, INC.
Chicago

Library of Congress Cataloging in Publication Data

Covin, David, 1940–
  Brown sky.

  1. World War, 1939–1945—Fiction.   I. Title.
PS3553.0875B7   1987   813'.54   87–2545
ISBN 0–910671–11–7

Published by Path Press, Inc., 53 West Jackson Blvd., Suite
1040, Chicago, Illinois 60604

Distributed by Chicago Review Press, 814 North Franklin
Street, Chicago, Illinois 60610

Manufactured in the United States of America

To Mom, in Memory of Dad and Edward

"All journeys have secret destinations of which the traveler is unaware."

Martin Buber

Prelude

1

Stephen Wenders was frightened. He tried to look out the bus window as a distraction, but the light was wrong and all he got was a glimpse of himself in the glass. Complexion so dark it hardly showed up, eyes unnaturally large and white. That's because I'm scared, he thought. Long nose.

The bus emerged from the shade and he could see clearly the elegant, stately houses, the spacious lawns, and behind them Lake Michigan rippling in sunlight.

Ordinarily, the thought of where he was going juxtaposed to the sight of such obscene wealth would have amused him. Ordinarily. But he was too preoccupied, too uneasy, too fearful to be his usual self. He had scarcely any sense of irony or humor at all. The spaces those feelings normally occupied were filled with quaking misgivings.

Still facing the window he closed his eyes, his elbow propped on the bottom of the window ledge, his chin between his thumb and forefinger.

Too late, now, he thought. Too late.

The shuddering of the bus grinding to a final halt and the squealing and expelled air sounds of its brakes re-opened his eyes. He turned away from the window. Right next to him and all around him men were getting to their feet. He wanted to stay in his seat a little longer. He didn't want to get up. He didn't want to get off the bus. Somehow he knew that outside the bus door . . . was another world, one where he did not belong. He felt that. He knew that. Even though the only other thing he knew about the place was its name.

Fort Sheridan.

Taking his suitcase and his laundry-bag down the bus steps was awkward. When Stephen stepped heavily off the last step to the ground, he did not pay much attention to his surroundings, he just kept his eyes fastened onto the back of the man ahead of him. He followed him.

A hand chopped into his shoulder.

It spun him around.

Anger, unchecked, sprang up in Stephen.

He looked up into a ruddy face with a mouth that seemed too full of teeth, a pair of eyes that seemed too small and squinting, a forehead that seemed too deeply lined, the top part of which was covered by a campaign hat poorly designed for such a head.

"Boy! Where you think you goin'?"

For an instant Stephen could not answer. He could not focus his rage. His features contorted with it and his mouth began to work, to get the words out.

A broad, heavy palm smacked across his mouth knocking him back to the bus and slamming his head against it.

At first Stephen felt no physical injury at all. He felt mental violation.

His eyes sparked wide open, a bewildered fury jerking at his features and snatching his large motor muscles into involuntary spasms.

"Don't say a damn thing unless I tells you to talk, boy! You in the army now!"

Stephen felt the dullness in the back of his head. He felt as if large, wooden blocks collided with each other inside his skull. He tasted blood in his mouth.

The rough hand shoved him in the opposite direction from that taken by the man he had followed off the bus.

"Over there," said the voice, booming out of thin lips under the narrowed eyes and a big, meaty nose.

The push from the soldier, coupled with the weight of Stephen's suitcase and laundry bag, sent him staggering off, pointed the way the army man had intended.

Stephen, stunned and suddenly alert to the impotence of his fury, felt his knees going loose. He tottered in the direction he had been pushed to stand beside another man who, like himself, was in civilian clothes, his luggage lying in a pile at his feet. The man looked uncomfortable and stared straight ahead. Stephen put down his own baggage. He struggled with himself. He had never felt such sudden, overwhelming hatred. He tried not to look up. He did not know what he would do if his eyes lit on that soldier again. Each hand grabbed the opposite sleeve of his jacket and held onto it tightly, twisting and twisting and twisting.

Jesus. What the hell have I got myself into. Jesus.

Gradually it dawned on him as he recovered from shock and as men kept getting off the bus that the Negroes were all being sent to stand with him and that the whites were all going off somewhere else. His ears started to burn. He felt a constriction deep within his stomach.

We are not in Florida, he thought. We are not in Georgia. This is Illinois. This is my home state. We're only forty minutes away from my house. What the hell is going on here? What kind of damn-fool Jim Crow shit is this?

The bus pulled away. No one remained in the asphalt area except the line of Negro men. Some looked at the ground. Some stared off into space. Some glanced miserably at their fellows.

"They gon' tell us they made a mistake and send us back home," said one man.

Many of the others chuckled.

3

They stood a long time.

Stephen felt more humiliated than he had ever felt in his life. He felt . . . conspicuous. Here we stand, he thought. Here we stand. The niggers. The dumb niggers. He wanted to get his hands around someone's throat. But there was no fitting victim. He wanted to cry standing with the other Negroes, a forlorn line of men, alone on a vast stretch of pavement.

At last a man appeared striding smartly towards them. He was a sergeant, a Negro sergeant.

Stephen's first reaction was relief. Relief to see someone who looked like him in a uniform. Relief that this Black man was clearly in a position of authority. It was genuinely elating to know that he would not have to spend every instant under the heel of a prejudiced, white bastard. Oh, God, a friendly face, he thought. A friendly face.

It was not that the sergeant's face looked friendly. It did not. It looked stern. It looked hard. Nor did he have a friendly walk. Proud. Purposeful. Commanding. He carried a swagger stick. Nothing in his expression or carriage suggested friendliness.

Only his color. That is what Stephen saw. That is what he riveted on. A friendly face.

His name was Wades, Sergeant Ephraim Wades. He was a career army man. He had been a soldier in the old all-Negro 92nd division.

Sergeant Wades faced the line of colored men. He could sense their welcoming him, their thankfulness that he had appeared. He felt the tension lift from them on his approach.

He knew that this moment was very tricky. It was important that he keep their loyalty to him, engendered by their common race. At the same time they had to recognize his absolute authority over them.

He stood at attention, his swagger stick protruding

4

from under his arm. He stared up and down the line of men . . . for a long time.

They were nervous. They didn't know what to do. Some of them looked around. Some of them smiled at him, trying to get his attention, trying to get him to smile back.

He knew that his standing at attention, not a ripple of movement in his presence, would command their respect. None of them could do it, and they would feel an odd kind of pride, a racial identity in his ability to do so. In this moment they would imprint on him without ever realizing it.

His mouth was fixed in a downward curve at each end. His bottom lip was thrust forward. He stood flagpole straight. Motionless. His eyes roved up and down the line.

One man stuck out his right foot and drew it back.

"Don't move!"

They all jumped.

Every man concentrated completely on the tall, black sergeant.

"My name is Sergeant Wades. To you—'Sergeant Wades, Sir!' Is that clear, boy!"

He pointed his swagger stick at the man who had shuffled his foot.

The young man mumbled an unintelligible reply.

"What!"

The swagger stick struck the man's stomach so swiftly that its stroke through the air, its impact, and its return were almost invisible. Its force was evident; the youngster doubled over.

The "whack" sound the blow made stuck in every man's consciousness.

Stephen winced in shock and disbelief.

"I said—and this is the last time I ever will repeat myself," said Sergeant Wades, "to you—my name is, 'Sergeant Wades, Sir!'

"Is that clear, boy!"

He stared at the offender.

The man's knees shook visibly. Tears stood in his eyes. He gathered himself and answered in a tremulous but loud voice: "Yes, Sergeant Wades, Sir!"

Sergeant Wades nodded.

Stephen was so glad he hadn't shuffled or moved a foot he didn't know what to do. He looked straight ahead and trembled. He was so scared he wanted to pee his pants. He wondered if he were the only one in a panic, but he was too terrified to look at the men next to him. He concentrated on holding in his urine.

"You boys is now in the army," the sergeant said. "You ain't soldiers, you ain't nothin' but recruits. But you in the army. My job is t'make yo' raggedy asses inta soldiers. Colored soldiers.

"And the first thing any colored boy got t'learn before he can be a army man is that there's two armies—a colored army, and a white army. And it ain't no doubt about which one you is in!

"Each one o' them armies has got its own set of rules. You got t'learn yo' rules—by memory—and obey them. And we startin' right now, with base regulations."

He gave them a list of every place which was off-limits. The whole base was off-limits except for their barracks and their drill areas. Negro troops were not to mingle with white soldiers. They were not to set foot in areas used by white soldiers.

That night, on his cot—exhausted—but too wired to sleep, Stephen lay with his eyes open, staring unseeing into the dark.

Somehow the world had gone crazy with him in it. His mother had been right. He should have found a way to stay out of this lunacy. The world outside the army was bad enough, but at least he knew how to get by in it. This! This! He shook his head.

He knew what it reminded him of. *Through the Looking Glass.* Alice in Wonderland. Everything was crazy. Upside down. The Mad Hatter. The Red Queen. The Cheshire Cat. Off with their heads! Oh, god. Oh, god.

He woke before reveille but lay motionless with his eyes closed. He was afraid to open them. He knew that everywhere around him, waiting for him to awake, waiting for him as a witness and a participant, waiting for him to claim as its own, hovered rampant insanity.

Sergeant Wades drove the men relentlessly. He drove them incomprehensibly. He drove them to break them. He drove them so that individually they could no longer make sense out of their world, were no longer masters of themselves, had to rely totally on him to survive each day. His purpose was to conform them to his discipline. When he said, "right face," he did not want the flicker of a question to cross anyone's mind, he did not want the slightest delay in the translation of the command to a response. When he said, "right face," he wanted the reaction to be automatic and instant. That meant there was only one mind in the little group, only one will. His.

He also wanted to mold them into a group, counting on each other, taking care of each other, supporting each other. He knew that mutual suffering would drive them together, forge them into a bond like heat from a fire. He was the common target for their hatred. He was strong enough to accept that role. They did not have to like him to submit to his authority.

He was from Mississippi. He was not used to a lot of Northern Negroes. But he figured that was not his problem. It was theirs.

Stephen changed along with the rest. From a nightmarish sense of reality he stumbled into a schizophrenia

7

of hating and being totally dependent on Sergeant Wades. Doing what he told them became a natural response, a herd response, the only path to certainty, the sole security in their world.

The more Stephen acted like an automaton, the more secure he felt, the better he felt. He was becoming, he realized in a fleeting moment of insight, just what Sergeant Wades wanted him to, a soldier.

Discipline was swift and brutal, but when the men started fitting his mold, Sergeant Wades became the very picture of benevolence and joviality. He still pushed them. He knew as they could not that one day their lives and the lives of others might depend on how automatically they reacted to a seemingly meaningless command.

Being a soldier had given Sergeant Wades his place in the world. In the First War he had been overseas. He had seen France. Decorated with the Legion d'Honneur and the Crois de Guerre, he had learned in places like Bois d'Hauze, Minancourt, and Maison-en-Champagne that his measure of being a man and that of his fellow colored troops was no less than that of any man in the world—from France, or Germany, or England, or the white U.S.A. After his return he had been stationed all over the country. He was a traveled man, a worldly man, a knowledgeable man. And he owed it all to the army. He didn't have to walk behind a mule or owe his life, put his family in bondage, to some cracker landlord. He was a soldier. And if he could instill that sense of pride in self in some of these boys, they, too, might be able to live a better life. If not, it was better that he broke them right here and now. They wouldn't be no good to nobody nohow.

Stephen developed a reluctant respect for Sergeant Wades. Under his tutelage Stephen realized what it was to be in the army. He also realized—contrary to all Sergeant Wades' aspirations for his men—that he did not like the army. There was first of all the mortifying certainty that the army was Jim-Crow from top to bottom. Stephen had seen Jim-Crow life as an adult for the first time during the previous summer. Those features of Southern life which he had despised were now imposed on him with the full authority of the military hierarchy. And he was being trained and prepared to surrender his life in order to preserve them, not only to preserve them, but to do so while totally immersed in them and subject to them.

At first he and his fellow recruits had neither time nor energy to express their feelings except as muttered curses and cynical rejoinders uttered *sotto voce*. But Stephen could see in his companions' faces and in their bearings what they felt. They felt what he did. They hated the army and hated even more the irremedial condition that they must be part of it.

They learned to make their beds and stow their gear and shine their shoes and fall in at attention and march and double-time only because Sergeant Wades was a master disciplinarian and because he literally held the power of life and death over them.

Each day stretched interminably. Sleep slipped stealthily through the nights leaving no sign of its passage.

Stephen had been prepared physically by an autumn in the country. He was not crushed by the rigors of basic training. He was one of the few who had the extra energy to help others get their gear ready for inspection. He liked doing that. It gave him some satisfaction in a life he saw as increasingly pointless.

Stephen had not internalized the extent to which the army had regularized and institutionalized lunacy. Intellectually, he had recognized its dyed-in-the-wool segregationist character, but what that abstract recognition meant for his daily life continually surprised him.

He had decided since he was in the army and not getting out soon, he might as well make the best deal out of a bad thing. He had come to admire the work of the signal corps company at Fort Sheridan and signed up for it. As training went on and on and he received no orders posting him to the signal corps company, he approached Sergeant Wades one day after a hard forced march.

"Sir, recruit Wenders, requesting permission to speak, Sir!"

The sergeant glanced up at Stephen.

"Go ahead, Wenders. What's on your mind?"

"Sir, I was wondering when we get posted to our regular units, Sir."

A puzzled, troubled look came to the sergeant's face.

It hit Stephen at that instant that he was never going to be posted to the signal corps. The signal corps company on the base was white. As was the engineers battalion. As were all the units except one. Only the quartermaster company (trucks) was colored. Stephen was going to be a truck driver because it was the only colored company in the camp.

Fred Harvey bunked on one side of Stephen and Wilderness Jones bunked on the other. One night after taps the three of them conversed in hushed tones.

"How you figure," said Fred, "right here almost as far North in Illinois as you can get, we got an officer corps full of Georgia crackers?"

"Don't you know," said Wilderness, "they understands us."

"What?"

"Yeah. That's what the army believe. You see, it ain't too many Negroes up north. And most of 'em what is lives in big cities like Chicago and Detroit. And they lives with each other. So the fays up north don't get that much of a chance to be around us. I mean, for real, how many fays does you know on a buddy-buddy basis? But in the South—niggas is everywhere. You cain't get away from 'em. So the rednecks and crackers is around niggas all the time. They knows niggas. They understands us. So it stand to reason they should be the ones to be our officers."

"Even if that faulty logic had some semblance of truth," said Stephen, "the Negroes our officers used to live with are Southern Negroes, and we're from Chicago. What possible experience have they had in dealing with men like us?"

"The first thing you got to understand," said Wilderness, "which you don't—is that a nigga is a nigga. Period. That's number one.

"Number two, Steve, which you still ain't learned after all these weeks and I'm surprised at you cause you s'posed t'be a college boy, is that the army got its own rules of logic. Once them rules is set, they's set in concrete. It do not matter if them rules say the sky is brown. Once they is set, the sky is brown. It don't matter worth a damn what yo eyes be tellin' you. Army rules."

"So the army rule is that southern fays understand Negroes? Period?" asked Fred.

"That's it," said Wilderness.

The three of them were silent for awhile.

Stephen felt sleep beginning to creep over him. He heard Wilderness' voice but he lost the meaning. He felt himself start to drift.

After the fifth week of basic, Stephen's company commander called him in.

"Have a seat, Wenders."

"Yessir."

Stephen sat erect, nervous. What the hell is this about? he wondered.

Captain Miller studied him.

"I've been looking over your AGCT scores," said the captain.

"Sir?"

"Classification scores—the tests you took when you came in."

"Yessir."

"You damn near scored off the test, Wenders." He looked probingly at Stephen for a long time.

"You didn't cheat, did you?"

"No sir."

"Mmhmm. I see by your records you're a college boy. Three years. Why weren't you in school last semester?"

"Uh . . . well, uh personal reasons, sir."

"Huh. I see. What'd you do—knock up one o' them l'il ol' gals? Nevuh mind. I tell you what, in South Carolina where I'm from, I've had my share. Frisky, ain't they? I don't blame you boys for havin' your fun.

"Well—back to these damn AGCTs. I've got to recommend you for OCS when you finish basic training. Anybody in Grades I and II on the test is eligible for OCS. With colored we often has to scrape down into III t'get officers. As a rule you people don't score too high on these tests. But, Wenders, you damn near done gone through the top of grade I. So I got t'recommend you. We need colored officers, and we got t'get most of 'em from you northern boys, cause I'm tellin' you the truth, you can have a whole camp full of colored boys in Georgia, or Alabama, or Mississippi, and not one of 'em higher than the bottom of Grade IV. Can't get no officers out o' that. Can't hardly get no soldiers out of that. So most of our colored officers is gonna have to come from northern recruits like yourself. Though, to tell you the truth, I don't see why we need no colored officers at all. Men don't like to follow 'em. They prefer white. We could make those of

12

you with high scores and the like NCOs. That would be the best plan. All white officer corps. Colored NCOs in colored units. That's the best leadership strategy. But with colored troops you can't go by what's best for the army. You can't run 'em like you would any other troops. You got t'worry about fool organizations like the NAACP and nuts like A. Philip Randolph and all other kinds of clowns who don't know a damn thing about running an army.

"I'm recommending you, Wenders. We should get all the colored officers we need for a whole quartermaster battalion out of this company. We've got some high-scoring Negroes here.

"I just want you to know one thing."

"Sir."

"Putting bars on your shoulders doesn't make you a white man."

When Stephen left Captain Miller's office he had to be alone. There was a place a few of them had discovered, he and Wilderness among them. A stack of empty crates had been heaped up next to the tall, chain-link fence which ran along the base-boundary. Whoever had unloaded them had been lazy and there was a space between the crates and the fence where it was possible to be alone. It was necessary to crawl through a small opening to get there, but once inside a person could be alone, private.

After Stephen had squirmed into the hiding place he stood up. He leaned against the fence. He hooked his fingers through the links and pressed his face into the cool wires.

He tried to think of how he had arrived in such a goddamned place, how the hell he could have arrived at such a place as this nightmarish army.

Nine months ago he had been a junior at Roosevelt College. Just nine months ago. A College kid. An innocent.

How the hell did I get here?

He remembered. He believed he remembered the very first steps he had taken which had led him to Fort Sheridan.

2

Alone at the cafeteria table he raised his eyes from the newspaper. He scarcely dared believe what he had seen.

He was afraid to read the ad again. It was too perfect. But he did.

Cook wanted. Summer cabin. Apply in person. Mrs. Whitterson. 79 Gladding Lane. Winnetka. For appointment call: Evergreen 3226.

On a grey wooden house with white trim, a huge front porch running across the width of the house, a dozen broad steps leading to the porch, and the house festooned with turrets, steeples, and gables, the number 79 gleamed in brass beside the heavy door.

Soon after the doorbell chimes had rung a uniformed maid opened the door. The briefest alarm flashed across her forehead and showed in her eyes before she set her face. Stephen saw it, read it.

Uh-oh, he thought.

She stood staring at him.

"Hello," he said at last.

"Yes." Her face did not move.

"Is this the Whitterson residence?"

"What do you want?" She had some kind of accent. German or Scandanavian, Stephen thought.

"I'm sorry," said Stephen. He smiled.

She did not.

"My name is Stephen Wenders. I have an appointment with Mrs. Whitterson this morning."

Her eyes, which had been pointed at his face but not seeing it, registered on him.

"Just a moment," she said. She closed the door.

Stephen stared at the heavy brass knocker inches away from his face. With all the world open behind him, he felt stifled, penned in, pressed against the door. He felt unable to shift his eyes from the indented, heavily-polished surfaces of the brass fixture. Beads of sweat collected along his hairline. A few began to roll down his forehead.

Oh won't I make a grand appearance now, he thought. He could feel himself shining.

The maid opened the door without looking at him. "Come in."

Once Stephen had stepped in, she closed the door and started off. "Follow me," she said with her back to him. She walked rapidly.

Stephen followed her down the hall until she stopped in front of a pair of large, sliding doors. She slid one of the doors open.

"Mrs. Whitterson will see you," she said.

Stephen stepped through the door and heard it close behind him.

At first he was conscious only of himself. Perspiration popping out all over his face. Shining. His clothes too small on him, the buttons on his suit-coat pinching. Soggy armpits. Don't I look a sight.

The room was light, full of sun, with a soft grey carpet, stuffed chairs and sofas, and low, dark-grained wooden tables. A massive, brick fireplace filled the center of one wall. The source of light and sun was the outside wall, all rectangles of glass, framing Mrs. Whitterson, who stood in front of a set of French doors.

Her tanned features were delicate, set off by a mass of reddish brown hair. She appeared to be in her late forties though she could pass for much younger. She wore a simple, light blue summer dress. Tall, slim but not angular, she bore a slightly amused expression.

She bore the expression because she was amused. My God a nigger standing right here in my sitting room. What would Whitney have said if he had been alive to see it? He wouldn't have said anything. The sight alone would have killed him.

"Good morning, Stephen," she said. "I did not know—on the phone—that you were colored."

"Oh, I see." Stephen felt his ears start to burn. He had known. Ever since he had looked at the maid he had known. But to hear it, to hear it so plainly. His ears were on fire.

"I'm afraid," she said, smiling, "that was the cause of Greta's consternation. We don't have colored callers—not at the front door." She laughed. She was enjoying this. He seemed pleasant enough—rather young—if she could tell anything about his age.

"Mrs. Whitterson, I answered the ad because it was not exclusionary. Usually, if an employer will not accept colored applicants, the ad will be appropriately placed and worded, 'whites only', or 'colored need not apply.' When the ad is in just the help wanted column, as yours was, and when there is no specification of race, then generally the employer doesn't care what race the applicants are. That's why I answered your ad. It was in the 'safe' category."

"How interesting," she said. "I'd never thought of that. Sounds all rather complicated to me.

"Well, Stephen, since you're here, and you sound like an intelligent fellow—rare enough in any race—can you cook?"

Stephen looked around the large, tasteful, comfortable room. He looked at the racing prints on the walls. He looked at the elegant lady against her glass-paned wall and he felt the heat in his head and thought about the wasted train-fare and the wasted time and the humiliation and she had never even thought of it and here

17

he stood colored and shining in the middle of her room where he was sure no Negro had ever stood and he had no chance at the job and now did not care and wanted to assert himself in some way and wanted to salvage a degree of self respect. Could he cook? What an absurd question.

"No," he said.

She burst out laughing. She took a few steps away from the French doors recovering herself. Merriment danced in her face. "But the ad says clear as day, in fact it starts with the word, 'Cook.' How could you—how could you apply for a job where you'd be cooking all summer and not even know how to cook?"

He felt better. Just for saying, "No", he felt better. He wanted to laugh.

"Well, Mrs. Whitterson, I didn't expect you to ask that question. Most people don't ask if a cook can cook. But if you had asked it and you had been expecting colored applicants as well as white, and I'd thought I'd had a chance at this job, I never would have told you I couldn't cook, but since it makes no difference anyway, it felt good to tell you the truth."

"But if you can't cook—supposing I had hired you—what would you have done? My dear boy, we would have arrived in Michigan and there would have been cooking to do. I don't go over there to starve."

"I don't know how to cook, but I do know how to read. There's something called a 'Cook Book.' I figured that as many blushing brides as there are who don't know how to boil water and end up with children who rave about Mama's cooking, that I could pick up that little book and have a grand summer. I mean the thing that appealed to me about the job in the first place were the words, 'summer cabin.' I would like to spend a summer in a cabin— making money. Not riding the 'L' to the loop, not surrounded by swarms of people—but in the country

18

somewhere. I figured it would be quiet, I could enjoy nature. There'd probably be a lake or a stream. And there'd be plenty of time to read and think. It wouldn't hurt me if I spent a little of my time reading the 'Cook Book.'"

She was surprised. She did not know Negroes could talk like that, or think like that. He seemed so . . . normal. But nice. And intelligent. She wondered about all the things she had heard her husband say, and the movies she had seen, and the articles. I like him, she thought. I like him very much.

She looked directly at him. "*Cook Book*, huh?" She laughed again. "How old are you?"

"Twenty."

"Well, at twenty years old, you've given me quite an education, and I'm fifty-three. I'll tell you what, if you'll give me your company for the summer, I'll teach you how to cook. In fact, now that I think of it, I'd rather have somebody I can teach. That way you'll cook things the way I like rather than some way you learned years before and I can't stand.

"What do you say to room and board and thirty dollars a week?"

Stephen blinked. He did not know anyone who made that much money.

"Mrs. Whitterson, you have just hired yourself a cook."

3

Quietly the oars dipped into the clear water. The boat slid over the calm surface and merged into the mists.

Stephen inhaled deeply. Cool air filled his nostrils. Mist droplets hung on his eyelids and freshened his face. He leaned back on the oars, loving the feeling of the water resisting his strength and then yielding, the boat gliding silently through the predawn shadows.

His heart fluttered as he shipped his oars and turned to his tackle. The boat began its drift past the spread of lily pads.

He noticed a commotion deep in the field of water foliage.

Something. Something big was thrusting its way between the plants' stems. Broad leaves and flowers submerged, water swirled.

What is it? Stephen fastened his eyes on the disrupted water. He could not tell. Large, circular leaves, torn from their stems, spun in circles.

Suddenly, the water erupted—and twisting, shaking, snapping, four and one-half to five feet of great northern pike burst into the air, showering water thirty feet in every direction. It landed on top of the lily pads with a great "thwack!", lay there for an instant, slid off into the water, and disappeared.

Stephen sat motionless while the boat drifted into the lily pads. It became entangled. Even then he sat—still—until the height of the sun told him he was soon due in the kitchen to fix breakfast.

Picking one oar from the lock, he used it to break the boat free from the plants. Once in open water he rowed hard, no longer trying to be quiet, but knowing that before he left Deep Cedar Lake there was one fish he was going to have to catch because no one would believe a word he said about it.

Stephen did not have to cook when Roger, the chauffeur, took Mrs. Whitterson to visit with friends around the lake. On the other hand he had to cook very large quantities when her friends dropped in to see her. Mrs. Whitterson had not entertained until after the first month. She had wanted to make sure of Stephen's cooking. After the first month, however, she was very pleased with his work. He fixed everything precisely as she liked because he knew no other way.

She thought of Stephen as her own creation and enjoyed him immensely. He not only learned very rapidly and very well, he was also not one dimensional. He had a wide range of interests which she attempted to pique. Of course, he went rather overboard on fishing, but all in all she believed that hiring him had been a stroke of genius.

Most of the time Mrs. Whitterson stayed home for meals, and most of the time there were just the three of them. She needed her little retreat. Her schedule was quite demanding during "the season" and she could not maintain the pace without an extended period of genuine recuperation.

Stephen was grateful for her consistent routine. It made the scheduling of his own time predictable and he had a great deal of it to himself since she required him to do only the meals and clean up, and to spend three evenings a week, after the dishes were done, reading with her.

It delighted her to have someone in the cabin who was literate. Roger was a solitary man who read only the sports pages of the newspaper and the comic strips. He was unobtrusive, but also uninspiring. Stephen, however,

21

was another matter. His presence excited Mrs. Whitterson.

They read in the study, each comfortably ensconced in an overstuffed chair.

"Stephen, you're not going to read to me what you told me you were going to read." She giggled.

"Oh, but I most certainly am."

"But why *The Hunchback of Notre Dame*—it's so, it's so . . . earthy."

"Yes. And that's precisely why I'm going to read it to you. You love that little earthy kind of thing—oh, how you relished the story of David and Bathsheba—"

"But that's—"

"And, besides, you have a certain repressed and libidinous fascination with the physically repulsive characteristics of Quasimodo."

"Stephen Wenders! How could you—"

"Because it's true. Because it's true. Now—quiet. Because I'm going to read, and you're going to listen. Just be careful to keep under control the tumultuous passions this narrative arouses in you.

"Ah, we turn to Esmeralda and Quasimodo . . ."

She loved the teasing. She loved it. It had developed gradually as they read to each other. It grew, without forcing, out of a sense of play which they shared. It had been so long since she had engaged in that kind of intellectual repartee, touched as it was by a hint of the sensual and the forbidden. Not since her days at Smith had anything remotely like it taken place in her life. Stephen read very well. He brought the story to life. She slumped in her chair and let her mind be carried away.

4

A thunderstorm kept Stephen in one morning after
he had cleared the breakfast dishes.

He strolled out on the porch to see the spectacle and
enjoy the breeze.

Mrs. Whitterson was there before him, her eyes alive
to the storm.

She leaned forward in her wicker chair. She turned
when she sensed Stephen's presence.

"Stephen, we're going to have a show."

"Yes, Ma'am."

She looked up at his profile. "Stephen, it's August
eighth. You've been here nearly two full months with
this old woman, and her chauffeur, and her poetry—are
you bored nearly to tears?"

He laughed. "No, Mrs. Whitterson. I love it."

"But you're young, and for a young man, this is a far
off and lonely place. Oh, it's alright for a week or two.
But I know. More than two weeks up here and the boys
used to get cabin fever. Two months. . . ."

"Everybody's not the same. Even if they do have age
in common. I like it here—very much."

"Well," she turned back to look at the sky, and the
lake, and the trees, "I've been enjoying this summer so
much, and I really don't have anything to rush home
for—the boys aren't going to be there. I've been thinking
that I'd really like to stay a month longer than I'd
planned."

Stephen sniffed the wind. He smelled the rain. He
drew the air deep into his lungs.

"What are you going to do for a cook," he asked.

She snatched a quick glance at him.

"I was hoping that maybe . . . you . . . would stay."

"Mrs. Whitterson, I understand that I'm colored and everything and therefore not to take education too seriously. However, I'm about to be a senior in college. Classes start the last week in September. If I were to stay here a month longer than planned, I couldn't even leave here until after the first week in October. Thanks but no thanks."

He said the words, still the suggestion caught him by surprise. How nice it would be, he thought. How nice it would be to stay here longer. If only I had the luxury of that choice.

"You know for a *young* man you can be most extraordinarily blunt."

"That's just because I got off on the right foot with you, Mrs. Whitterson."

"Let me try some of this bluntness, then," she said. "You're a young, single man, colored. Suppose we enter the war. How long do you think they'll let you stay in school?"

"About five minutes."

"My sentiments exactly." She stood up and walked to the screen, putting her hands on it. "If we go to war, you won't be able to finish the semester anyway. If we don't go, you can enroll next semester and lose only one semester in continuity—on top of which I'm willing to pay you forty dollars a week for the extra month and hire you at that rate for all of next summer. If you're going to teach, Stephen, you'll need a little nest-egg to fall back on."

He closed his eyes. It was very, very seductive. He was not anxious to go back to Chicago anyway. He remembered his cramped little room at the colored Y in Evanston. He thought about boring classes and studying late into the night until his head ached. He thought

24

about all that money. She was really talking about a lot of money.

"Let me think about it," he said.

A bright stilleto of lightning, popping the air, and a rolling crescendo of thunder like a kettle drum pounded with increasing intensity drowned out her reply. But she did not repeat herself. They both knew she would give him as much time as he needed.

* * *

Mrs. Whitterson watched Stephen carefully for a sign, but he did not give a sign and he did not say anything. He remained his efficient, cheerful self and he gave no hint that he was even thinking about her proposal.

He decided at last to write his mother. Maybe she could tell him something that would help him decide what he should do. He told her about Mrs. Whitterson's offer, about how it would interfere with college; about how it would enable him to go South, to see the relatives he had not seen since his childhood. He mentioned the possible effect of the war.

Her answer was more concerned with the war than anything else he had said.

Dear Stephen,

I received your letter, and I want to thank you for thinking of your Mama while you are cavorting around on that rich woman's country estate. I miss you and so do all your sisters, and your little nephew.

Stephen, all I can say is I hope they keep that war over there. It's got no business coming over here. You know your father served in the last war, that was before I met him, and you see what good it did him. You are my only son, you carry your father's name. Please don't take it off to some foreign land. Tell them your Mama needs you and you have to stay at home.

As for going South or going back to college in the Fall, you know I don't know anything about such things. Your Grandma Goodie and some of the others are getting up in age and I don't know how much longer they'll be around for you to go see whenever you take a notion. $200.00 more, that's an awful lot of money. You know I have to work almost three months to make that.

All I can say is stay out of the army, and as to your plans of travel or college, I figure that college is not going anyplace, but it's up to you.

All My Love,

Mama

5

In early October the fish were feeding ravenously. They tended to get active later in the morning than they had earlier in the season, and to become quiescent earlier in the evening. But while they were up and about they stuffed themselves.

Roger had taken Mrs. Whitterson into Witonkin for the day to settle her accounts for the year. Stephen knew he would be free to do as he pleased all day. He decided to settle his accounts with the Monster.

The day was clear and sunny with a light breeze. Deep Cedar Lake was quiet. The waters lapped gently against the dock and the boats. Fish did not splash. Insect noise had gone away. In the trees the wind sighed breathily.

Stephen had a deep sense of ritual. He did not know where it came from. He seemed always to have had it. There had been a ritual in the Baptist church his mother had attended but for a long time he had not recognized it. He had started attending Catholic mass because the ritual there was so clearly defined, so concrete. He had relished it all—the incense, the chants, the robes, the candles. Though he did not participate in the Communion, he delighted in it. When he had gone back to the Baptist church his discernment had been sharpened and he had picked out the ritual right away and cherished it. On what was to be his last day at Mrs. Whitterson's cabin on Deep Cedar Lake he wanted to consecrate the time. He carried out his preparations with ritual formality. He took a long time bathing. He dressed slowly, putting on long johns, woolen socks, and a heavy, scotch plaid, wool shirt. Up his legs and over his hips he pulled up a comfortable pair of blue jeans. He laced up a sturdy pair of hunting boots. Taking his time, he returned to the bathroom to pomade his hair, comb it, and brush it back, slick. Washing and drying his hands, he approved himself in the mirror, then went down stairs.

Cleaning up behind himself as he worked, he fixed a basket of food for himself, two fresh apples, two egg-salad sandwiches, five oatmeal cookies, a bunch of grapes, a thermos of hot coffee, and a canteen of cool water.

He packed his treats neatly in a wicker case. He walked it down to the dock and placed it in the storage box under the rear seat of his boat.

Back in the house he checked his fishing gear: the two best rods and reels, lines and leaders in good shape. The tackle box was full and in neat order. All the minnows he had netted the day before were still alive in the bucket. He took several trips to carry the gear to the boat and load it. Each time he stopped. He gazed across the deep-hued waters shimmering in the early light. He saw the far shore and all around the dark green shadow of woods splashed with autumn color. On his return trips to the house he stopped, too, looking at the even yards of lawn rising to the log-faces of the house, with its screen porch, its gables on the second story, and behind it the dense forest cover rippling with the slashing colors of fall.

At last he pushed the boat off from the dock and caressed the oars with the callouses on the palms of his hands and the insides of his fingers. His arms, his shoulders, his back, his body pulled into the rhythm of the stroke and the boat leaped forward, magically skimming almost effortlessly into the wind.

In the cove, thirty yards away from the lily pads, he set down anchor. Over the side of the boat he could see far down into the water before darkness swallowed all light. The boat rocked above a forty foot drop off.

He watched with an eye trained all summer as fish moved out of the hole towards the surface growth, and as they returned to sink out of sight.

He ate and watched and drank water. He saved the coffee for later when the chill would come off the land. Below him, in a seemingly noiseless world, the fish carried on their affairs.

Suddenly Stephen closed up the locker and put his hands on the rod. He tried to become motionless.

The fish cavalcade had stopped. Sunlight streamed into the water illuminating aimless moats until it vanished in opaque depth.

A shadow so long it seemed illusion, so broad it defied his credibility, loomed up out of the darkness and cruised without visible propulsion towards the lily pads.

Stephen did not know how long it had been present before he had seen it, how long he had seen it before he acknowledged it as more than a trick of light. His hand on the rod trembled but otherwise he remained motionless.

Stephen plotted the fish's path as it passed from his line of sight. He cast high and light. The lure was a giant, wobbling spoon with treble hooks behind, each streaming long, thin strands of pork rind.

Stephen began his retrieve, making it erratic, going from slow to fast, dropping it down and raising it up.

The hit felt as if he had been slammed across the stomach with a baseball bat.

The fish took the lure going up. It did not slow or divert its trajectory. When it broke water, Stephen saw the flash of the spoon against its mouth. It seemed that the body of the fish would never stop emerging, emerging from the water.

My God how big is it?

Suddenly it was free of the water and still rising—up and out. It shook its great body just once, the weight and force of its entire tail end whipped down on the taught line and snapped it off where it attached to the lure.

Stephen did not know whether the shock he felt was the line or his heart breaking, but he knew that he and the fish had come face to face and that the contest had been settled. He knew that the summer was over. He knew he had to go.

Deep River

"Deep River, Lord. My home is over Jordan.
Deep River. . . ."

Negro Spiritual
Traditional

1

Despite the mash of people pushing and pressing against him as they strove to get off the Jim Crow car, Stephen felt an immediate uplift upon the train's arrival in Jacksonville, Florida. If nothing else it was an escape from the three days and two nights on the densely packed and dilapidated car—hot, stifling. There had been so many babies on the car that no matter what time of day or night it was, at least one of them had been crying. The longer the colored passengers had stayed on the train, the more their body odors had risen. By the time they left they were individually ashamed of themselves and reluctant to look each other in the face. Stephen's clothes had grown sticky and clung to him. When he stood up he felt them as a particularly nasty part of his skin that showed. He felt as if he were naked in public, dirty and naked in public. Getting off the train was a definite boon to his well-being. It also freed him from the tortured journey to the dining car to sit, pointedly invisible, behind a green curtain, a pariah in his own land, a thing to be neither seen nor heard.

His elation upon arrival in Jacksonville had another source, too. Whatever had pulled him the thousand miles from Chicago was even stronger here in Jacksonville. It had been strong in the North; it had to be to lure him over such a distance. But now he could feel it as almost a physical presence. Close now. So close.

The bright outside light and the warm, humid air smelling of living water inundated his senses. He could not help smiling as he inched his way down the train steps.

There was such a gathering of people on the platform he did not know how he was to find whoever was there to meet him. He wove his way through the crowd, away from the car door, obeying an instinct to get to the edges of a crush of people. Once he was free of the concentrated humanity, he set his bags down and looked around.

Twenty paces further still, erect as a towering palm, strong bones set in a hard face, his Grand Uncle Tims stood next to the far wall of the railroad station.

Stephen grinned. He won't recognize me, he thought. I was only eight when I left—but him. He looks just the same as he did then. He picked up his suitcases and strode towards his late grandfather's brother.

"Hey, boy, slow down. You walks just like one o' them yankees." Uncle Tims held out the wide palm of his hand as he strolled over to his grandnephew.

"Uncle Tims, it's me—Stephen!"

"I know. Why'n tarnation ya think I'm walkin' over here to ya, boy? I seen you was a Wenders soon as you broke through from that bunch over there. Gi'me one o' them grips."

He took a suitcase handle with his left hand, and with his right, first shook Stephen's hand, and then reached around to embrace him and pat him on the back. "It's good t'see you, boy. It's good to see you."

Hugging his uncle with his free arm, Stephen rested his chin on his shoulder and struggled successfully to fight back the tears, all but two or three. Still it was a little while before he could speak. "It's good to see you, too, Uncle Tims."

"We won't be able to make it all the way to your Grandma Goodie's tonight," said Uncle Tims, as he led Stephen out of the station to the street way.

Stephen caught up with him and they walked side by side, each toting a bag.

"We'll get to your Aunt Alice's by this evening, stop off there over night, get our start by sunrise, and we'll be at Goodie's by dark tomorrow. I hope gettin' up at sunrise ain't gon' be interferin' with yo' city ways." Uncle Tims gave Stephen a little sidewise glance and chuckled.

"I've been living in the country all summer up to now," said Stephen. "I've been beatin' the roosters up."

"Is that a fact. I didn't know they had no country up North. I thought it was all cities like this here Jacksonville. I thought we had all the country down here in the South."

"Oh, there's a lot of country up there, Uncle Tims. Woods and farms and lakes and rivers. Now, you're right, there's not much country around Chicago. Just the city and the suburbs—places where some of the people who work in the city live. But up in Michigan there's plenty of country."

"Is that a fact. Well you could of fooled me. I guess nobody from here ain't never gone to that place. I ain't never heard of it before. Course now, Chicago, I done heard about that, and that place y'all lives in . . . Evanston, yeah, well Goodie tell everybody that's where y'all lives at. It's somewheres there about Chicago, ain't it?"

"Yes. Right next door."

"Is that a fact. My, my, my."

They reached Alice's house at dusk. She was delighted to see Stephen. She did not know how to react to him because the last time she had seen him he had been a little boy, but now he was a grown man. She wanted to hug him and squeeze him, which she did. But she wanted also to put her hands all over him and cover his cheeks with kisses and sit him down in her lap, which she did not. But wanting to do it and not doing it made her fidgety.

"I don't know what's wrong with you, Alice," said Uncle Tims. "Acts like you got ants in yo' britches."

She ignored Tims' chiding, but it embarrassed her that he had noticed.

"We don't have the electricity out here," she said, "but food taste just as good by the lamps."

She hurried them to sit down.

She lined up her five children and introduced them one by one.

"Don't you worry none 'bout them, they done already eat. Charles, too. He done gone out to fire up the ovens. He be back before morning."

Charles, her husband, worked in a charcoal furnace.

Stephen enjoyed watching his aunt. He could not remember much of her from when he was little, but he could see so much of his mother in her—not just in the way she looked, though there was plenty of Mama-Ruth there, too—but in her face and her build. He could also hear traces of his mother in her intonations and inflections, see them in the way she stood and her gestures. He marveled at how very personal characteristics he had believed belonged to only one special person could belong to someone else, too.

It surprised him. It frightened him a little bit because it was spooky seeing someone else put her hand on her hip like Mama-Ruth or make her voice rise in exactly the same way as if somehow she had captured part of Mama-Ruth and got it inside her, and it tickled him, too, because it showed how close family was, closer than you know.

Stephen fell asleep as soon as his head hit the bed. For three nights he had slept sitting up in the train. Lying down was a luxury he could scarcely believe. His stomach full, his face and body washed clean, he slept well, a smile on his face.

Slightly before dawn Uncle Tims woke Stephen.

"We got t'make tracks, boy, if we want t'make

Goodie's before nightfall."

Alice packed them some ham and biscuits and gave them a jug of cool water, and they were on their way.

They went straight to the river where Uncle Tims hired a skiff. Soon Stephen relaxed in the familiar rhythm of moving on water, though this time he was not responsible for the propulsion.

When the sun gained some height above the horizon, Stephen marveled at the river.

"When you was a boy I used t'bring you out on these waters. You was a pretty good fisherman. I guess you done lost all that."

Stephen smiled. "Time will tell, Uncle Tims," he said. "Time will tell."

They rode in silence for a long time, watching the dip and rise of the oars, watching the river and the birds and the sky. They watched the shoreline they could see; the other was lost to their sight. They saw a lot of heavy fish and heard many rise.

"How long will we be on the river?"

"It'll be into the afternoon before we leave the captain here," said his uncle, nodding at the boatman.

The boatman smiled and leaned back into his oars. He had to keep searching for the calmest stretches of water since they were working upstream.

More and more of the river came back to Stephen now, the times they had gone out in the pre-dawn hours to catch huge bass, the times they had gone shrimping along its banks. He remembered swimming naked in the river and the joy of a little boy in the sensation of skin and water.

"Of course you can get down to Jacksonville much faster than you can go up river," said Uncle Tims. He nodded at the truth of his observation.

When finally they did land it was early afternoon. The place looked like a jungle to Stephen, but as he searched the surrounding woods he made out a hint of a trail leading away from the beach.

The boatman did not tarry. He pushed the boat right back out again and headed for the main current.

"He gon' have it much easier goin' back," said Uncle Tims. "Once he get in that current he gon' just let her go. He'll use them oars mainly to see she stay in the main flow."

Stephen followed the boat until it vanished on the face of the water.

They sat down to eat up the ham and biscuits. They washed it down with a good portion of the water from their jug.

"That sure is some sweet water," said Uncle Tims. "I wonder how Alice come by that up in Jacksonville."

They picked up the suitcases and headed off into the little half-trail.

"Otha'll be waitin' for us about a mile and a half up this game trail," said Uncle Tims. "That's as far as the wagon ruts goes. It's other places where they goes all the way down t'the river, but none 'at can git you to Goodie's as soon."

Sure enough, Otha, the mule and wagon waited at the trail-head.

"Otha, this here's Stephen."

Otha, twelve years old, grinned and shook hands.

"Otha's yo Aunt Naomi's youngest. He stay with Goodie now that Naomi's gone crazy—off to Carolina or some such place.

"Get us home, Otha."

They loaded in the jug and the luggage and collapsed in the back of the wagon.

"Giddap, Hester," sang out Otha. "Hi! Hi!"

They rode into twilight before they approached Grandma Goodie's, though in the deep woods it was dark, darker by far than twilight. They could tell when they neared Grandma Goodie's by the dogs. The dogs heard them and set up their warning cacophony of sound. The dogs set off several roosters so that the closer they drew to the house, the more like bedlam the night sounded.

"Lucky them geese ain't in from the swamp," said Tims. "It would sound worse'n this."

"They be up soon, Uncle Tims," said Otha. "It be gettin' on to winter."

The trees were suddenly behind them and they could see windows alive with light and an open door.

2

Grandma Goodie looked exactly as Stephen had remembered her. It was as if time did not enter her world. Stephen had known he would be taller than she. When he had left, she had towered above him, a colossal figure. He had known he would now see her from a new height and he expected her to appear smaller.

Yet she did not. She retained her towering presence. She seemed the tallest person in the world.

She had the strong bones and stately carriage of all the Wenders who originated with her. Her complexion was the color of sawdust kissed golden. Despite her age her skin was smooth though it held permanently the deep lines of smiling and frowning and living. Her thick, white hair was twisted into a single braid which she wound around her head.

Her eyes were set so far back in her face as to seem absent, except for the light that reflected back from them, or when she opened them wide revealing their astonishing size.

As always, Stephen could not focus on her clothes. They hung on her, reduced to inconsequentiality, inadequate for the role alloted them—to clothe such a woman—as if someone had tried to stitch together a bodice to adorn a lofty cypress.

"Come on down from there and let yo Grandma Goodie look at you."

Stephen complied.

"My, my, my, you are a Wenders. Look just like yo daddy. Except fo' yo hair. Got a little Weatherin mixed in yo hair.

"Come on in, Stephen. Otha and Tims'll git yo things."

She did not let him get by her, though, without hugging him, almost crushing his bones and collapsing his lungs, and kissing him.

"You cain't grudge yo Grandma a good hug. I'm the one what raised you up, boy. You wasn't but five when yo Mama left here and you was eight befo' she come back to take you away. You one o' Goodie's and you always will be."

She guided him ahead of her into the house. It was smaller than he remembered, much, much smaller, and a good deal more cluttered.

Stephen slept in a small room off the main room. It had its own door to the outside. It was big enough for a narrow, slat bed and his luggage. As Stephen remembered there were several such rooms attached to the house.

Just before he went to sleep Stephen remembered that he had forgotten to ask about Uncle Solders. And he sensed then how close he was to whatever had called him from so far away.

41

3

During the first month that Stephen stayed with Grandma Goodie she had many visitors. Three were ladies wise and deepened by age like herself. One came by herself and stayed two days and two nights. Two came together and stayed one day and one night. When those ladies were visiting they worked with Goodie, did her chores with her, talked with her late into the night. But there was some work she did not share even with them. That she always did alone, though there is no doubt that she and those ladies talked about the mysteries involved in it.

There were many other visitors and kinds of visitors. Most came in small groups and stayed two or three hours during a day. People generally found the long tramp or ride to Goodie's too arduous to make alone so they waited until a group was ready to go. Also, it was easy to get lost along the way and a number of heads could usually find a way to stumble on the right track. Most visitors came to refill a long-time prescription, though some came for a special ailment or seeking advice for a life problem or interpretation of a dream. Some came as shoppers, for soap or lie or pitch or for commodities made available by Tims' skill—alligator or water mocassin skin, turkey and crane feathers, jerky, hides and fur.

Then there were family, who came and stayed as long as they liked, though usually not more than four or five days. Uncle Tims himself was present at Goodie's during that first month no more than two weeks. The rest of the time he was at his own little spread. Family members and Goodie's special friends joined immediately into the work of the place. Not a beat was lost with their arrival. During probably twenty of the thirty days of the month people other than family or close friends came about business with Goodie. She told Stephen that late fall and early winter were the times of the year when she had the largest number of visitors. Most of her clientele were country people and there was not as much work in the fields during those seasons. During planting and harvesting seasons, she said, sometimes as much as a month would go by without a single visitor.

Stephen was glad that he had fortuitiously picked such a busy time. He enjoyed seeing the arrivals in all their diversity. Most seemed genuinely awed by Goodie and her place and remained quite small and diffident during their visits. They were intimidated by the location of her domicile which seemed to them to lie beyond the bounds of civilization, the very furthest penetration of human habitation into the deep river country. Stephen delighted in being one of the enchanted cast who dwelt there.

Nevertheless, there were times of solitude with no strangers around. Usually the company came only for a short portion of the day. Most visitors were really frightened of the woods and wanted to be out of them before dark. When Stephen felt oppressed by their presence, all he had to do was step into the forest and in an instant he was alone.

He watched these visitors and he loved their eager country faces peering from their wagons or from their little, huddled groups. They wanted to see everything they could, but they were afraid to see some of the things they might. He watched them being torn between their human curiosity and fear of the unknown. He wondered if they could feel the pull. Sometimes it was so strong he tried to touch it with his fingers, but his slender digits only slipped through the air. Whatever had drawn him and drew him still had no material substance.

4

In dim morning light, followed by the dogs, Paul, Powhatten and Tone, Uncle Tims led Otha and Stephen into the bush.

The ground was soggy underfoot before either of the three spoke.

"We keep going much further, I think we're gon' need a boat," said Stephen.

"Don't worry," said Uncle Tims. "We ain't gon' git too wet. No, sirree, I'm just takin' us to some ground where these old eyes can do some dependable trackin'. Soon as we get some light, we gon' pick up some tracks."

"What about the dogs?" asked Stephen.

"Oh, they all right," said Uncle Tims, "but fo' what we after t'day, we gon' need a double-check and it's gon' take eyes t'do that. Yessirree, it's gon' take eyes. Though I do say Otha's is better than mines. They just ain't had as much trainin'."

"What we aftah?" asked Otha, eyes shining.

"Stag deer," said Uncle Tims. "I'm out t'find me a stag deer."

Otha laughed. He wanted to start running through the woods with joy, and if his uncle had permitted it, he would have. But he knew better so he just tried to keep his feet under control.

"We got us a turkey yesterday, didn't we," said Uncle Tims.

"Sho did," said Otha.

"He gon' be good eatin', too," said Uncle Tims. "Big Tom. But we need some meat we can strip and dry. Need some skin. And I need me some horn, too, and bone. And

45

it's a lady up the way I done promised some venison steaks. Yessuh. I'm gon' find me a stag deer."

Paul was the first to start whining.

"He done picked up somethin'," said Otha.

Fresh morning light filtered through the trees.

"Get down on the ground and see if you can read that sign where he's carryin' on," said Uncle Tims.

Otha moved carefully. He moved slowly to his knees. Soon he was lying flat, almost under Paul's nose. Powhatten and Tone tried to push him out of the way.

"It ain't no stag," he said at last. "Too small." He stood up.

In the period of half an hour the dogs picked up scent from three more deer. None of their sign held up to be stag under Otha's intense scrutiny.

Once, though, when they passed through a small clearing, the dogs acted strangely, laying their ears flat over the backs of their heads, putting their tails between their legs, making slight whimpering sounds, and trotting very rapidly away from the clearing.

"What's wrong with them," asked Stephen, "bear or something?"

"No. These dogs ain't scared o' no bear," said Tims, "many as we done hunted togethuh. Ain't that right, Otha?"

"Yessuh. They likes t'git right afta a bear."

"No," said Uncle Tims. "That ain't no bear. Solders been through here. Not long ago. Solders been through here."

Almost a sound then. Stephen seemed to hear it through his bones.

Close. So close.

5

Naomi came at last. She had to see her brother's oldest child, notwithstanding that her youngest was living with her mother.

Goodie had never understood Naomi, which produced a kind of balance in that Naomi had never understood nor been interested in understanding her mother.

Naomi stayed three days, most of which she spent discussing the provinciality of colored society in Raleigh and Durham but how she had been unable to abide life in Charleston because of the frightful geechies.

It was so good to get away to the country, she said. She just had to have a respite from the crush of being a woman whose presence was demanded at every affair, no matter how grand or trivial. How she missed her dear brother, she lamented, who had at least understood her, if not suffered her too well. But Stephen looked so like him there was some comfort in that—except for his horrid Weatherin hair.

Stephen, outraged as he was by his father's sister, was surprised that he regretted to see her go. She had spent scarcely five minutes with her son, had begged and wheedled and conned every penny out of Grandma Goodie and Uncle Tims they thought she might have a right to, and then late one morning had Otha drive her off to the river, refusing to accept Hester in the traces, declaring "I will not ride in a mule wagon." She had insisted that Pharoh, the horse, be hitched up, and off she had gone.

He missed her. After so short an acquaintance—he did not recall her from his childhood—he missed her

47

deeply. He understood why she would be *ne plus ultra* at all those parties and social affairs. Her presence was incandescent. And at over fifty she was still spectacularly beautiful.

"She never should of went to Jacksonville," Grandma Goodie said after she had gone. "Went to Jacksonville and all those boys fell on the ground for her and it went to her head. Never got over it. Should of kept her here with me. Could of made somethin' useful of her life. As it is the only good thing she put in this world is her children. Would of been a disgrace still havin' children up in her forties if Otha wasn't such a good boy. But his sisters is old enough to be his mama—and then some.

"Yessir, she come back here after her first trip to Jacksonville—her and yo daddy went—and she was changed then. Never was the same afterwards. She had to get back there. Did, too. Every chance she got. Till finally she stayed."

Light of the World, Stephen named her for himself, and then he laughed because she was. Light of the World. She had to be where someone could see her. What good would it do for her bright light to be shining in these deep woods, where no one could be illuminated by its radiance?

He missed her. He missed her very much.

6

A week later when Stephen stepped outside his door Grandma Goodie passed him on the way to the pump.

"Stephen, heft a couple of them buckets over yonder and help me bring in some morning water for the cookhouse."

Stephen was quick to comply and soon joined his grandmother at the pump.

"Solders is back," she said.

Stephen felt a quickening.

"Been back two or three days," she said. "He's settled now. We'll pay him a call after breakfast."

Stephen would not have believed it possible but they took off from his grandmother's yard in a direction he had never gone in all the while he had spent there.

Stephen did not see the house when it was directly in front of them. But he felt it. He felt the terrible weight of it.

"Here we is," said Goodie.

Stephen stopped because his grandmother stopped. He himself could not see where they were except surrounded by leaves and tree trunks and bushes and vines as they had been since they left her yard.

Grandma Goodie stood about six feet in front of Stephen. A dense clump of bamboo filled the space between the trunks of two massive trees directly ahead of her.

She turned around, smiled at Stephen and stepped into the bamboo.

Stephen waited. He expected his grandmother to reappear, or to call him. She did neither. He felt the weight on his limbs. Unbearable. I know what it is, he thought crazily, centripetal force. He could not resist it.

He walked hesitantly forward, stopped, then stepped into the thick growth. He kept his hands out in front of him and his second step brought his palms hard up against a flat, rough, wooden surface. He brought his hands back and parted the fronds that blocked his vision.

He saw what appeared to be a weatherbeaten wooden wall or fence. Keeping the bamboo out of his face, he reached forward with his free hand and touched the surface.

Yep, it's there alright, he thought. He inched forward. Down below his hand he saw a greyed and frayed chord that resembled a latch string. He pulled it. The door swung inward.

The space in front of Stephen swallowed up his sight. He kept his hand outstretched before him and stepped forward.

Soft laughter sounded like shotguns in his ears. He almost buckled.

"Come on in, Stephen," said Grandma Goodie's voice, "ain't nothin' gon' eat you."

He heard gentle laughter from a male voice.

"So this the one," the voice said.

"That's him," said Goodie.

"Mmhmm. Well, he look jest like his father. Come on in, boy! What's wrong—you done pee'd yo britches or somethin'?"

"I can't see."

"You got room t'take a couple steps. Come on in. We ain't gon' let you bump into nothin'. Yo eyes'll adjust after while."

Stephen took two faltering steps forward.

He heard the door close behind him.

He felt absolutely blind.

"I'm gon' take some of the strain off this boy," said the man's voice.

Grandma Goodie chuckled.

Stephen heard movement. Where it was he could not tell. He heard the squeak of wood turning against wood. A square opened in the darkness and dim light from outside poured a long rectangle into the room, dust moats dancing in the rays of illumination.

For an instant Stephen thought he was somewhere else, looking at something he had seen before. Then he remembered staring into the silent depths of Deep Cedar Lake, sun beams streaming into dark water. He remembered seeing specks floating in the lines of light, remembered waiting for the monster to emerge.

He pulled his mind back.

Just beyond the light he discerned the figure of a seated man. He was dim, but visible.

Yes. I am here, Stephen thought. At last.

"Stephen, this is yo Uncle Solders," said Grandma Goodie.

Uncle Solders, like Uncle Tims, was Stephen's grand uncle, his grandfather's brother. Stephen nodded. "Glad to meet you, Uncle Solders."

"It ain't the first time," said Solders. "But you was a little boy the last time you seen me. Now you a man. Sit down."

Stephen noticed a chair to his right and took it.

Then he was able to see Grandma Goodie seated across the small room from him. He felt better.

"Goodie's the only one able to keep up with me," said Solders. "She use her woods spirits t'get reports on my whereabouts."

51

Stephen was trying to see what Solders looked like. His eyes were adjusting to the minimal light.

Here. All the time I was supposed to come here. To this man.

"You believe that, boy?"

"Sir?"

"Never mind. It make about as much sense to believe it as not."

He looks like Uncle Tims, thought Stephen. Like Otha will look when he gets older, like the pictures of my daddy, and like I, too, must look. Wenders. Wenders.

"Stephen's been dyin' t'meet you," said Goodie.

"Oh?"

Stephen could feel his great-uncle pick up.

"Why would that be, young man?"

Stephen did not know why exactly. Of course, he wanted to meet all his relatives that he could, that is why he had come South he had told himself. For so long he had discounted the tugging, not believing it. But it was real. And it led here. Why. He did not know why. There was another reason why he wanted to meet his uncle Solders. Uncle Tims and Grandma Goodie—and even Naomi—had made a mystery of his strange, reclusive relative. He remembered how the dogs had acted in that clearing. Chill bumps swept over his skin.

"I don't know," he answered.

They did not stay much longer. Goodie explained to Stephen on the way back that though Solders could stand some company, even enjoyed it for awhile, his solitude was important to him. After he had just returned from the woods he could take people in only small doses. She had wanted to get the introductions over, get Stephen and his grand uncle "tuned" to each other, as she put it. She said Solders would come over to the house when he was prepared for the press of human company in its natural state. Then there would be plenty of time to look into other matters.

Stephen wanted to know what other matters, but got no satisfactory reply, so he contented himself with marveling about how in his treks through the woods he might have passed Uncle Solders' house a hundred times and never known it, and at how all weight had been lifted from his shoulders, and how the incessant pulling had ended. He was now expectant. And afraid.

7

Stephen was wide awake when Solders spoke from the dark outside his window.

"Ready, boy?"

"Just a minute, Uncle Solders. I'm not dressed."

Three minutes later Stephen joined Solders outside.

"Is Grandma Goodie up?" asked Stephen.

"No. But she'll know where you's gone."

Solders handed Stephen the end of a knotted cord.

"You won't be able to see for awhile, so just hold on to this. Don't let go—or I'll be gone."

With that he moved.

When grey-light came Solders told Stephen he could release the cord.

Since they were on a broad rut Stephen had no trouble following the older man. It was not until the first actual sunlight began to filter through the trees that Stephen realized they were on the wagon track that Otha had driven him on to Grandma Goodie's.

Solders stopped.

"This where they jumped yo father," he said.

Uhn.

Stephen felt the impact and his knees gave way. He staggered. He leaned against a tree and felt the sweat explode from his clammy skin.

The place was nondescript. It looked like the rest of the trail. The ruts were no wider. There was no fork in the track, no sinister overhanging branches. Stephen wanted some kind of sign that he could latch onto, some kind of symbol. There was nothing. He looked at the ground. He looked at the trees. He took a hesitant step, his tongue rough in his dry mouth. He turned around, he reached out, touching the trunks. He had ridden past here before. He had not remembered it. Nothing about it had shouted out to him. It was just a place in the trail no different from any other.

Uhn.

He bent over. He felt he was going to topple to the ground.

"I found it that very next day, that Sunday after it happened. It was eight of them."

Stephen's mind peopled the scene with eight brutal men waiting in the dark.

"They had six horses which meant four of 'em was ridin' double-mounted. But they left they horses over back yonder."

There was a wall of growth where Solders pointed.

"He put up a fight. He put up a big fight. But eight was too much."

Weak. I feel so damn weak, thought Stephen.

"They couldn't tie his feet like they done when it was a whole crowd of 'em in Jacksonville. A man's legs is much stronger than his arms. They couldn't get no control over his legs, so they tied him by the arms and drug him off behind one o' they horses. I'm gon' show you the way they taken."

Solders started back down the wagon track the way they had come. Stephen dragged his shock-stressed body after his uncle. After about half a mile Solders took an abrupt turn off the track to his right. He wove through thick underbrush for about three hundred yards. Where dense growth ended a little deer-trail began.

"What we just come through was a cleared place then," said Solders. "They just galloped right on across that, yo father bouncin' off the ground behind 'em."

The deer trail was narrow, but much easier to traverse than thickened undergrowth.

"This the way they taken in to Long Swamp. I don't think they knowed exactly where it was, just knowed it was a place what was used for killin' niggers, just knowed this trail was a way to get there. It was dark and they was brandishin' lanterns and torches. They couldn't make good time so this part wasn't too hard on yo father. Most of the time he could get to his feet and walk or run behind the horse."

Stephen was following his father now. He saw each step. It became real to him. In the place where it had happened it became real.

After an hour on the deer trail Solders stopped.

"I'm gon' show you somethin'," he said, "somethin' I ain't never told nobody."

He walked about ten paces forward and stopped. "Come here," he said.

Stephen walked up to stand beside him.

Ahead of them the trail pitched slightly downward. They could see down it for about two hundred yards before growth screened it from sight.

"It go down like that for a total of about a quarter mile," said Solders. "When it hit bottom, that's Long Swamp."

He squatted down on the ground. "Look here," he said.

Stephen knelt down beside him. A thick, gnarled root with two thick appendages jutting from it crossed the trail at the top of the incline.

Solders ran his hand over the root. His fingers felt the knobby growths.

"When the lead horses got to the lip of this rise, the riders kicked them on.

"The last horse was pullin' yo daddy. His rider could see up ahead of him where the others was carryin' the light. When they busted into a gallop, he seen that and seen the way was clear, so he kicked inta his horse too.

That horse jumped to it and snatched yo daddy off his feet.

"That brought the rope back down on the ground, and just about the time that horse hit full stride, the little slack in that rope what come from yo daddy's bein' snatched forward and fallin', whipped around this root, and when that rope straightened out again, it pulled and it snapped. I found pieces of it wrapped right here," He caressed the protuberances.

Stephen reached over and touched the root.

"That rope breakin' throwed that horse forward like he was shot from a bow. The man couldn't stop him. He run down through them other horses and out into the swamp. Hit some quicksand and it taken him down. I hit him with my proddin' pole. The man got out though.

"By the time them killers had done rounded him up and figgered out what done happened, yo daddy was gone."

Stephen looked up at his father's uncle. In his throat he felt his wildly beating heart.

"They sent them horses right on back up the trail. They figured that's the way he would go. Two of 'em rode all the way to the head of the trail—where the clearing was. Didn't find him. They waited there till way past sunup. The others tried t'cover the ground off the trail. They didn't even bother lookin' round the swamp. They didn't figure nobody would go there alone—in the middle of the night.

"Didn't find him. I'm sure they planned to go home and get a bunch of they friends and come back Sunday t'find him. But ol' Avery Weatherin had got word of what done happened, and he dared a man jack of 'em t'come back lookin' for Stephen. They didn't come neither. Come Sunday wasn't nobody out in these woods but me."

Stephen was not able to take his eyes off Solders. Solders stood up. So did Stephen.

57

"I—you see—Stephen, all by myself I found out what I just done told you, what happened, but it taken a long time. I found out more, too, but it taken longer. This area up around here, with they horses and tramplin' around they'd done covered up all yo daddy's prints and all his signs. I couldn't find which way he done gone. Me—I'm thinkin' just like them—ain't nobody—specially not colored—in his right mind gon' go into Long Swamp and I wanted to stay away from there myself. So I like told myself Stephen wouldn't be there.

"I got this far Sunday and seen what happened. And I scouted round here, but I couldn't find no sign—nothin'.

"But, you see, I knowed from the old mens—the Seminoles who used to talk with us when we was boys—all of us, yo grandaddy, Tims, and me—not every print, not every sign could be covered up or brushed away—not even by a troop of cavalry. So I knowed it was somethin' here and I was missin' it.

"I spent the night here and first good light I was lookin' again. That was Monday morning. I never did find nothin' round here. But let me show you what I did find."

Solders took off straight into the trees.

After about half an hour the ground became soggy underfoot. Stephen heard the cries of swamp birds and saw pockets of water.

Sand and swamp grasses and stretches of film-deep water replaced undergrowth. Spanish moss hung down like veils. They waded in knee-deep water stirring up a gassy smell. They tramped onto sandbars.

Solders stopped and climbed up on a giant cypress log lying on its side in shallow water. So long had it been there that the horizontal seemed its natural position.

Stephen climbed up beside Solders.

"We in Long Swamp," said Solders. "We been in it awhile."

Stephen blinked. He looked around himself apprehensively.

"We just kind of on the edges of it. It's big. Long Swamp. They named it right. But it's long like a snake. It turns and twists and loops around—so it ain't just straight long—it's long and windy long, too.

"I want you t'get a idea of what it can do to a man. Like I said, we been in Long Swamp awhile. If you wasn't with me, you'd most likely be dead. I don't know how, but unless God was takin' you by the hand, you'd be dead. We done bypassed three pools of quicksand. I done counted five cotton-mouths I done kept you away from. I seen one coral snake and this is broad daylight. What has you seen?"

"Your back."

They both laughed.

"Yo father come to this swamp," said Solders. "Maybe you don't want to admit it . . . but I know you hope he got out of here alive, or maybe that he's living here—somewheres.

"I know he was lucky for awhile. Stephen was a city-boy. He was raised in the country so he knowed creeks and woods and swamps, but when he got to be a growed man he went away to the city and never did come back in a for real way. He went all over—up North workin' for white folks—traveled wherever they traveled.

"Ruth had y'all here, but Stephen was gone most of the time. He spend a few months of the year with y'all—nights mostly, worked days in Jacksonville for those people he worked for. We used t'say he stayed here just long enough t'make another baby and then he was gone again. So he wasn't no woodsman like me or Tims, or even like his own daddy.

"That's why I never thought he'd go to the swamp. He had enough wood sense left in him to know where it was, and to know he had no business in it. I believed he would stay away from it.

"But after I couldn't find no sign at all in the woods, and as much as I hated t'do it, I started searchin' round the edges of the swamp.

"Wednesday evenin' after that Saturday I set right here on this log. On this very spot. I taken a notion to look down by my hand, and there on a wood splinter was a piece from yo daddy's trousers."

Solders reached into a little pouch that he wore on a string around his neck, fished in it with his fingers, and brought out a scrap of dark cloth. He handed it to Stephen.

"Keep it. It's yours."

Stephen cried.

For a long while they sat silently.

"He got this far," said Solders. "I couldn't tell how much before me he'd done been here. I feared all I could do of any use was to pray.

"I stayed in these swamps for two weeks. I found his underwater prints right around this log leading deeper into the swamp, but they was the last sign of him I found.

"I never told yo Grandma Goodie about this log. I never told nobody. I feared it would give 'em too much hope. They ain't never been in this swamp. They don't know what it's like. But you is Stephen's only son and the one most likely to carry the worry all yo life. So I'm showin' you.

"Now, I ain't never told Goodie, but it's a lot o' things that woman know without bein' told, and she knowed it was somethin' out here in these wilds what I could show you that nobody else could."

They sat.

"Thank you, Uncle Solders," Stephen said at last.

"It's your due."

Neither of them moved.

"Well, I done said my piece. We gon' have to spend the night, but we can go back in the morning—now that you knows all that anyone living will ever know about what happened to yo daddy. Or . . . if you really has to see to believe . . . I can take you into Long Swamp to see the truth . . . awful . . . and naked."

Close. So close. Too close. Far too close. Far too much ever to see.

When they broke their light camp in the morning they headed straight into the heart of the dark waters and they did not emerge for two weeks.

* * *

When Stephen returned to Grandma Goodie's he learned that the country had been at war for two days.

He took two days to get ready to leave.

Otha drove off down the wagon-track. Stephen sat in the back beside Uncle Tims and waved to Grandma Goodie, who stood at the edge of her clearing, waving back, tall and straight and full of life, a long braid wrapped around her head.

We Are Soldiers
in the Army

*"We are soldiers in the army, we have to fight
although we have to die. We've got to hold up
the blood-stained banner. We have to hold
it up until we die."*

Traditional

1

After basic training, while the bulk of Stephen's company went to Camp Robinson, Arkansas, to become part of a truck battalion, Stephen and fifteen other men from the company rode a military train to Fort Benning, Georgia, for OCS. Stephen was returning to the deep South. He did it with foreboding. There was good reason. The train was segregated from the time it left the base. Unlike a commercial train the Negroes did not have to wait until the Mason-Dixon line to change to jim-crow facilities.

As they lined up in the aisle waiting to disembark, Stephen and Charles, his seat partner, heard the soldiers from their car who were deboarding ahead of them being greeted.

"Niggas!"

"Git yo black asses outa Jojah!"

"Coons and clowns in uniform!"

"Gotdamn, they'll let anything wear a uniform now!"

"That skin-head nigga right there is mine!"

Charles looked over at Stephen. "I can hardly wait 'till it's my turn," he said.

2

Soon after their arrival in Georgia, the men from Fort Sheridan's Quartermaster Company (truck) 4748 Battalion had run into a condition representative of what Wilderness Jones, since shipped off to Arkansas, had labeled "brown sky." Stephen remembered that Wilderness had said that army rules had no connection to reality and sought none. If army rules said the sky was brown, so it remained, the testimony of anyone's and everyone's eyesight notwithstanding.

Wilderness had said that the way to keep in touch with reality was by clearly labeling those army rules and definitions which contradicted reality. Just call them brown sky he had said.

Deep in Southern Georgia, in OCS, though the colored candidates lived in their own barracks, the mess, the classes and the drills were not segregated. The heart of the army in the heart of Dixie was integrated. Brown sky.

Ahasuerus Paine, a graduate of the University of Chicago, whom his colleagues called a Communist but who himself professed only to have studied Marxist philosophy, had a theory about OCS brown sky.

"They can't segregate us," he said, "because they want to teach us a sense of class. The army is based on class oppression and they want us to assume our identity as part of the officer class.

"Now, they say that if you don't make a clear distinction between officers and enlisted men, you can't have military discipline. But that's not true. First of all, NCOs are not officers, and I never heard of anybody having a hard time obeying them, and, secondly, we've all heard of instances when all the officers, even the NCOs, were killed and an enlisted man took over and military discipline was followed to the t. We've all heard the stories, and they're true. No, the officers represent the interests of a distinct social class, and that's what's being protected in this demarcation between officers and men. And we have to learn it. We have to learn that our first loyalty is to our brother officers, so that when those spooks in the ranks start acting crazy, we side with our superior officers and don't provide leadership to those mutinous Negroes.

"They want us to believe that we have been selected into their elite corps, and that such acceptance makes a difference between us and our men—so that when the deal goes down, there will be no question as to where our loyalties reside."

Stephen had never heard anyone make that kind of analysis and he did not know what to think of it. He was convinced, however, that whatever the army's explanation for the desegregated conditions at OCS it was purely brown sky.

Nevertheless, as the OCS class progressed it became increasingly integrated, significant numbers of the white candidates spending nights in the colored barracks. One result of the OCS selection process was that the colored candidates tended to have more academic background than the white ones. In Stephen's group all the colored candidates had some college and most were college graduates while many of the white candidates had ended their formal educations at high school graduation. When the white soldiers saw the Negroes consistently having the answers for class assignments and doing well on tests, they did not hesitate to integrate the study sessions.

This integration of the officer corps, however, had

very strict limits. Like vanishing ink, it disappeared when exposed to the light of Georgia society. It went no further than the boundaries of the military compound. The residents of South Georgia had no idea of the heresy perpetrated within the inner-most precincts of their state. They did everything within their power to see that not the slightest ripple disturbed the proper order of things.

For this reason, passes were a difficult matter at Fort Benning. Stephen and most of his friends, out of a sense of prudence, did not avail themselves of them except at the greatest extremity. The good citizens of Columbus, Georgia and environs were simply not anxious to have colored soldiers strolling around in their midst. What was true for colored soldiers in general was doubly true for Northern colored soldiers, and what was true for Northern colored soldiers was true in spades for Northern colored officers. Even without the humiliation of the buses, the Georgia populace did not make a weekend pass an occasion to be desired.

There was also the legacy of Private Felix Hall. In April of 1941, in the woods that constituted part of Fort Bennings' vast reserve, he had been found hanging from a tree, his hands tied behind his back. The army had labeled his death suicide.

This feature of the local tradition was quickly impressed upon every Negro arrival at the base. Those few soldiers who had any doubts about the truth of the incident were quickly disabused of them. Such individuals were invariably eager to go to town and strut their stuff. That is when they learned why buses had become a symbol of humiliation to Negro troops. They found themselves waiting at the back of a long line to board buses. No matter when they arrived at the line—and being so eager many of them arrived first—they were always at the end of the line when the buses arrived. They were

68

not allowed to board until all the white soldiers had boarded. Sometimes this meant that five or six buses would leave before a single colored soldier got on—standing in the back, all the way to Columbus. Some buses would not mix soldiers by race, so that even if the last bus in a group had a dozen empty seats on it, if the other soldiers on that bus were white, colored soldiers had to wait for an entirely empty bus, and if any white soldiers came before that bus arrived, the Negroes had to wait until another empty bus came along.

The upshot of all this was that after standing in line for five or six hours, several hundred Black soldiers would not get to town. The last bus would leave, sometimes half-empty, leaving them standing.

Many times while they waited, friends of theirs who had been fortunate enough either to cram on the back of a bus or to get onto an all colored bus, returned to camp. Often such returnees were ashen. Usually they were bloodied, sporting black eyes, prominent bumps or bruises, torn uniforms, sometimes broken limbs or missing teeth. They had been met by the welcoming committee of Columbus' white citizens. Such sights discouraged many soldiers from attempting to board the outbound buses. They also removed any doubts about the reality of Private Felix Hall's death.

The hundreds of battered, tired, and angry Negroes thus left involuntarily on base were a potential source of great disruption. The MPs, aware of such possibilities, always waded into them in massive pre-emptive strikes. They busted heads, busted arms, arrested many and dispersed their gatherings. Many soldiers were preemptorily relieved of any further military responsibilities as a result of such farsighted MP action. Their resulting permanent injuries made them unfit for soldiering and they were given medical discharges.

Many were simply sent to base hospital where they

were healed up and sent back into the fray, purple heart recipients without benefit of combat Stephen called them.

Stephen channeled all of his energies into learning everything he could about the army, the officer corps, and every leadership theory the army had to offer. Even the other colored candidates began to think of him as a grind. He knew he had no alternative. If he truly opened his eyes and looked about him, if he let himself see, he would react. He would mutiny and be court-martialed. He might be shot. Instead, he worked very hard. He challenged himself on every exam, every assignment.

Everybody thought he was gung-ho. They did not know that his hatred of the army was growing deeply, like a wound. It was as if every minute he spent reading, memorizing, analyzing, and drilling was spent with a spade digging the wound more deeply into his soul. His hatred for the army was surpassed only by his revulsion for the South, the side of the south he now saw, no longer cushioned in the bosom of his family, when he had to look at it from the outside and see the place it had reserved for him.

Nine of the fifteen Black men who came with Stephen from Fort Sheridan passed the OCS class and were commissioned as second lieutenants. Stephen graduated first in his class. Of the total class of 550 men, 225 passed.

3

By misadventure Stephen disembarked from the train at Prescott, Arkansas, several miles from Camp Robinson. He knew right away that he had made a dreadful mistake—arriving alone in a strange southern town. He knew that the consequences for such stupidity were monumental and he could do little except to try to remain inconspicuous. That was hard because he felt huge. He felt gaudy. He felt like the Washington Monument walking around the tiny Arkansas town.

The other Negroes noticed it too. They saw him coming and disappeared before he got to them. But he had to talk to one of them. He had to know when the next train came.

The shoeshine man could not escape. Stephen bent down to talk to him. He felt like the Statue of Liberty bending over from the waist. The shoeshine man felt it, too. Stephen read it in his eyes.

The shoeshine man told him that there would be no train through that he could board until morning.

That puts me in a hell of a pickle, Stephen thought. Either I can spend the night alone in this town, or I can walk the road to Camp Robinson alone—nothing between me and the 4748th except Arkansas pine woods and deranged crackers. Oh, Lord, the devil and the deep blue sea.

Stephen did not want to be seen too long in any one place. He was afraid of attracting a crowd. On the other hand, if he moved too far he would attract attention to himself just by passing too many pairs of eyes. It was not safe even to stick close to the railroad station. It had its habitual loungers and idlers.

Damn my stupid hide, he thought as he walked away from the train station. He was furious with himself for getting off the train in the wrong place, but he was further galled because when he had been asking the shoeshine man about the trains, he could have asked him where the colored part of town was, and he had not. Now the shoeshine man had gone. His speaking to the Washington Monument turned into a talking Statue of Liberty had been too great an affront to the good white citizens. The shoeshine man should have known that such a garish, walking and talking statuary obelisk was imaginary and ignored it. He had to vanish so that their wrath would not settle on him. Stephen had to find another Negro to ask or find the colored neighborhood on his own.

"Hey boy!"

Oh no.

"Gotdamnit, nigger! Don't you hear me talkin' t'you!"

Stephen looked over his shoulder.

A large man wearing a cowboy hat and khaki clothes stood behind Stephen, his face beet-red. Just as Stephen was about to turn his head back around, maybe, he thought, he could walk away from this too—disappear as the other Negroes had—just as he was thinking that and starting to turn his head back around, the glint of the badge on the man's shirt caught his eye. Stephen turned around and stopped.

"Nigga! I expects t'be spoke to when I speaks!"

How to behave. Stephen did not know how to behave.

The man's hands gripped his belt. Stephen saw the holster and the billy club.

Stephen did not know what to say. What should he say?

"Sir?"

The word enunciated crisply, clearly, infuriated the sheriff.

The lieutenants bars by themselves had been provocation enough. But then waiting for the customary, drawled, "suh," and hearing the sharp, finely pronounced, "Sir," drove the sheriff over the edge.

Stephen saw the explosion in the sheriff's face. He believed he could see the blood vessels etching themselves as little red lines across the white's of the sheriff's eyes. But he did not know how to behave. He did not know what he should do. He stared in confusion as the man seemed to turn rabid before him.

"Goddamn it, nigga, when I wants a answer, I wants a answer!"

The sheriff snatched his billy club out of his belt and aiming for Stephen's temple, caught him across the forehead. Kicking furiously, his boots slammed into Stephen's knees.

Stephen tumbled backwards, falling on his back in the street.

O Jesus what now? O Jesus what now?

"Git up, Gotdamnit! Git up!"

Raising his torso up on his elbows, Stephen froze. He could move no further. His heavy limbs would not budge. His tongue swelled up in his mouth. His body trembled, shivering as if struck by a winter gale. His eyes bolted open, enormous.

"Shit," said the sheriff as he drove his heavy boot into Stephen's stomach. He kicked again, grazing Stephen's chin.

Stephen rolled over onto his stomach, collapsing. He lay in the full grip of terror, shivering, hideously paralyzed.

A small crowd gathered, standing around Stephen's prostrate form.

"Ah see you got one o' them niggas in you-nee-form, Sheriff," said a voice.

"Smart-ass nigga, walkin' on the sidewalk," said the Sheriff. "And then wouldn't speak back when I raised my voice to him."

"Impudent, slimy filth," said another voice.

"Don't he know we don't 'low no niggas on the sidewalks," said yet another.

"Well, if he didn't, he do now."

The crowd broke into vicious laughter.

A head wearing an army captain's campaign hat peered through at the edge of the crowd. He wanted to see what the fun was about.

He saw the freshly laundered, crisply pressed khaki uniform sprawled out on the asphalt.

"Is that man alive?" he asked.

All heads turned towards the speaker.

"I'm stationed at Camp Robinson," said the speaker.

"Well, this is one of yo colored dogs," said the Sheriff, "you betta keep them in that camp o' your'n. They don't know how t'behave around decent folk."

"Sho don't."

"Nigga scum."

"Is he alive!" the captain repeated.

"See fo' yoself," said the Sheriff. He kicked Stephen in his ribs. Several rough hands turned Stephen on his back.

Stephen's eyes diminished the rest of his face. They looked like small, dark-centered moons placed below his forehead. Not only had his tongue filled his mouth, but also his throat had constricted, rendering speech impossible and breathing difficult.

The captain heard the breathing and saw the bars simultaneously.

"What's your name, lieutenant?" he asked.

74

If possible, Stephen's eyes opened a little wider, but he said nothing. His breathing rasped the air.

"What did this man do?" the captain asked the Sheriff.

"The nigga walked on the sidewalk," said a voice from the crowd.

"That's right," said the Sheriff. "The nigga walked on the sidewalk, and we don't 'low that in Prescott. Then he resisted arrest."

"Alright," said the captain, "I'll take care of it. He doesn't fall under your jurisdiction. I'll send for the MPs."

Captain Anderson had not gone quite far enough to be called a nigger-lover and attacked in his turn by the crowd. All the same he was relieved for himself as well as for the colored lieutenant when the MPs came.

That is how the MPs brought Stephen into Camp Robinson.

4

A week later, on a Sunday afternoon, a thunderstorm caught Wilderness Jones and Stephen on a hill about a mile away from their barracks.

"We better beat it off the top o' this hill," said Wilderness.

"I'm right behind you," shouted Stephen. "Move it!"

They dropped down the hill easily, bounding on rocks and clumps of grass. The soles of their shoes found dry surfaces. The rain had not had time to make them slick or soggy.

Still, the big rain drops, falling heavily, drenched the two men in less than a minute.

"Hey—look! Over there!" called Wilderness, veering off to the side.

Stephen followed.

They arrived under a wide outcrop of rock. A little shelf under the massive overhang was entirely dry. Lightning flashed, filling the air with eery light.

They both slumped to the ground, panting.

Stephen looked out away from the hill. He saw the sky twilight dark from storm clouds. Rain showed—lines against the gloom.

"Whew," he sighed.

"Look like we gon' be here for awhile, lieutenant," said Wilderness.

"Sure does," said Stephen, "plenty of time for you to tell me about that something special you mentioned in the barracks after you saw the MPs drag me in."

"You ain't forgot, has you?" said Wilderness.

"Does a snake have tits—hell, no, I haven't forgotten. You lay something like that on me, drop it, and don't mention it again—you think I'm going to forget? Come on, Wilderness, give me a little credit."

Jones smiled. "I give you a lot of credit, Steve. That's why I'm gon' talk t'you about this. I mean, my plan. I done talked to a whole lot o' cats about what I feel about the army. That ain't no secret."

Thunder rolled across the sky.

"I mean I knowed it all along, but I done decided—real clear like; I done said it out loud—who the real enemy is. I know that now. Clear. No confusion. Like I know pussy's good. Like I know water's wet. I cain't be fooled about it no more. Our real enemy ain't no Japs or Germans. Our real enemy is right here. I mean the Japs and the Germans might be bad. I mean the Japs might be bad—they killed a lot of people at Pearl Harbor. But they don't really be fuckin' with our people—you know what I mean? And they colored, too, so they couldn't be all bad. And the Nazis, they preach race-hate and that's bad shit. But they ain't doin' shit to us. Maybe later. Maybe if they win the war they'd fuck with us. But they ain't doin' shit to us right now.

"Somebody is. Somebody is fuckin' with us everyday. Everyday. They don't has t'preach race hate. They practices it. Practices it on us. Everyday. They is our real enemy. Our actual enemy. The almighty white man. 'Cept I done found out he's so simple and childish-acting I call him the white boy. The white boy. Civilian or military. It don't make no nevermind. He's all the same. And he's the enemy."

"Brilliant deduction," said Stephen. He realized that before his trip to Florida, before he was drafted, before OCS, before he had lain in the dust of an Arkansas street, it would have been—for him—a brilliant deduction. Now it was a common-place observation.

"I know that a lot of cats think the same thing," said Wilderness, "but it don't make no difference unless you does somethin' about it. Then it do make a difference. It make a real difference. It make the difference between me—and I hope you—and them other cats like the difference between night and day."

"What," said Stephen, "what do you propose to do about it?"

"What you do to the enemy," said Wilderness. ". . . you fight him. We's bein' organized and disciplined and trained to wage war. Well, I plan that we do what we been taught. I say we should wage war, we should use all what they done taught us about organization and discipline and training—to wage war. But against the real enemy."

Wilderness looked out into the storm.

"We can fuck with the white boy, Steve. All we need t'do it is the best truck unit produced by this damn army. We can fuck up his maneuvers. We can lose his supplies. We can burn up his fuel. We can run through his damn peckerwood farms and fuck up his crops. We can just wage war against the mother-fucker and we don't have t'fire a damn shot.

"The way I sees it, there is two things that's gon' be required from the officer in charge of this mess."

"Mess is right," said Stephen.

"He got t'be damn good, cause he got t'train a crack unit, and he cain't give a damn about his efficiency rating, cause it's gon' be fucked to hell."

"So you think I'm good," said Stephen smiling.

"Well, let me put it this way. With me as your first sergeant you cain't lose."

"So it was no accident that we're both assigned to third platoon," said Stephen.

78

A big grin spread across Wilderness' face. "The head clerk in the battalion office is my man," he said, "and that ain't the only thing that ain't no accident. How you think our platoon got assigned to Captain Fandley's C Company?"

Stephen narrowed his eyes at Wilderness.

A gust of wind blew a shot of rain on them. They shivered.

"Listen, Steve, I know you hate Fandley, but—"

"I don't hate him. He's just the most incompetent man—of any rank—in the whole army."

"I know. I know. That's part of the plan. See—he's gon' mess up so much and be so confused that we'll have plenty of time and plenty of chances to do our thing without being caught. You know, they'll just pass it off as one of Fandley's fuck-up platoons. That's why you cain't have no thing about your efficiency ratings."

They talked for a long time. The sky cleared. The storm moved on. The hilly ground remained wet and slippery. They waited for it to dry and talked on.

There was one note of central beauty in Wilderness' plan. He did not believe the army had any intention of ever using colored troops in a theater of war. Since he believed they were going to be kept in the U.S. throughout the hostilities, he felt their mobilization should at least be put to some good use. They would not be surrendering such vital years of their lives entirely in vain. But the critical element of his perception was that even in the unlikely contingency that the mighty U.S. army should stoop to using colored troops, the efficiency rating of their own company and their own platoon in particular would be so low that they would never be sent overseas. Hence, they would not only do something truly worthwhile during the war, they would also escape any chance of being blown to bits by the Japs or the Nazis.

By the time the sunset had tinted the sky with vivid pinks and purples they had sealed in finality their conspiratorial bond. They came down from the hills intent on working mischief.

Four days later they went to work. They threw their men into total preparation. The men studied their trucks. They drove their trucks. They took their trucks apart. They loaded and unloaded their trucks. They winched and hitched and piggy-backed their trucks.

Stephen and Wilderness marched them and drilled them and held them at attention. They had them clean engines and grease axles, and change tires and align wheels. They had them drive through obstacle courses.

Stephen specialized in map reading. He spent every night studying maps of the Camp Robinson area. He drove the whole area day and night, matching what he had seen on the maps with what his eyes and headlights showed him. He drove on roads, cow paths, and deer trails. He drove up creek beds across fields and over ridges. He started knowing the country the way he had come to know the forest around Grandma Goodie's. He found errors on the maps and corrected them on his copies. He drew his own maps. He took his men out into the country day and night. He had himself blindfolded on the way out and used mapreading to get them back home.

For a solid month not one of his men got a pass or furlough. They were too tired to complain. But at the end of a month they felt for sure they were the drivingest outfit in the camp.

At the end of their month of intensive training they were alerted. Their company was to go on maneuvers in support of the 88th infantry and the 139th artillery regiments.

5

True to form, within two hours after his lead jeep pulled out of Camp Robinson, Captain Fandley had his whole company lost. He called a halt on a two-rut dirt road just before it plunged into an unbridged stream.

Stephen told Fandley he knew a way across the stream. Stephen rode in the captain's jeep and under his direction it took the company forty minutes to turn around and reach a fording place that Stephen had picked out on the map. When they reached the ford, Stephen left the command jeep and went back to his truck.

Captain Fandley led his company across the stream and up the cow path.

Stephen had done as the Captain desired, he had found a way across the stream. That, however, did not place them any closer to their assigned position than the dead end. In fact, by the time the company bivouaced for the night, they were eighteen miles away from their assigned area.

* * *

The battalion commander was furious. He had sent scouts out all over the woods. They had found no trace of C Company.

* * *

Captain Fandley was perplexed when he woke up after the first night on bivouac to find most of his men suffering hangover symptoms, and many of them smelling distinctly of alcohol. After his initial surprise at their condition, he took it as a matter of course that their performance the rest of the day was unresponsive and listless. Nevertheless, by the time they pitched camp that evening he had managed to get them eight miles further lost.

Stephen and Wilderness, who were delighted at the success of their plan to pilfer liquor from the base and sell it on maneuvers, knew that with the company lost they would have an unlimited opportunity to unleash their profit-making schemes and enrich the platoon's coffers. By the third day Captain Fandley was hopelessly confused, and the first, second, and fourth platoons given over to a grand debauch orchestrated and capitalized on by the third platoon.

The battalion commander, beside himself with rage, had called off all searches and written off finding C Company. He split its assignments between B and D companies.

* * *

By the fifth day Captain Fandley was no longer concerned about reaching the 88th infantry and the 139th artillery. He was worried about ever getting back to Camp Robinson. He was scared of dying in the wilderness. When he was a child many of his Sunday school lessons had come out of the book of *Exodus*. He kept dreaming of Moses never reaching the promised land. He felt that he was a kind of Moses to these poor, colored troops. Would he perish before he could deliver them to the land of milk and honey? It began to prey on his mind.

Sunday night when C Company's trucks came streaming back into Camp Robinson, supplies exhausted, not a single objective accomplished, hours after everyone else, the men of three platoons in a profound stupor, no one was prepared to receive them.

It did not, however, take long for Major Atcheson, the commander of the Negro truck battalion—all four companies—to get ready for the offending officer. He held a private reception for Captain Fandley in his quarters.

6

Captain Fandley was not exactly relieved of his command. That would have been too much of an affront for a commander of colored troops. It was more as if he were put in limbo while the army searched for a replacement and for some safe place to ship him. He kept his quarters, and nominally his command. Everyone knew, however, that his exec was supposed to be acting in his stead. Since Lieutenant Freeman was incapable of acting on his own behalf, much less anyone else's, actual command devolved upon the two line, white, first lieutenants who were themselves so busy trying to get reassigned that each platoon was left to its own devices.

The 88th and 139th were shipped overseas. Fandley's replacement had still not been named when the 4748th was called on to support the 112th infantry, the 451st artillery and the 87th armored regiments in battle maneuvers.

Major Atcheson attached C Company to B Company. He did not want C Company operating alone. He figured if nothing else they could learn by association.

Stephen's and Wilderness' main problem was how many drivers they could pull out of their other operations to go on maneuvers with them.

They had rented garages in several of the larger towns around Camp Robinson and in the two big cities of Little Rock and TexArkana. In each of those garages they had assembled trucks out of replacement parts. They used the trucks to run a bus service for colored troops. They had a schedule which they circulated by surreptitious means. On rates varying from five cents to twenty-five cents, depending on the distance, a colored soldier could walk a quarter mile past the main gate and at a scheduled time catch a truck that would drop him off dead in the middle of the colored section of town. For the same fare he could get a return truck on schedule which would drop him off 100 yards from the main gate.

Colored soldiers no longer had to suffer the humiliation of the bus wait, and Third Platoon had a steady and lucrative income. Often Third Platoon's passengers hooted and jeered as they roared past the regular camp buses.

For a rather stiffer fee the platoon also ran an AWOL service in which it transported men to the railroad outside Little Rock where they could depart—out from under the watch of MPs—for distant points.

Faced with the necessity of maintaining a maximum number of drivers during maneuvers, Stephen and Wilderness had to decide which of their routes to suspend and which to keep going. It was clear that they would have to keep the service going in the greatest demand areas, but the question they struggled with was where the cut-off point should be. They finally settled on keeping open Little Rock, TexArkana, and two shorter runs. They would spare four drivers from the military exercises.

There was one huge advantage Stephen's and Wilderness' platoon had in being with the whole battalion on maneuvers rather than with C Company alone. Third Platoon would have a much bigger market for its illicit wares. Stephen and Wilderness were aware, however, that under the watchful eye of Major Atcheson no shennanigans would be possible. Therefore, for three days before maneuvers began the leadership of Third Platoon spent the time war-gaming alternative strategies. By the time they rolled out, they were ready to put their plans to the acid test. Their scheme called for them to wreak havoc and make money on an unparalleled scaled.

Major Atcheson was a good commander. He was thorough in his preparations. The one possible weakness in his command demeanor was that although he anticipated normal bumblings, even gross errors, and incompetencies, he was not conditioned to look for the active malfeasance which had become Third Platoon's specialty.

Slightly after midnight following the first day of maneuvers, camouflagued for night action, Third Platoon dispersed its tricksters throughout the operations area. They changed, removed, and redirected every single road sign and marker in the war games area. Long before dawn the culprits had returned to their bivouac undetected.

The problems arose on the third day of maneuvers when trucks started returning to Camp Robinson, which was being used as a staging area. None of them got back. Some ended up in dead-end gulches. Some ended up in the middle of creeks. Some ended up in farmyards, cowpastures, and one string of twenty trucks ended up surrounding an isolated, rural, Southern Baptist Church.

Major Atcheson stayed in the forward area and was not aware of the dimensions of the fiasco until twenty-four hours after the fact. By then he had lost contact with 7/8ths of his command. The profit-taking ventures of Third Platoon were in full swing.

On the morning of the fifth day, after having notified the infantry, artillery, and armor commanders of his difficulty, under a full head of fury, with his first sergeant driving, Major Atcheson took off in his jeep in search of his battalion.

He came first upon the scene of almost two dozen trucks parked haphazardly around a once-whitewashed, shabby, little church. Not a man was in sight. Nothing stirred.

Major Atcheson had the sergeant bring the jeep to an abrupt halt. The officer hopped out. He looked around. He listened. Nothing. He walked around the trucks. Scattered willy-nilly around the whole area were beer bottles, wine bottles, and whiskey bottles. Empty. All empty.

He looked inside trucks. Empty.

He approached the church. From the outside it smelled like a tavern. He flung open the front door and stomped inside.

He gagged on the smell. A coughing fit recovered him. The linoleum floor was sticky with spilled liquid. Soldiers in various stages of dress lay everywhere—on the floor, draped over pews, along the pews. Mingled among them were women in similar stages of deshabille. Major Atcheson averted his head time and time again at obscene sights.

One soldier, stark naked, sat propped against the foot of the pulpit, a ripe, curvaceous woman without a stitch on sprawled across his lap. The choir stall was filled with still-life visions of fornication. The room smelled of flesh and body secretions. It smelled of alcohol. It smelled of bad breath.

As Major Atcheson stepped slowly, but gingerly, around the room he recognized that every soul there, every one, was asleep. Snores competed with the buzzing of flies in a chorus of insufferable sound.

Before him on a pair of thick lips—wide open, emiting a loud, abrasive noise—a fly paraded, stopping occasionally to feast on a pasty scum that ringed the lips.

Major Atcheson turned and bolted for the door. Tripping, stumbling, falling forward, yet keeping his feet, he charged outside.

"Sergeant! Sergeant Gripper!"

"Sir!"

"Get in there! Clean up that sty!"

No wonder VD is endemic among them, he thought. My God, I've always tried to think the best of my men, but this takes the cake. Amidst all his revulsion was the recognition of an almost irresistible lust that had surged through his body. It had been all he could do to turn his eyes away from the fecund woman under the pulpit. He had felt like wallowing in sin. He jammed the memory back into the dark recesses of his brain. It fled, but it did not go away. For the first time, though he had always thought of his command as a trust, and though he had always prided himself on feeling the companionship of a fellow-soldier for his men, he began to hate them.

It took Major Atcheson fifteen hours to locate and form up the rest of his trucks. He never learned what had precipitated the disintegration of his battalion. By the time he mounted his hunt every road sign or marker was perfectly in place. He was beside himself. With the exception of C Company after the maneuvers the preceding month he had been proud of his men; he was confident in them. He believed that this set of maneuvers would prove that they were ready to go into a foreign theater. Now he despaired that they would ever be ready for actual military service. He was coming to see that the scorn his superiors had felt for colored troops, scorn that he had believed was the product of ignorance and bias, was well-deserved. He wanted a chance to serve abroad. There was no sane alternative for a career officer. He had wanted to take his battalion with him. But beginning to feel as he was towards the men, he concluded that there was only one responsible thing for him to do, to seek a transfer. Perhaps another officer would be content with stateside duty, or would find something in these poor, despised souls that he had not. But he owed it to himself, he owed it to the diminishing allegiance he felt towards these troops, to get out.

7

Friday night in the barracks' dimmed lights Wilderness and Stephen sat on Wilderness' cot playing Gin Rummy.

Wilderness studied Stephen as Stephen meditated on his hand.

"Lieutenant," he said, "I got a question to ask you."

Stephen looked up. "Aw, shit," he said. "When you start with that lieutenant stuff I know you got a load of rocks to dump on me."

Wilderness smiled. "Now, Steve, you know it ain't like that."

"Cut the shit, Wilderness. What have you got on your mind?"

Wilderness put down his cards. "Well . . . you see, I've got through channels a very serious request. We ain't never got one like it before. . . ."

Stephen put down his cards. He looked into Wilderness' face. "Wilderness, I don't want to start talking about your mother, so why don't you get to the point?"

"Alright, Steve. It's just that, I mean, we ain't never done nothin' like this—"

"Like what?"

"Well, it's these splibs at Fort Polk who done heard about our services on the grapevine and it seem like they is just in a sack full o' bees.

"See, where they go for they passes is Alexandria and the crackers in that town been beatin' up on them somethin' pitiful, then the MPs comes and they wades in on 'em, too. If that wasn't so bad, when they gets back t'base the white troops start fuckin' with 'em, and the MPs gits in on that action, too.

"Well, the shit has done got so bad, that the members just ain't gon' take it no more. They figures the next time they goes t'town in a big group, and somebody fucks with them, they just gon' kick ass. There won't be enough MPs t'handle them.

"The trouble is, they knows when that happen, after they gets back to base—prob'ly the next mornin'—the white troops gon' be sent in full combat gear to arrest they ass."

"How many colored are we talking about?" asked Stephen.

"Well, those what contacted us is a infantry regiment, a battalion of engineers, and a battalion of anti-aircraft.

"See, the problem is. They just like us—or just like we supposed to be. They ain't got no weapons—not even the infantry. The engineers and anti-aircraft ain't got no weapons at all. They been took away and locked in a armory under twenty-four hour guard. And the infantry had all they ammo confiscated and the bolts removed off they rifles."

"So they want us to ship them some rifles and ammo," said Stephen.

"That's right," smiled Wilderness, "grenades and machineguns, too. Anything we can get our hands on."

"So we are supposed to be the ones to supply the arms for the outbreak of World War II on American soil?"

"Steve. Who's the enemy? Who's the real enemy in this war? Who's the real enemy of our people?"

Stephen looked off into the darkened corner of the barracks. Wilderness was right. This was, "a very serious request." Talk about understatement. Like saying, "I heard about a battle they're getting ready to start. It's called Armagedon." Wilderness had been right to stall before telling him about it. He should have kept stalling.

Maybe I should stall, he said to himself. Maybe now I should stall.

8

Stephen took his first pass since he had been in Arkansas. He was careful. He rode in one of their own trucks. He rode it all the way to Little Rock.

He dropped off the truck not far from the campus of Philander Smith College, and though he did not know he was going there, that is where he found himself. The campus was fenced and locked but such a barrier was not formidable. Stephen quickly clambered over it onto the grounds. It was a small campus, but it was a true campus, not just a collection of buildings on a Chicago street.

Though it was late November, the night was not frightfully cold. The air and grounds were damp from a recent rain. A few night lights turned water droplets silver as they hung on the ends of pine needles. The lights silhouetted the old brick buildings. Stephen enjoyed creeping cautiously across the deserted grounds. The darkness seemed to give him an extra sense for the age of the structures. They felt ancient.

He was an interloper, an interloper in a world that was alien to him yet somehow seemed to claim him as bones of his bones and flesh of his flesh. The campus had a feeling of being separated, set aside from the world.

Sudden light blazed in front of Stephen. A door had been flung open. Stephen froze. A figure stood framed in the light. A white disc, hurting Stephen's eyes, shone from the middle of the figure. Stephen felt weak. The man—he could tell it was a man—turned and went back inside. The door closed on the light, bringing back the welcoming dark.

The night watchman. Yes. The night watchman.

If I had been raised in the South this might be my school, he thought. A colored college.

He trotted along the campus walks, pit-pat on his toes, touched the trees, inhaled the air. In the seclusion of the impenetrable shadows he felt like slumping against a tree and spending the night, but he did not. The ground was too wet.

A few blocks away he found a string of clubs and joints. His uniform got him into one though it did not bring him a lot of pleased stares from the civilian men in the place. The other soldiers acknowledged him respectfully. None of them were officers. Several of the women seemed literally to light up.

He met an intriguing girl named Evelyn. Her home was Fort Smith. She had come to Little Rock to work and save up enough money to go to Philander Smith. She wanted to be a school teacher. This was her second year in Little Rock and she believed that by the next fall she would have saved up enough money to pay tuition and buy books. She lived in a rooming house and her job would bring in enough to pay the rent, buy some meals, and keep putting enough away to meet her ongoing college expenses. She was pleased with her life and excited about her future.

She was so captivated by Stephen's uniform and his lieutenant's bars and his northern accent that he did not have to say much about himself. He smiled, and smoked, and looked at her, and drank. The juke box played songs which were totally foreign to him. But she liked the music and her pleasure in it animated her.

She was very pretty. Her skin, much darker than any wood Stephen knew of yet not as dark as India ink, seemed to glow as if it held some inner light. It looked as if it would be as soft to touch as velvet.

He watched the expressions playing across her face, and the shining, heart-catching beauty of her smile. He loved her accent. A lot of his men had accents, so he was used to the inflections. But the tones—he had never heard tones like hers. They made him want to laugh and smile and stare forever into her eyes while listening.

She could not have men in her rooming house, but Stephen learned after a few questions to a soldier about a house where rooms were rented by the day. They went there.

Her skin was as soft to touch as velvet and her mouth as sweet as the nectar of pomegranates. He could not have enough of touching her and seeing her and hearing her mouth make sounds that were never meant to be words.

He did not return to camp until early Monday morning. The following week was far too busy to enable him to continue his conversation with Wilderness. He left the first thing Friday evening to be with Evelyn.

* * *

Stephen and his leadership war-gamed Wilderness' proposal of rescue at Fort Polk. They discovered that if they were ever to make the run to Louisiana they would have to be able to count on forty-eight to seventy-two free hours at their disposal. That finding relieved Stephen of the need to make a decision. He could continue his weekends with Evelyn. He could continue to mark time on such a fateful choice. There was no possibility of attempting a delivery until the platoon was once again assigned maneuvers.

Thankful for being saved from making the decision— with either choice there was no way to avoid being wrong—almost out of sheer relief, Stephen fell ever more in love with Evelyn.

9

Twenty-four hours after maneuvers began, Third Platoon became irretrievably lost.

A long, circuitous route kept the platoon from being observed by other units as it made its way to the weapons cache. The trip to the cache took four and a half hours. It had to be done in daylight because the trails they had to use were too vague and poorly marked to be serviceable by night.

Loading was accomplished in an hour. By twelve-thirty in the afternoon Third Platoon had started its long roll to Fort Polk. They drove slowly and carefully through the maneuver area, kicking up to top speed only when they were well outside the exercise zone.

The convoy made very good time. Stephen and Wilderness together knew each dip and grade in the route. The gearing was a wonder of precision and artistry. The loads were so perfectly balanced that they enhanced the trucks' performances.

The long, drab green line passed out of Arkansas and plunged into Louisiana. The northern parishes fell away rapidly. The drivers took the trucks through central Louisiana and entered the southern part of the state.

"Fort Polk cain't be far away," sang out Wilderness. Then he saw before them, spanning the entrance to the bridge across the Dugdemona River, a phalanx of wooden barricades. Behind that barrier stood a line of armed men, and behind that cars, pick-up trucks, tractors, and state-trooper cruisers.

The acknowledging glance Wilderness gave Stephen

was quick, almost imperceptible, but Stephen caught it. He was proud of it despite the paralysis he felt afflicting his body.

Farmers, troopers, roughnecks, deputies, quite an assortment, maybe if he just concentrated on them he wouldn't freeze up. Relax, Stephen, my boy, relax. You're not driving. You don't have to do a damn thing except retain your power of speech.

He inhaled. Leaning forward to try to encourage circulation to his head, he exhaled slowly.

Easy. Easy. Nothing but terror.

Wilderness was trying to identify the weapons: Shotguns. Thirty-ought sixes. Forty-five pistols. Thirty-thirties. Ah—some double barrels. Submachine guns. Yes.

The truck stopped.

Both men looked into their mirrors, watching the column stopping behind them.

Stephen still had enough presence of mind to look out of his side window.

There was enough room for the second truck to pull up beside them.

"I wonder if all this is for us," said Stephen, his voice high and tight, his breathing hard. He was amazed that he could speak at all. Despite the chattering of his teeth, the very sound of his creaky, tremulous voice heartened him.

"Got damn it, Philbert," said a man on the left side of the line of armed men, "will you look at the niggas in the government issue trucks. Ain't they a sight!"

"He, he, he, he, Philbert," said another man, his hands clenched on a shotgun, "should we blast 'em out o' them trucks or wait till they gits out?"

A short, thin man stepped forward, very neat, clean-cut features. He wore a broad-brimmed hat. His heavy,

97

brown coat was unbuttoned, just showing the top corner of a badge which emitted a dull gleam in the late afternoon light.

"I'm Sheriff Overton," he said, "Why don't you boys come down out o' your truck?"

Stephen cleared his throat. He was now more confident that his voice would not fail him. He was glad he did not have to stand up since he knew his vibrating knees would never support his weight.

"Good afternoon, sir," he said. "I'm Lieutenant Robert Evans, 2328 Quartermaster Corps. We're on maneuvers. Would you like to move aside and pass us through, or do you have some special reason for stopping us?"

A chorus of laughter, hoots, and catcalls answered Stephen's question.

"You a yankee sombitch, ain't ya," said a big man next to the sheriff.

"Gon' be a dead, yankee sombich, soon," said another.

Much laughter and derision followed the remark.

"I don't like to repeat myself, boys," said the sheriff. He raised his shotgun, pointed it through the windshield at Wilderness and cocked it.

All the other weapons on the barricade were brought to firing position. Without moving his head, Stephen said to Wilderness, "See, this is why we war-game—and this is why you listen to your lieutenant no matter how cracked he may sound."

"Oh, don't you know I'm in your corner now," said Wilderness.

He swallowed, then honked his horn once, very, very lightly.

The sound caught the line of armed men by surprise and they flinched back for just a few hundredths of a second.

That's all the time it took for the tarp to be yanked

back on top of the truck revealing a fifty calibre machine gun trained directly on the line of men, manned by a gunner and an ammunition feeder. That's all the time it took for the second truck to start to pull out, enroute to coming on line with the first, showing the same armament, focused on the same target.

Everyone had heard the bolts slam, putting the machine guns in firing position.

The second truck stopped abreast of the first one.

Not a man on the line moved.

Stephen inhaled slowly, deeply. He let it out gradually.

The sheriff pulled down his shotgun.

"Listen, here, uh soldier," he said. "Uh ya see we uh got a report—fellas put your guns down!" He gestured at the men flanking him. They all lowered their weapons. "See, uh, we got a call from Dodson—that's a town y'all passed a few miles back. We's up at Winnfield, down the road a bit. Well, uh, see uh the folks at Dodson said a heap o' ni—uh, colored just went through their town in trucks. Said it looked like they was lookin' for trouble. Said Winnfield better watch out. So we thought we'd just stop you boys, have a talk. Didn't mean no harm. They's the ones—back at Dodson—said y'all looked like you was lookin' for trouble. If you want t'go back there—"

"We would like to pass through," said Stephen.

"Yes, well, boys, you heard the soldier—uh, clear the way."

Rapidly men pushed wooden barricades aside, jumped into cars and tractors and trucks, backed them up, drove them forward, got them out of the way.

Wilderness honked two short, clear blasts. He shifted into gear and started his truck forward. The second truck stayed in place, its weapon insistent.

The line of trucks passed one by one, under the protection of the gun.

The last two trucks also had their tarps pulled back showing the same deadly fixtures. As they pulled up even with the broken line of vigilantes, their air-cooled barrels swung around keeping a fix on their adversaries, allowing the number two truck to pull in at the rear of the column, its gun also swinging around as it came abreast of and then passed the tattered assembly. The gunner kept them in his sights until the road took them from his field of vision.

A mile later, tarp back in place, the number two truck pulled out to move up the column and regain its place in line. A steady cheer and a pounding on the metal doors issued from each and every truck it passed.

* * *

Wilderness talked and laughed as they covered the few remaining miles to Fort Polk.

Stephen sat very quietly.

He had still been afraid. Despite all his preparation, the fear had still come. Terrible, heavy fear. He could not lift it off himself. Fear.

He shook his head.

God.

What the hell is wrong with me?

Still . . . he had been able to speak. After a fashion he had been able to act . . . able at least to say enough words, to move his head enough, to get them past the barricade.

That was something.

That was something anyway.

Not much, Lieutenant Wenders, he said to himself, not much.

He looked at Wilderness, thankful for him, dependent on him.

10

The weapons and ammunition were delivered and sequestered at Fort Polk without incident. By six-thirty in the evening the mechanics were going over the trucks before refueling, making sure they were ready for the run back to the war games area.

The lieutenants who had negotiated the deal with Wilderness were in seventh heaven.

Lieutenant Taylor got Wilderness and Stephen off to themselves.

"Hey, we owe you cats our lives," he said. "Let us take your whole outfit into town tonight. On us. Let's celebrate together. You're one hell of an outfit. We want to acknowledge that. We want to let you know that we won't let you down."

"So . . . where's town," asked Stephen, "Alexandria?"

"Where else?"

Stephen and Wilderness both laughed.

"Hey, look, Taylor," said Stephen. "Maybe almost any other place. But we already had one little date with destiny on our way down here. We don't want to push it. Alexandria is off limits to our whole platoon."

"Says who?"

"Says our commanding officer," grinned Wilderness, pointing at Stephen.

"Alright," said Taylor. "But we're going in. This is too good not to celebrate. Look, your men can sleep in our quarters. We won't be back until sun-up. So stay here. Don't leave while we're gone. We want to give you a righteous send-off."

"Well, it won't be hard to convince us to spend the night," said Stephen. "We're beat."

"Good. Let me show you to your quarters."

* * *

Reggie Taylor bent down to whisper in Stephen's ear. "Wenders."

Stephen was instantly awake. He touched Taylor's arm to let him know.

"Light sleeper, huh?"

"When I'm on duty, yes."

"Look, man, I don't know how you want t'handle this, but you may want t'get your cats out quick. As I figure, there won't be any send-off."

"Why? What happened?" Stephen sat up.

"It's started," said Reggie. "We went to Alexandria and as usual the crackers were fuckin' with us. As usual, we didn't take no shit and we kicked a few of 'em up the ass. As usual, they called the MPs. But not as usual, this time the MPs couldn't handle us. See, we knew what we had waiting at home—thanks to you cats."

Stephen nodded. O God. O God.

"So," continued Reggie, "there were about twenty MPs. There were about 400 of us. Twenty of us for each one of them. So we just surrounded them and took their stuff. Their clubs. Their guns. Their jeeps. We arrested the MPs." Reggie giggled uncontrollably for a few seconds. "I'm sorry, man, but it was so funny. We drove their asses out halfway to camp in their own jeeps. Then we kicked them out. We told them we were tired of their messing with us when they should have been taking our side against those peckerwood civilians. We told them if they thought they were in bad shape now, they hadn't seen anything compared to the next time they fucked with us.

102

"Then we drove off and left them there, left them standing in the road without any guns, ammunition, clubs, or handcuffs. We drove a few more miles, ditched the jeeps—took off the distributors and yanked the fuel lines. Then we made it on back to camp."

Stephen stood up. "Well, you're right," he said. "It's going to happen."

"What are you cats gonna do?"

"I don't know," said Stephen. "we'll have to call a staff meeting."

"Well. . . ." Reggie extended his hand. "I wanted to let you know so you'd have plenty of time."

"Thanks."

Stephen took his hand. They both gripped hard.

"I've got t'go spread the alert," said Reggie.

They parted.

* * *

Directly in front of the rectangle of buildings which was the home of the 6666th Infantry Regiment stood a huge parade ground. On either side of the parade ground were the sidewalls of the barracks belonging to the 1333rd Engineers Battalion and the 5432nd Anti-Aircraft Battalion respectively.

When Stephen brought his trucks to the edge of the parade ground, except for his platoon, there was no motion visible in his whole field of vision.

He sent half of his trucks to the far side of the parade ground. The other half he kept with him. The trucks were parked at thirty foot intervals, facing the parade ground beginning at the second half of the parade ground from the 6666th's quarters. Both ends of both lines of trucks were anchored by vehicles with machine guns mounted on top. Each weapon was responsible for covering half the line of hostile troops which might appear before it. The guns stayed covered as the men of the third platoon sat and waited through a cool afternoon.

Around four in the afternoon a strange stillness descended on the area.

After a while, Stephen realized that the effect of stillness was produced by a vast, muffled sound, somewhere else.

The white commanders of the 6666th must have realized what produced the effect about the same time, for they went scrambling out onto the parade ground. They lined up in the middle of the field, facing the infantry's quarters. The junior officers among them ran back to the barracks banging on the respective doors, shouting:

"Fall in on line! Fall in on line!"

The noise they made screened the sounds Stephen had heard earlier. From his vantage point high in the cab of the truck, he surveyed the approach to the grounds, but he could see nothing. Everywhere except for the 6666th's barracks and parade grounds, immobility greeted his eye.

The white officers had returned to the field, facing their respective company and battalion positions. The regimental officers held their positions in the center of the field. Rigid. Erect.

The men of the 6666th began spilling out of their barracks and racing for their places.

Stephen still had his ear cocked for the slight rumble and clank of tanks. Then it dawned on him. Base command did not expect these men to be armed. They would not send tanks.

Surprise is always an ally. He remembered the axiom from OCS. They will meet more than they reckoned on, he thought. We have pitched our first strike.

He turned back to the infantry piling into their formations all across the field.

What struck him was not the quick and orderly arrangement of the men as they spilled from the streams issuing out of the long, low barracks. Though it pleased his eye he was not jolted by the neat little rows and columns into which the disorderly flood of men transformed itself.

What caught him was the shock, the disbelief, the stark fear on the officers' faces.

They too had harbored not the slightest suspicion that their men would be armed, armed not only with operable weapons, but also with full complements of ammunition.

When the anti-tank platoons and the cannon company also arrived armed to the teeth with regulation hardware, the officers' incredulity assumed a nightmarish quality.

The lines of officers stood facing their men as if they faced an alien monster hatched on some far off world of terror and destruction.

Stephen looked across the ranks of steel-helmeted men. They stretched across the width of the whole parade ground. Deep, they reached from the middle of the field back to the regimental headquarters building. Row, after row, after row, they ordered their arms, rifle barrels slanting past their shoulders. They stood rank on rank, battalions, companies, platoons, sections, squads.

Their company guidons fluttered in the wind. Their faces were set. Arrayed before him Stephen saw more than sixty armed platoons on combat alert.

He heard then, clearly, the sound which had come to him so faintly earlier. Marching boots. Many marching boots. Then he saw them. His vantage point showed him each flank of men in full battle gear as it swung by column march onto the parade ground.

A quick glance through his field glasses told him

that the commanding officer was a colonel.

A regiment, he thought. They've sent a regiment to arrest a regiment and two battalions. What happened to concentration of forces?

I guess they just figured—a bunch of niggers, who needs overwhelming force? Unarmed niggers at that.

Surprise. Surprise.

Strike two.

As the flanks of the arresting infantry, the 111th Regiment, trod onto the field, the officers of the 6666th, at command of their colonel, about-faced and presented their ashen faces to their oncoming counterparts.

The commander of the 111th, not yet having recognized how the troops facing him were equipped, passed off the ghastly palor and stricken expressions of his colleagues to the disgrace of men about to see their whole command arrested and probably court-martialed.

Another element which had entered the awareness of the 6666th's commanding officer and which contributed even further to his discomforture and no less to that of his other white officers was that now all those rifles were at their backs.

Here was no time to do or say the wrong thing.

Incongruous against his bloodless face, sweat began to slide down his temples and cheeks.

The commander of the 111th brought his men to a halt and stepped forward.

Moving forward after having momentarily stopped, his eyes reoriented themselves. They picked out the gunbarrels.

Without thinking he looked for the bolts.

Present.

His eyes leaped to the face of his opposite number. He understood now, fully, the real reasons for the drained complexion, the widened eyes, the tortured face, even the sweat spreading on his collar.

The words he was about to utter froze in his throat.

As he swallowed he realized that his men were defenseless.

"Lock and load," he bellowed.

He heard the reassuring sound of 5,000 men complying instantly to his command.

"Lock and load," yelled the commander of the 6666th.

The response, just as quick, was louder.

The men on top of Stephen's four armed trucks slammed home their bolts.

Wilderness touched Stephen on the shoulder. "This is where the deal go down," he said.

Stephen nodded. He could not stop his hands from shaking, but they did their work. He pulled his service pistol out of its holster and checked the clip.

The 111th's commander had started to sweat.

The men in his command had heard the answering loading of the men facing them. Their reaction had been almost visible. They had been told the niggers were unarmed. The men in the front ranks could see not only the determined expressions on the faces of the men opposite them, they could also see the leveled anti-tank guns on the flanks.

Hey—we didn't bring our anti-tank men. As if by spontaneous generation the thought raced simultaneously through scores of heads. We're understrength!

The men of the 111th found their rifles slippery in their grasps.

They had been told to come over here to scare the shit out of a bunch of unarmed niggers and to arrest them. Nobody had told them to get ready to die.

The commander of the 111th felt his uniform getting too small for him. He recognized the symptom. He knew about fear. He had fought in the Ardennes in World War I. He had been serving as an observer in Paris when the Germans had made their armored thrust across northern France in 1940. He knew that he could not wait on it or it would take him over. He stood, as the commanding officer, ahead of his men—alone—his chest a target for a volley of over 5,000 bullets.

He thrust his right arm forward. Pointing with his index finger, he shouted.

"Arrest those men!"

The guidons fluttered in the breeze.

A tarp on top of a truck rustled.

Not a soul moved.

The commander of the 111th did an about face. He looked at his men.

A long time leader of men, what he saw was clear.

They were not going to move.

Strike three. You're out.

He turned them around and marched them off the field.

That night, when Stephen was sure that the controls around the base had been lifted, he led his little convoy back to Arkansas.

11

Once Stephen stepped inside the armory, he knew the jig was up. Taking up an appreciable amount of floor space were piles of gasoline cans, stacks of tires, heaps of canvass, and unopened cases of brand-new carburetors.

He recognized the haul right away. It formed the contents of one of Third Platoon's dumps. Stephen walked over to the other officers.

"Ten—hut!"

The officers snapped to attention.

The base commander, a brigadier, strode in.

"As you were," he said. "Senior officers on your left, junior officers on your right."

All the white officers moved to their left, all the Black ones to their right.

"At ease, men."

The general glared at the group.

"Gentlemen, your battalion has the most disgraceful record it has ever been my displeasure to oversee.

"I know it is not your fault, Major Atcheson. For your information, gentlemen, Major Atcheson has one of the most distinguished service records in this man's army. The blame must rest squarely where it belongs—on his subordinate officers and on the men of this battalion.

"I have determined that this reprehensible state of affairs cannot and shall not continue. Especially after the vaudevillean performance of the past ten days.

"If that had been an actual combat mission our armored infantry would have been wiped out for want of ammunition and fuel. Do you understand that!

"And then, we had a reconnaissance platoon here for special training and what should they find, but this—"

He pointed to the heaping mounds of material behind him.

"I had not the slightest idea where it had come from—or put more accurately—who had put it there, since it had to have come from our supplies. And after long and detailed questioning of many, many soldiers, what unit should appear as the only possible culprit—C Company, C Company of the 4748th Quartermaster truck battalion—the very worst truck company in this entire Corps Area!

"I am flabbergasted. You are not only incapable of following the most elementary assignment, you are also guilty of pilfering from your own government!"

Captain Fandley and Lieutenant Freeman turned bright red. They had not the slightest idea of what the general was talking about. But they felt deep shame. They were guilty. They had to be guilty because of the way he was hollering.

"I could call for a general court-martial of the whole, rotten, shit-pile of you. But I'm not going to bother. It would waste too much time and money on the part of the army, and in this kind of thing, after all that effort—the evidence is usually inconclusive at best. So you're spared that. I have a better solution for you stinking son-of-a-bitches!"

Lieutenant Lang, the weak-link among C Company's Negro officers, flapped his lips silently. He had an almost irresistible impulse to speak out, but flanked as he was by his brother second lieutenants, he did not dare. He slapped his lips together and trembled with humiliation.

"All this is over," the general roared on. "I'm breaking up this stinking mess.

"Tom, you'll finally get something you deserve. You're being transferred out of here for Airborne train-

110

ing at Fort Benning. Your next command will be Airborne."

Major Atcheson could not repress his smile. His face flushed. He nodded to the general.

"The rest of you assholes," the brigadier glared at the white officers, "you never did these troops any good and you're not going to start now. You all have orders posting you away from this unit."

The lifting of tension among the white officers was almost visible. They wanted to shout for joy.

"The junior officers of the 4748th will stay attached to their respective platoons," said the brigadier, "but the 4748th as an organic unit will no longer exist.

"A Company, B Company and D Company will become training cadres. You haven't learned a damn thing, but you've been in training long enough yourselves to qualify as cadres. We need truckers bad, so we've got to activate more training cadres, and at least in training units you won't cost anybody's life.

"But C Company—you're such a scummy outfit, I wouldn't trust you to train a pig to eat. You are a disgrace to the country, the army, the uniform, your outfit, and your race. I would *never* put you in a position of training other men. You are incompetent, and I believe, irredeemable.

"You will be shipped to a POE for embarkation to the MTO. Maybe the Nazis and Wops will blow your asses up in a hurry and save us all a lot of worry—because with your record, within three days after your de-embarkation you should be lost miles behind enemy lines, your equipment broken down, and no longer our burden.

"At any rate, I shall be held faultless for sending you there, as they are so pressed for truckers over there that they are now pulling men who don't know how to drive into trucking units as drivers. I think I can say without equivocation that your incompetence cannot be greater than theirs—at least at the start of their training. In any case, you shall now be the problem of the MTO, not ours. They have enough problems so that one more small, company-sized problem should not be too much of a burden for them to bear.

"Goodbye to your whole, filthy battalion, and good riddance.

"Dismissed!"

12

Members of C Company were furloughed for two weeks before they were to report to their next duty post, Fort Dix, New Jersey.

The evening before they scattered, Stephen called all the members of Third Platoon together in a secluded pine grove.

They sang a chorus of "We Are Soldiers in the Army," and laughed, and their eyes watered, and they hugged each other and felt warm together, Third Platoon, thirty-odd men in the Southern twilight.

Then with Wilderness standing beside him as first sergeant, Stephen brought them to attention.

He could not explain it, and if asked to describe it, he would have failed, but as his eyes rested on each man, he knew how that man laughed and how he frowned. He knew the way he carried himself and the set of his shoulders. He knew the timbre of his voice and whether he was quick or slow to anger.

"Gentlemen," he said, "tomorrow we'll separate for a short while. We will go to friends and family. Many of us will go home. We will go back to the lives we knew before. For a time. For a time. We will do what we have talked, and dreamed, and planned of doing for so long. And we will do it with great intensity. Because we will not have long before we're back together again. Back as a unit. Back as Third Platoon of C Company. Because that is what we have become.

"We are different men from what we were a year ago. And when we go back home, when we go back to our friends and families, we will not see them as we did before, because we have been changed.

"We have been changed by the United States Army. We have been changed by Camp Robinson. But most of all, we have been changed by what we have been through together and what we have meant to each other.

"As I said, we have become a unit. Together, we have stood up against this army. Together, we have stood up against the prejudice and hate and humiliation of our fellow citizens. Together, we have become the best trucking outfit in this man's army and we know it!

"We have needed each other. We will continue to need each other. Because though others may talk about it, we live up to it—we live by it—the fact that *No Man is an Island*. No man stands alone. We count on each other. We trust each other. And that trust has never been broken.

"I don't know what we'll be in for when we come back, but I know what we've been through. I know where we've been. I know what they've tried to do to us, and I know that they have failed. We have left our tire tracks on every highway, every road, every path, every trail in Southern Arkansas. We have hauled material the army didn't know it had to places it still doesn't know exist. We have fooled generals, and colonels, and majors, and captains, and red-necked cracker farmers. We have brought arms to our brothers across every obstacle the devil could devise and stood beside them, arm in arm, while they faced down a regiment!

"You can't tell me that we're not the best trucking outfit in this army. And you can't tell me that we haven't seen combat!"

Stephen paused. He looked over his men. He loved them. It was a strange way to feel about a bunch of men he had not even known a year earlier. But it was true.

He loved them. He nodded to Wilderness who reached into the satchel he held at his side.

"I have called you together this evening because although the army may not recognize it, we recognize that we have already been at war, and we believe that our service should be commemorated.

"The U.S. Army is supposed to award a battle star for service in a field of operations under enemy fire.

"Since the army has been negligent in this instance, we are making our own award."

Wilderness placed something in his hand.

Stephen held his palm out vertically so that the object could be seen clearly in the middle of it.

It was a small, black cross, each end of which was pointed, like the end of a battle star.

"This," he said, "is the Southern Cross, awarded for combat duty in hostile territory in the STO, the Southern Theater of Operations.

"Sergeant Bynam. Will you please step forward."

Each man who stepped forward, saluted. Stephen returned the salute, looked into his eyes, pinned on the Southern Cross, and shook his hand.

"Congratulations," he said.

I know you, he felt.

Farewell, they saluted.

13

Stephen spent the first week of his furlough with Evelyn. It was a very hard time for them both because they knew he was going away, but that was not what they wanted to think about. They wanted to know only that they were together and to live every moment of being together and for there to be nothing else in the world and no other time, past or future.

Stephen loved to let their lips cling together and peel off each other slowly, like tape from a wound. It seemed to stretch the kisses out so that they lasted almost without ending. Though pleasurable time does appear to go faster than normal time, Stephen and Evelyn crammed so much living and doing and feeling into those days that they hoped to reverse the process, that in retrospect those days would seem to have lasted 500 years.

They were afraid of the separation because it might mean they would never see each other again. It was their great fear, but they did not mention it, neither of them. Instead, they held each other and felt each other and touched each other and kissed each other and listened to each other and talked to each other. They knew that Stephen might never come back but they did not say that, they breathed each other's breath, and fed each other, and slept late in the mornings on top of each other's arms.

He marveled at the darkness of her eyes and tried to will them inside himself because he knew he might never see them again. And she, too, wanted them to become one person as a guarantee that they would not forever be parted. But they both knew that he might die, or he might think less and less of her until he almost forgot her, or he might meet someone else, or she might simply write him for any number of reasons to tell him never to return, so that the wilderness was full of dangers which might keep him away and never permit him to come back.

The morning he left on the train he was glad it was a jim-crow train because he would not want white people to see him crying, a grown man, a soldier, a lieutenant, a leader of men decorated with the Southern Cross and crying over a little girl so beautiful she hurt your heart.

She neither knew nor cared that the train was jim-crow. She hated it because it was taking the insides out of her life. She did not care who saw her crying because she was not conscious of her tears, the pain that filled her from the inside was jealous and would admit of no other awareness.

* * *

Stephen arrived in Chicago on Christmas Day. Everyone was at Twelfth Street to greet him—Mama, Virginia, Wynfried, Electa, and Electa's little Gabriel, now two years old.

Stephen went out a few times to see friends, and three or four people came to see him. But he spent most of the time closeted with his mother, sisters, and nephew. It was cold outside and ice and dirty snow covered all walking surfaces. The house was warm and cozy, and the company, though over solicitous, was fun and tender.

He waited until his last night to drop his big news. His sisters had all gone off to put Gabriel to bed and to read him a bed-time story.

Stephen and Mama-Ruth sat alone in the living room.

Stephen knelt down and looked through the glass

door at the fire. He picked up the hand shovel, scooped up a shovel-full of coal from the coal-bucket, opened the door and slid the coal expertly to just the right place at the back of the fire.

He put the shovel back in the bucket.

He closed the door and slapped his hands off. He peered into the fire.

"Mama," he said. "They're sending our unit overseas."

He could not tell if the silence lasted long, or if it were the sharpness of it that made it seem that way.

"What," she said. "I thought you were going to New Jersey. You'd be near your sister. What's the name of that place. . . ."

"Fort Dix."

"Yes," she said. "Fort Dix. You said that's where you were going."

"We are. But after that we'll be going overseas."

"Oh," she felt relieved. If they were going to be there for a while anything might happen. Everyone said they were always talking about sending colored overseas, but they never did. Stephen had stayed in that Arkansas camp five months and at first he was always writing back saying they were going overseas. They never did, though, and after a while, he stopped writing about it. She felt better. They were really going to Fort Dix, not overseas. Overseas would come later, if it ever did.

Stephen was getting hot, kneeling so close to the fire.

"It's true this time, Mama," he said. "Fort Dix is a place where they send soldiers before they leave from an Atlantic port—because it's on the east coast. Our unit has already been ordered overseas."

She could not stand the thought. She tried to put it away from her.

Stephen stood up. He could not take the heat anymore. He walked back to the couch and sat down.

118

He looked at the Christmas tree. It was beautiful. Some of the decorations were old, from his earliest recollections of Christmas in Evanston. He had put many of them on the tree in earlier years. A few were his favorites; he had always coveted them and made sure he was the one to hang them on the tree. A few times he had even been required to fight one of his sisters to retain the honor. There were new decorations that he did not recognize, recently purchased. One had been brought ostentatiously by Wynfried from D.C. Stephen did not know how many times she had pointed it out to him in all its garish glory.

He smiled. A tree in the house. It never failed to surprise him—every year. It was gloriously irrational—a tree in the house. Trees are for outdoors. How absurd to have one inside, how magically absurd.

Mama-Ruth was thinking. Last week for the first time she had seen one of those service flags with a gold star in a window. It had scared her so she had stood on the street and stared at it in front of a stranger's house. It was real. It was hard for her to accept what that flag said. How could it be true?

Their son had been pulled out of their house, that very house she stood in front of, pulled out and sent across the oceans to some country he probably never even heard of, and he was killed. Why? Why?

She had stared at the window, but it had not answered her.

Why?

How could such a thing happen?

What sense did it make?

She, too, had a son.

That was not ever the kind of homecoming she could bear for him: a gold star on a service flag in the window.

"I thought you would want to tell the girls," he said. "I wanted you to know first."

Return to My Native Land

"No, we have never been amazons at the court of the King of Dahomey, nor princes of Ghana with eight hundred camels, nor doctors at Timbuktu when Askia the Great was king, nor architects at Djenne, nor Madhis, nor warriors. We do not feel in our armpits the itch of those who once carried the lance."

*Return to My
Native Land*

Aimé Cèsaire

1

Captain Barley did not assemble his officers until his exec had reported for duty. That was three weeks after C Company's arrival at Fort Dix.

When Captain Barley met with his new exec the captain's only concern seemed to be that the men got good food and plenty of it. "Chow, that's the key," he said. "See that the men eat well. Yessir, our chow times are going to be good times."

The exec was a first lieutenant named Acorn.

Captain Barley ran the first meeting of the company's officers through Acorn.

Acorn stood in front of the six seated officers and talked while Barley sat behind him in a chair, staring at the lieutenant's back.

"Good morning, Gentlemen," said Acorn. "I want to introduce you to your new C.O., Captain Thomas Barley." He stepped to the side so the officers could see Captain Barley sitting in his chair.

Barley promptly moved his chair to the side so that he stayed behind the lieutenant.

"I am First Lieutenant Acorn," Acorn continued. "And the company has two new first lieutenants— Lieutenants Overmayer and Havershram." He nodded to the two very young, very green, very inexperienced gentlemen in question who both blushed.

"I think everyone else has been with the unit since its formation and are familiar with one another.

"Captain Barley has prepared a statement which he has asked me to read."

"Ordered," said Barley in a low and barely audible voice.

"Excuse me," said Acorn. "Ordered me to read."

He looked down at the sheets of paper which he had all along been holding in front of him.

"I have been called to this post because I am the best man for the job," the statement began. "I did not seek it. It was thrust upon me because of my excellent record. I do not intend to stay here long (it is my belief that no officer should be required to spend more than one short tour of duty with Negro troops—a view shared, by the way, by two of my uncles in the War Department who are pressing this view on the Department and the Army at every turn)."

Very interesting proposition, thought Stephen. The statement presumes there is no such thing as a Negro officer since I'm sure the good captain did not mean to imply that Negro officers should spend one short tour of duty with Negro troops and spend the rest of their time commanding white troops. Serving under this man is going to be a thing of beauty and a joy forever.

Acorn continued to read, "I do not intend to stay long, but while this company is under my command, I expect it to do an about-face and turn in a superior performance rating.

"I can say categorically that you junior officers have established a record for which you can feel only shame. And I am here to tell you that you'd better ship up or I'll bust you all back to private. Therefore, it is mandatory that you follow my instructions to the letter. No exceptions.

"Now, we are not authorized here to engage in military exercises, but we can and will establish military discipline. Every day we will have inspection, drill, and parade. We will continue that routine shipboard. By the time we reach the MTO I expect this to be the snappiest troop in the Quartermaster Corps.

"You can tell your men that they will be rewarded for their effort. We will eat well, very well.

"All my orders shall be issued through the executive officer. Any communications or questions you may have for me shall be directed through the executive officer. Do not speak to me unless you are spoken to. I maintain a closed-door policy at all times.

"You are dismissed."

Stephen wanted to get one, good, clear look at the captain before he left the room. He wanted to know what a genuine asshole looked like. But as the captain remained squared up behind the exec, all Stephen's twisting and peering and dipping and craning proved to no avail.

2

The sun was high by the time Stephen managed to wangle his way on deck. He stood against the railing sniffing the fresh sea air, enjoying the way it felt on his face, and watching the seemingly unending run of waves.

The sounds of the ship crashing against the water drowned out his thoughts. He became entirely a column of sensory receptors, at one with the rhythms and sights and sounds and sensations and smells of the day. He stood thus transformed for a long, long time.

The breeze that came off the land caught him by surprise. But there could be no mistaking it, the breeze was blowing out from shore. It was warm and it brought with it scents that had never touched Stephen's nostrils.

Africa.

He sniffed the winds to be sure.

Yes. Never in my life have I smelled that.

Africa.

He strained his eyes on the horizon for a long time. He did not know how much time had passed before he was sure that the light line at the end of his field of vision was land.

He locked his eyes on it. Land. He stood transfixed. His head was very light.

Without warning, without his understanding at all, he was sobbing. It came on him so swiftly that before he could arouse himself to fight it, the great tearing insight that swept up from somewhere so deep within him that it had lain hidden even from himself had taken hold of his body, shaking it, had seized his tear ducts, opened them, and poured water down his face.

Caught as if by a sudden breach in a dyke, he gave way to the power of his emotions.

For a long time he stood grasping the railing, shuddering under the force of his ancient pain. He could not raise his head. Until his consciousness spoke to him and told him no matter how sweet the hurt, it could not be long endured.

He squeezed in hard on himself. It was a while before he could wipe his face and eyes, sniff in the dribblings from his nose. He looked down at the water for a long time and held on. He had to keep bearing down. He knew if he relaxed for an instant he would be swept away again.

When at last he raised his eyes again there was no question that the unanswering horizon stretching from North to South was land.

Someone stood at his elbow.

Stephen turned his head to see who it was.

Ahasuerus.

People had thought he was a Communist at OCS. A University of Chicago scholar. Sensitive. Analytical. Like all the other platoon leaders in C Company, he and his men had been victimized by the Black Cross' ventures—sent out of the safety of training duty in the U.S. to foreign war. Stephen felt a responsibility for his friend. And hurt. He's African, too, he thought.

"I should have known you'd find a way to get up here," said Stephen.

"I see I'm not alone."

Stephen smiled.

They both stared at the distant edges of the great continent.

"Do you know the poem by Countee Cullen?" asked

Stephen.

Ahasuerus did not answer directly. Instead, he recited.

> " 'What is Africa to me:
>   Copper sun or scarlet sea,
>   Jungle star or jungle track,
>   Strong bronzed men, or regal black
>   Women from whose Loins I sprang
>   When the birds of Eden sang?
>   *One three centuries removed*
>   *From the scenes his fathers loved,*
>   *Spicy grove, cinnamon tree,*
>   *What is Africa to me?*' "

They heard the water smashing into the ship and rushing along the hull. The strange smell, now, was very strong.

3

Stephen had seen Casablanca from the sea, a beautiful, whitewashed city with long breakwaters and a lighthouse. On shore he encountered its living realities and plunged bodily into the pungent odors no longer diluted by wind and ocean swells.

Dark men assaulted them on all sides, men of all ages. Boys, teenagers, young men, middle-aged men, old men ran up to him, ran after him, begging, complaining, wheedling, selling. For the most part he could not understand their words, but he understood their elaborate gestures and expressions. They wore raggedy clothes and smelled foul. Though most of their heads and bodies were covered with rags, their faces were not and they exhibited a wide variety of colors and features, just as would the population of any Negro neighborhood in the states. It was only later that Stephen learned the Americans referred to all these people as Arabs. Some were clearly no more Arab than he was. Others were obviously mixtures of Arabs and Black-Africans. But the Americans in their racial chauvinism could see no differences between these dark-skinned peoples. The old cliché, "They all look alike," was in full force. Foolishly, Stephen had assumed that his countrymen would be able to see that just because all these dark-skinned people spoke Arabic did not mean that they all had the same racial origins. He thought that any fool could see that many, many of them shared a heritage with him and were no more Arab because they spoke Arabic than he was English. It was so plain. These were probably the people his Grandma Goodie referred to in her lineage as Moorish Africans.

It amused and fascinated Stephen to think he might be related to the surging crowds of beggars, cheats, thieves, and louts. Except for a freak of history I might be they, and they might be me, he thought. He could not help staring at them. This only excited their interest, as the best way to avoid them was to ignore them. To pay them the slightest bit of attention was to invite their overtures.

Ahasuerus caught up with Stephen. "Come on, Wenders," he said, "stop standing around goggle-eyed. They're going to steal the clothes off your body before you've gone half a mile.

"Just think, if the white man had not already done so much for us, we'd be just like these poor souls. Ragged, filthy, poor, illiterate, good-for-nothing heathens, unable to speak the English language. But as you see, due to the intercession of the Great White Father, we are well-housed, well-clothed, well-fed scholars—and you and I in particular have the advantage of being officers in the American Army, with men at our command and able to drive monstrous trucks. By the way, Wenders, where are our trucks?"

The men of C Company learned three days later that while they had been off-loaded in Casablanca, their trucks had been sent around to Oran.

This news was not terribly distressing to Stephen who wanted to stay away from areas of active hostility as long as humanly possible. It did, however, leave him with grave doubts about the efficiency of the command to which he and his men had been committed.

Ever since Third Platoon had shown up at Fort Dix wearing their Southern Cross decorations, the other platoons of C Company had nick-named them the Black

Cross Platoon. The men liked the name and it stuck. In Casablanca, while the other platoons of C Company allowed themselves to be exhausted and prostrated by the heat, through Wilderness' wheedling the Black Cross was on port security, guarding army supplies.

As tightly disciplined and as well trained as the men of the Black Cross were, army losses were cut considerably. As vast as the storage area was and as diverse as were the arrays of supplies, there were still some losses. Nevertheless, the weekly totals of identified pilferage were reduced by eighty percent. At the same time, the special treasury of the Black Cross developed a new source of revenue.

The pilferage which continued was strictly regulated and administered through the apparatus of the Black Cross. The platoon was not greedy. It kept losses minimal, but even so, a tiny portion of such a vast flow of goods resulted in a prodigious windfall.

The commander of Port Operations eventually discovered that C Company was lollygagging in his jurisdiction, enjoying unseemly privileges, and got them busy unloading ships. The Black Cross had to take its turns on this miserable duty with the rest of the platoons. Never one to be undone, Wilderness found a way to turn even that back-breaking agony to his unit's advantage.

"See, the shit come in with code numbers and letters on the crates," he told Stephen. "Well, for security they always changin' the codes. But the port operations, they don't know what the new codes is. They changin' them at the other end. So ships full of stuff comes in and don't nobody know what it is. They just says, 'store it.' By the time the code done come in they done forgot where they put the stuff.

"Sometimes they sends the stuff without no invoices."

"What do you mean?"

"Mean just what I said. Sometimes a whole ship will come in without no sign of what the cargo is. They just unloads it. Don't have the leastest idea what they unloadin'. Just says, 'store it.'"

"Well, where are the invoices?"

"Oh, they be sent somewhere else. I don't know. Nobody do. Maybe Oran. Maybe London. Maybe Texas. We gets invoices, too, without no cargo. Don't have no idea where the cargo is at. Just a big list of code numbers and letters and no ship with nothing like it in the harbor."

"But, now the Black Cross know what's in every one o' them crates we unloaded," said Wilderness.

"How?"

"We just rips one of 'em open and takes a look."

"That's all?"

"Uh huh."

"Then why doesn't the port command do that?"

"It's security regulation. They cain't."

"Oh, you mean security keeps changing the codes on them, the result is they don't know what they're getting. The purpose of this comedy of errors is to thwart enemy espionage, while enemy espionage can do just what you've done and rip a case open, but operations can't do that because it would violate security?"

"Now you're talkin'," said Wilderness. "Plus, it wouldn't do the port authority no good to know what the cargo is noway."

"Why's that?"

"Without the code and without the invoices they wouldn't know where they was supposed to ship it. So what if they got fifty crates of truck rear-axles? Where they supposed to send 'em? Without them invoices or code instructions they just gon' sit up here anyways. Even the food. They don't know who's supposed to get the food, so it's just gon' sit up here and rot. 'Course, they don't know which cases is food and which is axles cause they ain't op'nin' none. But we takin' care of all that now."

"Good," said Stephen. "It's all been worked into the operation?"

"Uh huh. Ain't another box of K-rations gon' go bad."

4

Occasionally, the Black Cross was assigned to guard POWs. Stephen could not get over how they looked like all other white boys he had seen—whether in Chicago, Winnetka, Witonkin, Florida, Arkansas, or even Frenchmen from Casablanca. They looked the same. That does not mean that he believed they all looked exactly alike and were indistinguishable, but that if they were not dressed in the drab, green uniforms with the big PWs in white on the backs, and were dressed instead in U.S. army uniforms or street clothes and he had seen them on the streets of Casablanca or Evanston or Jacksonville he would not have been able to tell they were not Americans. Some of the prisoners were Germans and some were Italians, but all could have passed for Americans. That amazed Stephen and he frequently stared at them. He could not understand why they were so busy killing each other. He could not understand why they had gone to all this extravagant effort—creating vast, inept bureaucracies; erecting whole industries to create continental arsenals of redundant hardware; conscripting, deluding, rendering imbecilic whole populations in order to kill each other inefficiently in vast numbers.

Why?

They could trade places with each other and nothing would be changed.

He stared at them. White antagonism towards Black people was more comprehensible to his sensibilities. There was that basic physical difference. People seemed to have an irresistible need to feel better than someone else and in race providence had provided a ready-made excuse. But in these whites—all of European extraction, whether in Morocco or America—there were no such physical distinctions. Yet, they were remolding the world, the better to exterminate each other, albeit with a great deal of incompetence.

The enigma was one which dumbfounded Stephen and the sight of the prisoners with their huge PWs on their backs never failed to throw him into a prolonged state of consternation.

He could not believe, as much of the propaganda averred, that they were fighting for various principles, because as far as his observations had revealed, none of them had any principles. He also could not believe, as many cynics proposed, that they were fighting for the wealth of the earth. In the first place, they were too busy destroying it; and in the second place, many of those who were fighting would be killed and never enjoy such wealth, and it was unlikely that they would pursue even great wealth when the risks were so final.

Therefore, Stephen remained in a quandry. The war became a greater mystery to him the closer to it he came, particularly when he saw the primary antagonists face to face.

Private McCauley of the Black Cross was not beset by Stephen's singular anguish, but the whole movement overseas had thrown him into great disarray.

Private McCauley lived for women. He thought only about women. He dreamed only about women. All his wishes, hopes, dreams and aspirations were about women.

His few recorded AWOLs had been over women. His occasional fights were over women. His rare drunken sprees were caused by women. He lived for women.

When he ate, he ate only that he could have more energy for chasing women. When he slept, he slept only that he could grow stronger to chase women. When he read, he read only that he could learn better ways to chase women.

He was not so much a gourmet as he was a gourmand. He loved beautiful women. He loved ugly women. He loved fat women. He loved skinny women. He loved women with hour glass figures and he loved women whose figures defied description. He loved old women and he loved young women. He could not live without them.

That is why he nearly went crazy on the troop transport. McCauley was one of the few members of C Company who did not get sea-sick. He prayed for sea-sickness so he could be relieved of his misery. To no avail. The grotesque days and nights without women stretched out before him interminably. He tried to force sea-sickness upon himself, eating mountainous quantities of food and drinking vats of hard liquor. His digestion remained as smooth as a well-oiled machine.

He decided he would sleep himself into oblivion but he kept being awakened by frightful nightmares that he was trapped on a ship with hundreds of men and no women. By the time the ship reached Casablanca, Stephen was very close to putting him on medical report for hysteria.

Five strong men were required to hold McCauley back from racing down the gang plank and out into the streets of Casablanca. When McCauley finally got ashore his euphoria over being on land, where women resided, was short-lived. He discovered to his horror that in Morocco, a Muslim country, women were secluded. They were not allowed out of their homes unescorted, and when they did appear, they were totally covered, even their faces. After that revelation, McCauley's deterioration was rapid and almost complete.

What saved him was his detection of Vansen's Woman. Private Harvey Vansen was a white infantry private who had been stationed in Casablanca for three and one-half months because his orders had gone astray. He knew where his outfit was. He knew where his buddies were. They had been in the Kasserine Pass before Rommel's troops came through, and afterward they had been running very fast—away from Rommel—across Tunisia. He knew they were in a place called El Guettar and in contact with the enemy, though trying to avoid it as much as possible. None of them had been as successful at avoidance as he, though his winning ways were not due as much to his own skill as to the bungling of the U.S. Army. But though Private Vansen knew where his unit was, he had no intention of attempting to join it until he got his orders. With a little luck that would never happen because it was unlikely that the army even knew his orders had been lost.

After Vansen had been in Morocco about two weeks, he had found His Woman. One of her brothers had been about to kill her for some offense, the nature of which Vansen was never able to understand. Vansen had been wandering through the Arab quarter when he had come upon the spectacle which was about to occur. By gesturing and mimicking with people in the crowd, Vansen had finally raised someone who spoke English. This new-found acquaintance explained the thrilling event they were all about to witness. Hating violence, being naturally chivalrous, and also being in desperate need of sexual fulfillment, Vansen got the English-speaking Arab to intercede on his behalf and he was able to buy the woman. Apparently selling her to a foreigner took the onus off the family, placed there by her earlier actions.

She did not cost much—thirty-five dollars, U.S.—but after that Vansen had the responsibility as well as the joy of owning her.

He knew that when he finally got his orders—if he ever did—he would have to sell her. He could not take her with him and she could not go back to her family. He doubted that would be a problem. There were plenty of slave-traders around as well as G.I.s. She knew she would be sold when he left and this was no problem with her. She was simply happy to be alive. Regardless of what might have been expected of her, she had not been looking forward to sacrificing her life for the family honor. She did not understand English when Vansen met her, but she was intelligent, learned quickly, and she understood signs and gestures very well. They lived in a small house just on the edge of the Arab quarter.

McCauley found them like a hyena finds bad meat. One woman in the city had great potential for accessibility to an American. McCauley found her. His frenzy carried him into every section of the city. There were women available, of course, but the language barrier and unfamiliarity with the city and its customs made them invisible to the newly arrived American Negroes. One day, as McCauley roamed crazed through the city, he came across Vansen and His Woman shopping in a bazaar. The incongruous sight of the American soldier and the Arab woman clicked in his demented brain. He zeroed in on them then and there. Race made no difference to him. Though Vansen had never known a Negro personally, he had no strong racial antipathies. In McCauley's maniacal condition, all of his guile sprang to his service, and in a matter of minutes he had charmed Vansen and become his most intimate friend. He managed his seduction of Vansen with such legerdemain that Vansen did not recognize that McCauley was physically incapable of taking his eyes off Vansen's Woman.

McCauley quickly learned what would happen when Vansen got his orders and he lived for that day. In the meanwhile he spent every second he could in Vansen's house. Although Vansen did not notice, His Woman could not help recognizing the naked lust in McCauley's eyes. He literally drooled in her presence.

He brought them things, wondrous gifts which Vansen could never have managed. He came always with gifts, and extra little things for Vansen's Woman, because he was already thinking of her as his woman. He was living in the future since the present was unendurable.

McCauley learned to eat couscous and other exotic dishes. He loved them. He loved them all because he loved Vansen's Woman. He even learned to love Arab music because she loved it and he became a devout Muslim without knowing what a Muslim was.

McCauley had only one serious concern. Vansen's orders did not come. The non-arriving orders developed into an obsession with McCauley. He began to believe that there was a conspiracy not to send Vansen his orders so that he could never have Vansen's Woman. He brooded and wept over the non-arriving orders, twisting in anguish as he lay on his lonely bed.

Finally, desperation seized McCauley. He knew he could not last much longer. His hand had begun to reach out surreptitiously towards the folds of Vansen's Woman's flowing garments. He had not been able to stop it. The hand had never touched even so much as a hem, but he had not been able to control its relentless advances.

McCauley wrote up orders for Vansen and had them delivered by courier. Vansen was not surprised. He had been amazed that his good luck had lasted as long as it had. He had never seen the kind of paper the orders were typed on. For some reason it reminded him of the Quartermaster Corps, but since they had been delivered by an official courier, he never questioned them. He accepted the inevitable. He was also surprised that the orders called for him to leave the very next day, early in the morning. They provided no means of transportation but instructed him to get over to Ben Chebka as fast as he could the best way he could, as he was long overdue. Vansen rushed around and found some Arab merchants who were going in that direction to do business with the U.S. troops and arranged passage with them. After taking care of that critical matter he returned home to make arrangements for his personal effects, including selling his woman to McCauley. McCauley had long ago secured that right by paying Vansen $100.00 for the option to buy her. Vansen sold her to McCauley for $250.00, making a net profit of $315.00 on the transaction.

Vansen retained the right of his last night in town with His Woman. This was distressing to McCauley who could not bear to leave his new possession. Nevertheless, they were the only terms under which Vansen would conclude the deal. McCauley had no alternative but to agree to them. He spent the night sleeping on the street outside Vansen's door. He could not force himself to go any further.

Vansen left with his merchants early in the morning. McCauley was in bed with His Woman before the sheets had settled from Vansen's departure. It took him less than thirty seconds to confirm in carnality why he was absolutely and irrevocably crazy about women and to affirm that he was categorically and indisputably correct to be so.

Vansen was killed the first day he joined his unit by a British plane providing ground support for the American troops. This was a fact which McCauley never learned, nor which had he learned would have troubled him, as Vansen's purpose in life ended for McCauley as soon as he had provided him with His Woman. It took less than one second for McCauley to forget that Vansen had ever existed in an existential sense, though he did often refer to His Woman as Vansen's Woman. That appelation, however, was just a name like Jones or Smith, with no active referent.

* * *

Not long after McCauley acquired his amazing property C Company got orders to move out. The allies were preparing for a major offensive in Tunisia. The Americans had to replace many of the organic trucks for II Corps (which was the American Army involved in the offensive). By mistake a large number of those trucks had been off-loaded at Casablanca instead of Oran, their intended destination. Someone would have to drive them across Morocco, Algeria, and into Tunisia. Since the trucks were going to have to come in any case, they could be loaded with supplies. C Company just happened to be in the wrong place at the right time and the task fell to them.

McCauley came to Stephen adamant. He had to take His Woman with them. Stephen tried to be reasonable with him. He explained to McCauley that he could not "own" another person. That was slavery. People were not property to be bought and sold. Since they were going to have to go and there was no question of taking the woman along, the best thing McCauley could do would be to find some Arab family she could stay with and be sure she was comfortably settled.

McCauley looked at Stephen as if he were a lunatic. Patiently, calmly, McCauley explained to Stephen, word by word, how yes he could buy her because he had. Paid cash. And yes she could be sold, because she already had been—twice—the first time by her brother. He realized that she was not a piece of property and that is why he had to keep her with him. She was not a chair or a shoe, something that could just be discarded. She could not be sold to the highest bidder. She was a human being. She was His Woman. But he did own her. She was bought and paid for.

Purchasing His Woman had provided McCauley with a great sense of security. He realized that he need never, ever be without a woman again. Ocean voyages could hold no terrors for him. Days or even weeks without passes would be painless. He would always have His Woman. No matter what. She couldn't divorce him or leave him because he owned her. Wherever he went, she would go, a constant reassurance, a constant woman presence.

That is why he had to have her now. They were going to go out across the desert, where there were no women. McCauley knew he could never withstand another drought such as he had just been through.

In measured, hushed tones he told Stephen that if he had to be without a woman again he would go crazy. He would not be able to stand it. He had to take her with him.

All Stephen's remonstrations about the inconceivability, the impossibility, the absurdity of such a scheme sounded to McCauley like the howls of a madman. The lieutenant could not see reason.

Finally McCauley said that if the lieutenant could not open up his mind and see the light of day, he would have to take the only course left open to him. He would have to go AWOL. He was never going to be high and dry again. He was never going to leave His Woman. He had found the solution to all his problems.

Stephen listened. He knew that McCauley was serious. He knew McCauley's priorities, and the army was not number one. It was far down on the list. Even the Black Cross, as important as it had become to all its members, could not challenge what McCauley held as most dear. Women. Now all personified in this single woman. But taking her in an army convoy across the desert just so he could keep her with him? The very suggestion was preposterous.

Unfortunately for Stephen, McCauley was an excellent driver. He was also a first-rate mechanic. He drove well because it provided him with more opportunities to see women. He could fix anything on wheels because he never wanted to be stranded away from women. Not only that, but McCauley was an excellent shot if they ever needed protection on their flanks or needed to hunt down a sniper who was impeding their progress. He believed the skill would be handy for rescuing damsels in distress.

The men of the Black Cross would not take kindly to his absence. They would miss more than the considerable talents he brought to the platoon's work. He had certain other incomparable assets. When the men had a pass all they had to do was follow him and they would invariably end up where the women were—and in record time. It meant very few wasted minutes.

"I'll keep her in my truck," pleaded McCauley. "Don't nobody even need t'know about it. She won't be no trouble."

Stephen thought about it. What was it Uncle Fends always said, he thought: "You study long, you study wrong."

Stephen shook his head.

"All right," he said. "You can take your woman. But I don't want to hear a word about her. No trouble, at all. I don't want to know she's there."

McCauley almost split his cheeks grinning. But he could not waste any more time on Stephen. He rushed off to His Woman.

* * *

Acorn gathered his officers around him. He had maps spread out in front of him.

He pulled an ink pen out of his pocket, took off the cap and drew a circle on the biggest map. "Casablanca," he said. "This is where we are."

He drew another circle on the far side of the map. "Tebessa. That is where we have to go.

"In planning our routes we'll want to take into account mountain driving, probable washouts and muddy areas, and plot our estimated rate of progress—across the whole route.

"Any questions before we start plotting?"

There were none.

They worked long and hard. When at last they finished, the two first lieutenants were asleep, mouths probiscus-like, latched onto index fingers. Lang was awake only in the sense that his eyes were open. His brain had lapsed into unconsciousness hours earlier.

Acorn raised his bloodshot eyes to Stephen's.

"Wenders," he said, "I'll want you to be the lead platoon."

Ahasuerus and Charles smiled in relief.

"Yessir," said Stephen. He felt good about that. He knew what his men could do. He stood up.

As they walked away from Acorn's quarters, Ahasuerus and Charles walked slightly behind Stephen.

Ahasuerus reached out and put a hand on Stephen's shoulder.

"Whither thou goest," he said.

144

5

As the Black Cross rolled out of Casablanca, Mc-Cauley's Woman sat in the cab of his truck. A big American helmet covered her head in case there should be any inquiring eyes. For Private McCauley there could not have been a lovelier day.

Past Fes they were told that they were in an area where they were likely to see enemy activity. They had seen none. In particular, they were alerted to be on the lookout for air attacks.

Very shortly they saw signs of war. Bomb craters. Indeterminant scraps of metal strewn about the landscape. Engineers working on torn-up stretches of road. They tooted, yelled, and waved at the one section of Negro engineers they passed. The engineers saluted them with an equally enthusiastic greeting.

Further along, a torn wing pointing skyward like a ragged obelisk, a downed plane lay on its broken side 100 yards from the highway. The soldiers stared as they rode by. Death and destruction. Mute testimony. Death and destruction. Here we come. War. The land of the outlaw.

In Algiers fifty calibre machine-guns were mounted on top of a dozen trucks.

They were two and one half hours out of the city, cutting inland towards Oulded Rahmonn, when the Stukas and Messerschmidts jumped them.

The planes came in from the Mediterranean.

They were hard to hear above the noise of the trucks, but their engine sounds were different.

"Do you hear that?" Wilderness asked.

"Hear what?" exclaimed Stephen, gripping the bottom of the window and canting his head out of it.

He heard it.

"Maybe they're friendly," he said.

They have to be friendly, he thought. He tasted a terrible, metallic bitterness in his mouth.

"Maybe," answered Wilderness. He tried to see the sky.

Stephen had his field glasses on and was looking for everything he was worth.

Suddenly he saw the first plane. It was getting ready to make a run by their flank. It did a fly-by and banked on its side to get a good look at them. It was a Messerschmidt.

I know what that taste is, he thought. It's the taste of death.

The roaring of the Messerschmidt filled his ears.

I don't believe it, is what Stephen thought. He did not want to believe it.

Then Wilderness saw the plane. "Hey, Steve, let's tell the gunner to open up on him."

Maybe if we don't shoot at him, he'll leave us alone, thought Stephen. He could not accept the fact of the airplane. He could not accept the reality of such a monstrous and unrelenting threat to his life. It seemed to occupy the whole sky, yet he refused to believe in it. Something in the back of his mind said, it's called denial.

Part of him even tried to convince himself that the pilot could not see them, him with his blue flag flying from his right front fender and the two and one-half miles of trucks stretching behind in full view in the middle of the road. Maybe we're invisible from the air, he wanted desperately to believe.

Stephen had not realized how fast those airplanes moved. He could see the pilot's head. He was very, very low.

Stephen closed his eyes. *Wade in the water.* He inhaled deeply. *God's gonna trouble the water.* As he let his breath out, he said, "Yeah. Signal. Give the signal."

The truck shook violently as the machine gun opened up. The smell of cordite enveloped them.

Stephen's instinct was to leap out of the truck and flee. Yet, he was relieved. He was almost elated. He had acted. He had overcome the paralysis. He still felt it wanting to edge back. But he could beat it. He now knew he could beat it. He struggled with himself. Think. Don't worry, it's just panic. Panic. Live with it. Live with it. Think.

He inhaled.

He let it out slowly.

O Jesus I beat it once.

Just keep thinking.

He scanned the dusty shoulder of the road. It looked stable. His trembling hands trained his field glasses on the road further down. It looked good, too. He reached over and got Wilderness' attention.

The truck angled off the road and disappeared in a cloud of dust. The whole column followed suit.

"Okay," said Stephen, "get your left tires on the road. We'll follow it that way."

They could not see the other planes when they came, but they heard them.

Deprived of individual targets, the Messerschmidts swung back and forth trying to dodge the machine gun bullets and shot blindly into the moving wall of dust.

The Stukas held back, trying to decide on a course of action. The squadron leader decided that if they could get the lead truck, they could momentarily immobilize

147

the whole column. Although they could not see the lead truck, they knew its approximate location by where the dust cloud began. The Stukas turned and climbed away, gaining altitude and distance for their bombing dive.

The Messerschmidts finished their first pass and veered away over the hills.

Stephen knew, as the lead truck, they would be the most vulnerable and would be the prime target. Thinking. He kept thinking. It kept him busy. It kept his mind away from the icy ribbons of panic. Thinking.

"They're gone, let's get back on the road and get some visibility."

The truck lurched as it gained the road again. In a few minutes the whole line of trucks was on the hard, narrow ribbon.

Stephen was scrutinizing the shoulder on the other side of the road. He stepped onto his running board and signaled the truck behind him what he wanted it to do.

When the Stukas came diving down out of the stark blue sky they found the seventy trucks in the convoy arranged in fourteen dust-concealed rows, each flanking the highway as it sped along. There was no single lead truck, no head of a column to pick out of the dust as a target. The lead plane pulled out of his dive, and the others followed. They were on a strict ammunition ration and they were not going to throw any away. They could find more visible targets elsewhere.

Before the airplanes could return, Stephen had located a massive overhanging rocky hill. The trucks lined up, bumper to bumper, flush against it, accessible from only one direction, and that at a terribly dangerous angle. Their machine-guns trained on every square foot of that approach, C Company waited for an hour, hopeful that the planes had used up their fuel.

As Stephen sat staring at the piece of sky he could

see, his ears straining for engine noise, he remembered the taste of death.

In deep, post midnight darkness, traversing rocky, eroded terrain between Ouled Rahmoun and Tebessa, a truck whose drivers had attempted to turn around and escape the column when the Messerschmidts attacked, and which Bynam had kept in the column on Stephen's orders, lost a pair of wheels on the edge of a steep-sided wadi. The truck flipped and tumbled fifty to sixty feet down the almost perpendicular walls of the gash. It carried ammunition and, with its detonation, threw the North African night open to yellow and orange flames and the shuddering blasts of multiple explosions.

Private Walker Johnson and Private Pete Dafney left no identifiable trace of themselves on this earth.

Throughout the rest of the journey Stephen was wrapped in thought.

Suppose he had not recommended that Bynam follow the column to police it.

Suppose he had not ordered Dafney and Johnson to be returned to the column.

Suppose they had done what they wanted, broken ranks and left.

Nothing worse could have happened to them.

Nothing.

Nothing worse.

Lang was their platoon leader and he would have to write the letters to their families, but Stephen was the cause.

He had not known the men well, but he remembered their faces. Young. Very young and he remembered how they had come to him and apologized for pulling out. They had been scared, they had said.

He remembered then that he had seen them once when he was on a pass in Little Rock and with Evelyn. They had been window-shopping. He had pointed them out to Evelyn at a distance and told her they were in his company.

Laughter. Laughter had been in their faces.

He had not heard them screaming that night. What he had heard had been the explosions and the flames roaring. He had seen the strange, pulsating, orange light in the pitch black desert and the way it reflected off Wilderness' face like the battle-paint of some demonic warrior.

He had not heard them screaming that night but he heard them every other night. They hovered at the edges of his sleep, and when he began to drift towards unconsciousness, they cried and howled as if to remind him that the peace of sleep was not to be taken lightly and that to gain its rewards each night he would have to run a gauntlet of horror.

Some nights he did not sleep. He was not strong enough to hold his eyes closed through the terrible sounds.

After C Company had delivered II Corps' missing trucks, the men were ferried, by land and by water, out of the combat zone, west, to Oran.

Although they received a two day pass when they reached Oran, they were depressed. They could not get the two companions they had lost out of their minds. They had not been prepared for their deaths. It was as if they were just realizing what war meant. They began to recognize somewhat belatedly how real and how very, very final it was.

Arriving at the American materiel center on the North coast of Africa did not enliven them any. The town was hot and subject to frequent air raids and full of soldiers and soldier's supplies. It was devoid of tree-lined streets and wooded parks such as they had seen in Algiers. It claimed none of the beauty of the cork coast or the cypress and pine woods that had delighted them until they passed a little west of Algiers. It reminded many of them of a great, baked, barren army base.

But what probably depressed them the most was the knowledge that once they found their trucks, the trucks that months earlier had been sent to Oran instead of being disembarked with them at Casablanca, they would have to turn around and drive over 500 miles back to Tunisia to support II Corps' role in the coming offensive. Riding in the boats and trucks and trains that had brought them back to Oran after they had delivered the trucks to II Corps had been such a luxury. They had delighted in it. Even so, they had realized that the trip was a long one. Now they would have to turn around and drive the whole thing, every lousy mile. They realized as they had not before, how much at risk their lives would be. Dafney and Johnson who had been so vital, so prankish, merely days before, were now only memories. To the East hundreds of miles of desert awaited each of them. And death, a wanderer on that barren landscape, was lonely, and in search of companions.

The men of the Black Cross were disheartened as they stood around in small groups wondering how they were going to find women without McCauley. Over time without realizing it, because McCauley had proved such an infallible guide they had become dependent on him.

"Straighten up and fly right, straighten up and fly right."

The voice was unmistakeable, even the slightly off-key tune. Heads spun around.

McCauley stepped into a group of men, effervescent, his fingers snapping, his feet seeming to dance.

"Are we ready mens?"

151

"McCauley!"

"Hey, McCauley, what are you doing here?"

"Same thing you are, jack. Ready t'hit the streets."

"Come on, McCauley. What about Your Woman?"

"Hey, man. Let's be realistic. I been with that woman all day and all night for three weeks. I need me some fresh insight."

"Fresh insight? What are you talkin' about, McCauley?"

"Talkin' about gettin' all I can—everyday in everyway."

"Are you cuttin' loose your old lady?"

"Man—is you CRAZY! I needs My Woman. Yes, I do! But looka here. Just cause I got one in the pot don't mean I cain't go out and look for some more ingredients for my stew. Yessir, she's my reserve. My mainstay. My emergency supply. But, you know, when you reach new feeding grounds, you don't use up your reserve stock. Uh uh. You lives off the fat of the land. Hot dog—off the fat of the land!"

McCauley smacked his lips and licked them with his tongue. He lowered his voice slightly.

"Now, gentlemens, you know with all the army they got in this place, it's got to be plenty of good time ladies. And we ain't gon' make but one stop before we jumps on 'em with all four feet."

"Where's that at?"

"At the pro-shop, my man. At the pro-shop." And at that McCauley was off like some strange pied-piper with a long string of full-grown men behind him.

* * *

Almost as soon as they arrived in Oran, Acorn set off to follow up leads on their trucks.

He found them at last, a full complement of brand new trucks, with four command jeeps, lined up neatly in dust-covered rows, four miles away from the port.

Ten hours of paperwork, fussing with clerks and Quartermaster Officers who seemed to be viewing the world from the bottom of a toilet bowl waiting for the shit to fall, finally got Acorn authorization for his company to claim the trucks. Almost simultaneously they got orders to load up and head back east, past Roum es Souk and Tabarka to Djebel Abiod. Except for their own gasoline supplies, the load was pure ammunition.

Stephen was writing letters when Acorn interrupted him and told him to round up his men. Stephen did so, but he took his time. He did not know when again they would get the chance to act as young men their age normally act. He did not wish to draw them from the normal world of carnality, sensuality and abandonment and into the world of organized madness any sooner than necessary.

After they finished washing their truck, Stephen and Wilderness stepped back from it.

"Come all the way across the Atlantic t'be with us," said Wilderness. "Even if they did bring it to the wrong port."

They laughed.

"Yeah, and that extra mileage brought it through the Straits of Gibraltar and into the Mediterranean, too," said Stephen.

Wilderness nodded. "Yessuh," he said. "It ought t'have a name."

"A name?"

"Yeah, you got a name, ain't you?"

"I'm not a truck."

"Well . . . that ship what we come on had a name—

they even names the coaches of trains. And this is our truck, Steve. It need a name."

"Maybe."

Stephen looked over the truck. He could not help smiling. "What kind of a name?"

"I don't know. You the college man. A name—you know—with power."

"One that would protect us from our enemies?"

He could not repress the thought of Johnson and Dafney. Lord, he did not want to go like that. Protection. Yes, they needed protection. They all needed protection—he and Wilderness, and all their men, too. That would take quite a name.

"Yeah, a name like that," said Wilderness.

"A lucky name, too?"

"Right, right."

Stephen reached inside his shirt and touched the piece of his father's trousers. He kept his fingers on the cloth and closed his eyes. Almost right away he saw Grandma Goodie. She was trying to tell him something but she was not using her own voice. She was using her old, black bird, Abraham. He flew very high. Then he folded his wings and dove. Stephen could see straight where he was going. Then he heard Grandma Goodie. She spoke with her own voice. What she said was unmistakeable.

"I know a powerful name," Stephen said, "one that would mean destruction for anyone who stood against us, one that would mean protection for us."

He caught Wilderness' eyes with his and held them.

"I mean what I'm saying," he said.

"I believe you, Steve," Wilderness said, returning his even gaze.

"My grandmother believes that a name is a tool of power if it is used right," said Stephen

"Yeah, your grandmother's a conjur woman, ain't she?"

"I don't know."

They looked at the truck.

"But power is a double-edged sword," said Stephen. "The name I know is dangerous."

"Well, I don't know too much about them kinds o' things," said Wilderness, "but it make sense t'me that if somethin' is powerful, it's gon' be dangerous. I mean, a bomb is powerful."

Stephen turned away from the truck and looked down the little, narrow street. He shrugged. "You might not even like it."

"It was my idea t'name the thing," said Wilderness. "I'll take whatever you comes up with—just as long as it's got a name—just so we don't be callin' it, 'truck.' "

"Then its name is *Long Swamp*," said Stephen.

Wilderness swallowed, then nodded his head. "Sound good t'me," he said.

Later, they painted *Long Swamp* in black on each door and on the hood. They christened it with a bottle of Algerian wine and toasted it with true French Champagne.

Long Swamp rolled down the streets of Oran and took command of the trucks of the Black Cross and C Company.

6

The Black Cross stood strung out on a long ridge overlooking the dry, wadi country. Stephen and Wilderness stood in front of Long Swamp and looked down into the rocky, rough-grained valley below them. The coating of spring flowers was deceiving. Sometimes it looked as if they were looking down on velvet, but up-close the flowers were often far apart, the stones and crevices dominating the earth.

They could see white puffs, like tiny clouds, springing out of the ground below the heights.

"You know what they call that," asked Stephen.

"The mousetrap," answered Wilderness.

A faint booming sound reached their ears.

"How much sense do it make," asked Wilderness, "to drive down inta somethin' called the mousetrap?"

"About as much sense as to drop your balls into something called the nutcracker."

The little white clouds kept springing up and dissipating.

"How far you say they want us to go?" asked Wilderness.

"Over there to the right, two miles. They want us to set up a dump over there."

"It don't make no sense to set up a dump in enemy artillery range, do it?" asked Wilderness.

Stephen looked at Wilderness.

They both laughed.

"Yeah, alright," said Wilderness.

Stephen studied the map then looked back down into the valley. "Actually," he said, "where they want to set

156

up the dump is outside artillery range. See that ridge there?" He pointed.

Wilderness nodded.

"Well, they want to set up the dump tight against the reverse side of the ridge. The ridge protects the dump site."

"Mmhmm. But it don't protect nobody drivin' in there with a truck full o' shells, mines, and gasoline."

"I think you're right about that," said Stephen. "I think that's why Acorn had us mix loads. That way if one truck gets hit, we won't lose all of any one item."

Wilderness shook his head. "And I was startin' t'think that cat might be alright," he said.

"He's got a job t'do. Like us forcing Johnson and Dafney back into the column."

"Yeah, alright," said Wilderness. He stared down into the valley where the tiny little clouds kept materializing and disappearing.

"How we gon' git down there and out without gittin' somebody killed?"

Stephen leaned against Long Swamp. "We're going to sit right here and memorize this little valley and that little track, and this map. And we're going to wait until dark."

When the sun rose a new and fully-stocked dump lay against the northeast base of hill 388 and there was no sign of how it got there and no sign of a platoon of Black truckers who had dropped blind into the valley and not alerted on either side a single man of the 3,000 tense and edgy troops who faced each other on pain of death in the darkness.

7

The German surrender in Northern Tunisia was a strangely disorienting experience for the men of the Black Cross. They had been bombed, strafed by airplanes, bombarded by artillery, raked by small-arms fire. They had risked their lives driving lights-out in dead of night along crevices and canyon rims that would scare the tits off a milk-cow. They had dodged mines and crossed open plains under threat of air attack in broad daylight. They had repaired flats on the edges of precipices and brought out living men blown in half. They had come to accept unrelenting terror as a fact of life. Suddenly the Germans and the Italians surrendered in great lines and crowds. They came down out of the hills and squatted in the desert in the thousands. Peace had come to North Africa.

The Black Cross acquired the tasks of transporting prisoners from east to west and helping stockpile the materiel that would turn the whole southern edge of the Mediterranean into an allied base.

They were given a short haul from Rabat to Fes and while they were in Fes they discovered an extraordinary phenomenon.

McCauley had come rushing back into the bivouac area, pupils dilated, mouth agape, rushing in every direction, making absolutely no sense.

Wilderness finally got him to sit down. He had him close his eyes and take ten deep breaths, exhaling each one slowly.

"Now," said Wilderness. "You went to town. What happened when you first got there?"

"I had this feelin'," said McCauley, "somethin' was in the air."

"You always got a feelin'," said Chivvers.

"Let the man talk."

"It was excitement in the air," said McCauley.

"Bitches," said Anderson.

"Yeah, and somethin' else, too," said McCauley. "Found out it was a great big party goin' on at some big-time Arab's house. You ain't never seen no house like that."

"If it was a party, McCauley would find it," said Hamilton.

"I ain't jivin' it was a party—guess who was the ring leader of the party?"

"General DeGaulle," said Warden.

"Mussolini," said Wilderness.

"Yo Mama," said an indistinguishable voice.

"Josephine Baker," said McCauley.

"Fuck you," said Brady.

"Why you got t'lie?" asked Sheperd.

"Hey, hey, if I'm lyin' I'm flyin'."

"Josephine Baker?" Wilderness looked at McCauley. "I know you run into some shit what the average cat wouldn't believe—but Josephine Baker?"

"I swear to God," said McCauley.

"What the hell is Josephine Baker doin' in Morocco?" asked Warden.

"I don't know, but she was livin' in Paris, wasn't she?" asked McCauley.

"Uh huh."

"Well, maybe she didn't want t'stay there under the Nazis. I don't know. But I know one thing—she's in Fes today."

159

"Goddamn."

"That's what I said," laughed McCauley, his excitement rising again.

"How does she look?"

"Good enough to eat."

They all rolled around laughing.

"But the other thing that got me," said McCauley, "the place was full of Negro officers."

"Oh, shit, here come another one."

"I ain't lyin'—but I know what you mean. I was there and I didn't believe it. I step into a room and there's Josephine Baker, and on top o' that a whole troop o' Negro officers. I sat right there in that Arab mansion, starin' at Josephine Baker with Negro officers all around me, and I didn't believe it either.

"Come to find out, she's the one givin' the party. This Arab's a friend o' hers and he give her the house for her party. And—catch this—she's throwin' the party for them Negro officers."

"What the hell is a whole bunch of Negro officers doin' in Fes, Morocco? They sure as hell wasn't livin' in Paris."

"That took me a while to figure out, but I should o' noticed right away."

"Noticed what?"

"They was wearin' wings."

"Oh, shit."

"Here we go again."

"What have the nigger been drinkin'?"

"Halos, too, I imagine," said Bynam.

"McCauley gon' tell us the niggas was dead, and they done found them a way into heaven."

Everybody laughed.

"I ain't talkin' about them kind o' wings," said McCauley. "I'm talkin' about flyers' wings. They's pilots."

"The Ninety-Ninth," said Wilderness.

Surprised, McCauley looked at Wilderness. "Right," he said, a note of disappointment in his voice, "the 99th Fighter Squadron. How'd you know?"

"Colored papers been writin' about 'em ever since they started. Far as I know they's the only one there is."

"Fighter pilots?" the question rang out in unison from the group.

"Fighter pilots," affirmed McCauley. "Negro fighter pilots. I ain't never seen nothin' like it."

"Could they fly?" asked Crown.

"I don't know. They was on the ground then, but I figure they can or they wouldn't be over here."

After that all the men in the Black Cross made it a point to get in town to see Josephine Baker and the Negro fighter pilots.

8

A persistent thought kept plaguing Wilderness. It was that the prisoners of war were lucky. He could not accept the logic of a world which left the Italian and German captives forever free from the risk of war, though they at least believed they had something to fight for, while he and his men were left in a deadly caldron which had nothing to do with their own well-being. Even when he sat up and rejoiced at watching and being introduced to Josephine Baker, even when he joined the gangs following McCauley on his wanton debauches, even when he and Bynam sat in a bar and tried to drink each other stupid the thought occasionally broke through into his consciousness that the POWs were getting away with grand theft, and he and his men were receiving their death sentences. While the POWs had escaped the war, Wilderness knew if the Black Cross were ever committed to the new front they were stacking up supplies for, the fate which had caught up with Dafney and Johnson awaited more of them. He thought about the 99th, too. They would be shot at. They would have to fly through anti-aircraft fire, and they were liable to be attacked by enemy planes. They could have mechanical failures and fall from the sky. They had been horribly abused and humiliated by the army. It was always in the Negro papers. Wilderness had become sickened by reading of it. Yet, they would be sent daily to face death, while the POWs were out of the war.

Ain't no way, thought Wilderness. Ain't no way it should be like that.

* * *

McCauley had been struck by the idea of possessing his own harem. He meant to find out the best possible means of his having a harem in Morocco and what would happen to the women when he left. He did not want to rule out marriage, but he did not think that was feasible. He knew he would not be able to bring a congregation of wives back to the states, and he did not fancy the idea of leaving a collection of wives permanently on the other side of the world. Having wives also raised the question of children, whereas if women one was not married to had children that was a horse of an entirely different color. Besides, Muslim custom—at least so far as he had heard—allowed only four wives and McCauley had a considerably larger harem in mind. The Muslims who felt the need for more than four wives, made up the other numbers through concubines. That was a possibility McCauley savored. His thoughts were definitely running along the lines of purchasing his harem. He already knew because of the acquisition of His Woman that it was possible to buy women. Buying a whole household of women, however, was a matter for investigation. McCauley had an affinity for languages. Living with His Woman he had become a passing Arabic speaker and he understood it very well. As a result, he did not hesitate to plunge off into the innermost recesses of every Arab community where the platoon spent any time.

Wilderness began to accompany him on these odysseys, but for reasons entirely his own.

Through McCauley as intermediary, Wilderness began to strike up a strange assortment of North African acquaintances from Algiers through Casablanca. At Tenes, Mascara, Mers-el Kebir, and in the native quarters of all the larger cities, a person here or there was likely to have made the acquaintance of the strange North American *noire* who above all things seemed to be a man whose word could be trusted.

9

"Lieutenant Wenders," said Wilderness, "uh there's somethin' I got t'tell you about. Somethin' I been thinkin' about for a long time."

"Oh, shit. Here he comes with that Lieutenant Wenders bullshit. Wilderness, the last time you pulled that on me, we almost helped blow away the whole population of the United States."

Wilderness sneaked a glance at Stephen.

"Hey, come on, Steve. It wasn't that bad, was it? It was the right thing, wasn't it?"

Stephen pulled out from under the hood and straightened up. "Don't drag it out, man. What is it?"

Wilderness stepped back and straightened up, too. They slammed the hood down together.

"Alright," said Wilderness. "Let's walk."

They walked slowly, heading out towards the edge of their bivouac area.

"It started with those POWs," said Wilderness.

"Oh, you mean when you were talking about how they got out of the war?"

"Yeah. That's it. I got t'thinkin' about how they got out of the war and we still in it and we ain't even supposed t'be here. I never did think we was gon' be sent overseas so I never did do too much thinkin' about what t'do about it—especially after the way we fucked up at Camp Robinson. This ain't our war and I liked it like that just fine. We had all these men and equipment and we could ride around the country fuckin' with the white boy. I loved that.

"Next thing I knowed we was over here. Stuck. Had t'depend on the white boy t'get back. So we's livin' in deserts, fryin' ourselves inside the cab of a truck; drivin' over places where no self-respectin' road would ever go, and ain't no doubt about it—these roads ain't got no self-respect; gettin' shot at by airplanes; and all so we can tote and carry for the white boy, bring him his stuff, help him fight his war.

"What business has we got doin' that—these crackers what kicked us off the sidewalk and made us walk in the street, who wouldn't even let us get on a damn bus, who whupped niggas' asses everyday and run us out o' town. And we totin', and carryin' fo' them, savin' they damn lives—what kind o' shit is this?

"It bothered me, Steve. It bothered me bad. It hurt me.

"You know, if that shit had worked out at Fort Polk, we wouldn't even be here. Crackas probably wouldn't be here either. They'd be too busy fightin' our ass. And the Germans and the Italians and the French would be doin' whatever they wanted to here in North Africa. Kickin' Englishmen all up the ass."

"Yeah, there'd still be a war," said Stephen, "but it'd be a different war."

"That's it," said Wilderness, "for us it would be the right war."

"But here we are," said Stephen.

"Yeah," said Wilderness. "That's what got me. Here we is. And those damn Italians and Germans is through with this shit. That got me t'thinkin'. Why does we has t'stay in it? Why cain't we get out?"

"Wait a minute, Wilderness—I'm not about to voluntarily become anybody's prisoner of war."

"Hold yo horses, hold yo horses, Steve. That ain't what I'm talkin' about. Just let me finish.

165

"Like I said, I got t'thinkin', why cain't we git out?"

"Who do you mean by 'we'?"

"I mean us—all of us—the Black Cross."

"Alright. Go on."

"But the one thing I couldn't figure out was . . . you know, we could just stop driving anytime. But so what? Then what would we do? How the hell could we get out of here? How could we get back to the states?

"Then I started thinkin', the Arabs must have some way t'get out. It must be some of 'em what doesn't want to get blowed up, or to run around lootin' Americans and Frenchmen and Italians and Germans. It must be some of 'em who doesn't want t'have nothin' t'do with stealin' or who already done stole enough and wants to get out so they can enjoy it. What does they do?"

"So that's why you started running around with McCauley."

"You got it. It took me awhile cause first of all didn't nobody trust me. And then after I met some people what did, it taken me a little while longer t'meet anybody what knowed anything. But after a while I did meet some."

"Uh-oh," said Stephen, "here comes the good part."

"We can git out o' here," said Wilderness, "the whole Black Cross can git out. But it ain't gon' be easy."

Stephen waited.

"Let me explain some things to you what I done found out. Now, the whole Atlantic coast of North Africa is blockaded. What make it so bad, it's blockaded by both sides. Mainly U-boats from the German side, but destroyers and cruisers and everything else from the U.S. and English side. It's some French boats, too. I don't know whose side they be's on. And Airplanes. Everybody's got his airplanes up in the sky watchin' the coast.

"So even if we could get on a boat somewheres along the coast of North Africa, it wouldn't mean much. We couldn't get far.

"But there is a way. Across the desert."

"Come on, Wilderness."

"I ain't talkin' about drivin' across the desert. It's caravans what runs out of Morocco across the desert and down into Black Africa."

"Black Africa?"

"Yeah, that's where yo peoples and my peoples come from. Black Africa. Where the peoples is Black like you and me. Where they taken our peoples from in slavery times. Like Europe is the old country for the white boy, that's the old country for us. You understand what I'm talkin' about? Black Africa."

Stephen remembered a passage from the *Old Testament*, "The land, shadowing with wings, which is beyond the rivers of Ethiopia."

"I can get us all passage on one o' them caravans," said Wilderness.

"And once we get to Black Africa?"

"We'll have contacts who'll take us anywhere we wants to go—you know—it won't take much for us t'look like the local peoples. We can find out the best place t'get a ship, go there and get on board. It's much easier t'get across the Atlantic once you leaves North Africa and goes South. We got way more than enough money in our special treasurey t'pay for anything we could need. Once we get to South America it's like stealin' candy t'get back to the states."

"Sounds possible," said Stephen, "I only see one . . . uh . . . difficulty."

"What's that?"

"How do we possibly explain our disappearances in North Africa and our re-emergence in the U.S.?"

"Shit. Ain't nothin' t'that," said Wilderness. "Everybody know how Arabs always stealin' shit from the troops. We just say we was hijacked. Our whole platoon

167

full of loaded trucks was hijacked by what looked like a army of heavily armed Arabs and they taken us South in a caravan. We gon' have plenty of time t'work up the details and make sure everybody study 'em. Then we say we escaped from them somewheres in Black Africa, couldn't find no way to get back North without bein' caught so we found a way to get on a ship goin' back across the Atlantic. Don't worry, Steve. When we gits back they ain't gon' be worryin' about how what happened happened, they gon' be too busy celebratin' our return. We gon' be heroes!"

Stephen thought about what Wilderness had said and realized that he was right. If they stayed in North Africa and did their duty and one day simply got discharged or got killed or got pitifully wounded they would be forgotten and discarded as so much Black fodder used up in the war effort. But if they followed Wilderness' plan and ran away from the war zone, escaped the agony of further participation in the carnage, they—thirty-plus Black men of all things—would be welcomed back to the U.S. as national heroes.

"How would we arrange our passage for the caravan?" asked Stephen.

"All we got to do is deliver our fully-loaded trucks with a certain cargo. That'll be our passage. The only bad thing about it, we got t'leave our trucks with them, even Long Swamp. They ain't takin' no trucks on this caravan. It's gon' be camels. Camels and horses. No trucks. No roads and bad fuel problems."

"No Long Swamp," said Stephen.

"Yeah," said Wilderness, "that's the only thing what bothers me. We lose our good luck charm."

Stephen looked at Wilderness bemused. What next, he wondered. What is he going to come up with next?

"All we got t'do is find a way to Marrakech," said Wilderness "That's the delivery point. That's where the caravan leave from."

Marrakech.

"What you think, Lieutenant? You the commandin' officer."

"Hey, man, when are you going to stop doing this to me?" asked Stephen. "Look . . . I need time to think."

"I know. I know. I just wanted to tell you as soon as I got it worked out—you know, so you'd have time to think about it one way or the other. Cause, you know, another thing I been thinkin' about—all this buildup we been haulin' for—and Cap Bon where they sent the 99th?"

"Yeah."

"Well, that Cap Bon, look at it on the map. It point at Sicily just like a finger. I think that's where they goin' next. I don't know if they gon' send us over there, too, but I know once we gets off this continent, our continent in a way—ain't gon' be no hope for us. Ain't gon' be no way out."

Stephen nodded. "Yeah," he said. "I need to think about it."

"No problem," said Wilderness, "I knowed you would. Whatever you decides—I just wanted you to know what's possible."

"Yeah."

* * *

On the day that the Black Cross decided unanimously for Marrakech they learned that the invasion for which they had been so busy building up supplies and personnel had taken place in Sicily, and that the 99th was flying support.

Wilderness, for his part, had become upset by the difficulty of finding an excuse to get the platoon to Marrakech. The U.S. Army simply did not have a significant

169

presence there. They wanted nothing in any considerable quantities delivered there, and nothing picked up, either. Though Wilderness had perhaps the best inside men in the Quartermaster Corps in all North Africa, and though he could through the largesse of the Black Cross' special treasury purchase any other favor he needed, there was no pretext on which to send a platoon of fully loaded trucks to Marrakech.

On the other hand, because of military security, an unauthorized run across the 150 miles of high plateau between Casablanca and Marrakech was out of the question. They had to have a legitimate reason for their excursion.

* * *

It was McCauley who made the breakthrough. Bosphore Club in Algiers catered to English officers. They enjoyed the dancing girls. McCauley spent a lot of time around the back door of the club, because he, too, enjoyed the dancing girls. They fit into a special category of women he had targeted as susceptible to his harem overtures. He tried to make as much headway as possible. Through one of the young women who found his proposal intriguing he learned about a whole raft of English officers who, as they put it, were "mad" to go to Marrakech. They had learned that it was Winston Churchill's favorite place in Africa and also that it had the most sumptuous and extensive brothels in the world. That last bit of intelligence was news to McCauley and steamed up his interest right away. He secured from his lady friend the name and unit of the leader of these young Englishmen and reported his findings directly to Wilderness.

Wilderness jumped on it. He knew that the Americans were embarrassed by an abundance of riches in the MTO and that they were continually favoring their impoverished English cousins with their surpluses. Whatever favors they could bestow they did. For the truth was, and the American command knew it, though the general public did not, the English had borne the overwhelming burden of combat in North Africa. Not only had they fought back across the desert from El Alamein, but also the landings in Morocco and Algiers had not been costly in lives to the Americans; and when the American II Corps had finally been committed to serious combat with the Germans at the Kasserine, they had broken and run. In fact, one reason the Germans had been able to fight as long as they had in Tunisia was because they had captured so many supplies and so much materiel from the Americans intact. The Americans had run away from their equipment and their dumps, not stopping to destroy them or render them inoperable. In fact, they had run in such numbers and in such confusion that they had hindered their own escapes by clogging up the roads. Many had fallen prisoner to the pursuing Germans because they could not get past the trucks, tanks, artillery, and other implements of war that filled the roads in the wake of their compatriots' flight. As a result of that performance, for the final offensive the Americans had been assigned a secondary role, merely keeping the Northwestern flank of the Germans engaged while the English launched the killing thrusts.

The English had no surplus trucks in which they might ride to Marrakech. The railroads had been disrupted as they were periodically and therefore the English officers had no means of consumating their earnest wishes. Through touching the correct buttons in the Quartermaster hierarchy, Wilderness alerted the command to the pressing need felt by a large contingent of English officers; to the splendid opportunity for the Quartermaster Corps to provide a favor; and to an excellent platoon which was available to perform the service.

10

As the Black Cross roared out of Algiers, the back of each truck loaded with singing, drunken English officers, General Montgomery landed over two divisions of the British Army in Calabria on the Italian mainland.

The men's mood lightened with each mile that took them away from Algiers and nearer Marrakech. They seemed to lose consciousness of their English passengers as they focused on what lay ahead of them. Sometimes they thought about their passage price, the one thousand weapons—brens, spandaus, brownings, and a thousand rounds for each gun—under the artificial floors they had constructed in the trucks, but mostly they thrilled at the prospect of escape.

They saw first the peaks of the High Atlas dusted by an early snow. Stephen pulled Long Swamp to the side of the road to stop and look.

"What is it?" said Chalmers and Johnson, jumping out of the truck behind them, and running to join Stephen and Wilderness who had left Long Swamp and stood in the road.

Stephen raised his arm to shoulder level and pointed straight away, above the horizon.

Rising from the haze at the vanishing point, a grey-purple massif, her crests white against a lapus lazuli sky, the High Atlas stretched from North to South across the whole heavens.

"My man tell me our caravan gon' take us over them," said Wilderness into the silence.

The city was a great meeting place, a great market place, a corner of the world where the inhabitants of the globe came together. The peoples on the streets were various and diverse. The truckers bugged out their eyes as they drove leisurely through the town. Many of the types they saw were familiar to them after five months on the top of the continent—Arabs and Berbers and Turks and mixtures of them all, East Indians and Europeans, Persians and Bedouins. They saw shepherds and peasants and merchants and sailors and craftsmen and warriors and the goum. They saw princes and slaves. They saw in great numbers—many, many more than they had ever seen before—people who had to have come from blackest Africa. The women's faces were uncovered, showing full, high cheekbones and dazzling smiles. They wore great earrings—some huge crescents of pure gold. Many wore a slender golden ring through a nostril. Their necks and arms gleamed and sang with jewelry. Elegantly they strolled through the bazaar.

The English soldiers, eager to be about their mission, debarked in the huge marketplace. They disappeared into the swarming crowds.

A vast palm grove marked the edge of the medina, the ancient part of the city. It was into that maze of narrow streets and red buildings that the Black Cross headed at last.

Long Swamp led them to a palatial walled estate which sat on a skinny, winding street not far from the Place Jema al-Funa.

Wilderness got out of Long Swamp and walked along the line of trucks.

"McCauley, come on," he said.

McCauley and His Woman got down out of their truck and accompanied Wilderness to a small door in the wall. There they stopped and talked for a long time to someone on the other side.

At last they got back into their trucks and Long Swamp led the column around two more twisting streets until they arrived at a very large gate which led into the same estate. The gate opened and the whole platoon drove in. They were guests for the night.

As soon as everyone was settled, McCauley wanted to know how long they would be staying.

"Short as we can, short as we can," said Wilderness, "but at least for the night 'cause I got t'make final arrangements."

A smile spread across the width of McCauley's face. He was going to have a whole night free to run through the finest bordellos in the world.

"But don't you worry 'bout it none," said Wilderness, reading the reason for McCauley's smile, "I needs a interpreter. You got t'go with me."

McCauley's face collapsed. "Man, you cain't be serious!"

"As a heart attack."

"Man, this city got the cat houses t'end all cat houses. You cain't expect t'keep me off the streets."

Wilderness patted McCauley on the shoulder. "Just long enough t'do yo job, m'man. Just long enough t'do yo job."

* * *

Long after dark, leaving Bynam in charge, Wilderness, Stephen, McCauley, and McCauley's Woman donned kaftans and burnouses and slipped into the serpentine streets.

"I got a map, folks, just follow me," said Wilderness.

Stephen could tell from the position of the stars that the time was close to midnight when they finally stopped by a door in a wall.

174

Wilderness spoke to McCauley and His Woman. Eventually the woman spoke into the grill of the doorway.

After a short pause, the door clanged several times then swung inward. The four stepped in. The door closed and clanged behind them.

Immediately Stephen smelled the animals.

Involuntarily he blew air out of his nose.

Wilderness giggled.

McCauley's Woman whispered to McCauley. He whispered to Stephen. "My Woman say it's a big caravan—many, many camels. Quite a few horses. She never smelled so many camels before."

They all tittered.

A large man appeared in the dark. Stephen could not see the man's face, but he could tell from the outline of his robes that he was very tall and broad. The man walked off. Wilderness followed with the others behind him.

The man opened the door in the wall of a building then spoke briefly to Wilderness through McCauley and His Woman.

When he had finished speaking, he ushered them through the door, then closed it behind them. They could not hear him as he moved away.

"My man's waiting in another room. This guy'll be back to get me in a little while," said Wilderness. The darkness in the room was so complete that they could not even sense each other's presence.

They felt around with their hands, locating comfortable divans and pillows and waited.

They could hear the animals stirring outside the door.

"Goddamn it, Wilderness," whispered McCauley, "you didn't say this was gon' take all goddamn night. I got t'find me the bitches."

"Patience, my brother."

"Patience my ass. I'm in the town with the best 'ho houses in the world and I ain't seen one yet—I'm about t'be patient upside yo head. Look—I'll tell you what. Use My Woman. She'll be yo interpreter. You don't need me."

"She don't understand me," said Wilderness.

"I'll MAKE her understand you."

"Be cool, McCauley, it ain't gon' be that much longer."

"How I'm supposed t'be cool when I'm so close t'all that pussy and still so far away?"

Wilderness did not try to answer him.

The tension built up inside McCauley.

As Stephen reclined in the oppressive darkness he realized that the other three must have spent a lot of time in similar places. He had never thought about the mechanics—all the clandestine meetings it must have taken to establish such a rendez-vous.

This is all outside my experience, he thought. Wilderness and McCauley and His Woman have been doing things like this all over Morocco and Algiers while I went about issuing my little orders and conducting my little inspections without a thought to what their efforts entailed.

He was very nervous. But he comforted himself with the observation that the others must be used to the situation and would know what to do.

They waited for a long time.

"When he comes for us, you wait here," Wilderness told Stephen. "We'll come back for you. He don't trust no face he ain't seen two or three times before."

"All right," said Stephen. He was wondering where in the city this place was. He was wondering what the room looked like. How many times had they done this— in strange cities, in unknown quarters?

He did not think he had fallen asleep, but suddenly he realized that he was alone in the room.

"Wilderness.

"McCauley," he whispered.

He was answered by silence.

Only a movement of air in the room told him the door had opened.

"Let's go."

It was Wilderness' voice.

"Everything taken care of?"

"Shhh. Let's go."

He felt the pull on his kaftan. He followed the pressure into the darkness.

The four of them were running down a street several twists and turns away before anyone spoke.

"What should we do?" panted McCauley.

"That's our ass," said Wilderness.

"What are you talking about?" said Stephen.

"His thote was slit," answered Wilderness.

"Ear to ear," said McCauley.

"That cat what opened the gate for us let us into a kind of outer room from where Hassan was waitin'," said Wilderness. "He said Hassan was expectin' us, he hadn't called for us yet, but we might as well wait for him there, then we wouldn't have t'go so far."

"My Woman said something was wrong," said McCauley. "She say she smelled death—and she got good instincts."

"I peeked through the curtain hidin' the room he was in off from our room. And there he was stretched out across some velvet pillows. Deep in blood."

"Good God—blood all over the place," said McCauley. "Thote split from ear t'ear."

"Well. . . ."

"Hey, Steve, we can forget about the caravan. What we better be thinkin' about is gittin' our ass back to our men where we is safe."

"Safe?"

"Yeah, safe. I don't know who killed him or why. But I know one thing—I don't want t'have shit t'do with it and we got thirty-some men sittin' on a million bullets."

"But...."

"Hey, Steve. He was my one contact, my main man. Everything went through him. I don't know nobody else in this operation and they don't know me. You know how long it taken t'set that up?"

"No, but—"

"Come on, man, we got t'book."

As they picked up the pace something bothered Stephen.

He swiveled his head around, unaccustomed to the burnous. Then he saw what he had sensed. McCauley's Woman ran beside them, but McCauley was gone.

11

They reached the walled estate slightly before dawn. They aroused the men, detailed what had happened, and explained the necessity to flee.

Sergeant Bynam wanted to know what they were going to do about the British officers.

"Leave 'em," said Wilderness.

"Yeah, but they our alibi," said Warden.

"Look," said Stephen, "they had planned to stay here at least a week. We didn't worry about how they were going to get back before, and this is not the time to start."

"Yessir," said Bynam, "but we wasn't plannin' t'come back ourself then, so we didn't need no excuse."

"First things first," said Stephen. "First we get out of here. As to an excuse—we try to concoct something on the way back. If it works, good; if not, we get court-martialed. Case closed. Let's move!"

The string of trucks pulled into the twisting street a little after sunup. They followed a maze-like, circuitous route for a long time before breaking free of walls and buildings, shaded parks and tunnel-like venues and emerging on a stark plain, a great wall on their left, the High Atlas commanding the sky on their right.

"Recognize anything," Wilderness asked Stephen, pointing to the blank face of the massive wall on the left.

"Nope."

"No reason you should. We's on the other side. But behind that wall is where we was last night."

Stephen stared.

179

"Now, look." Wilderness swung his arm around, pointing to the right.

Long Swamp topped a low ridge.

There, on the plain, close up, masking everything from view except the higher reaches of the towering Atlas, was a sight from *A Thousand and One Nights.*

Bawling camels carrying great, framed loads stood in three long columns whose beginnings and ends were indiscernible. About these standing beasts, alongside and in between the columns trotted mounted camels whose black riders sat high and arrogant on top of the animals' humped backs. The men called out commands and exhortations with accustomed authority.

Other, more humble persons, sat on camels in the inside column. They sat obediently on their still mounts while the strong-voiced drivers arranged the columns about them.

The spectacle sucked the breath out of Stephen. He asked Wilderness to stop Long Swamp.

Around the outsides of the seemingly interminable lines of camels was a sight Stephen had never imagined existed.

Black men, coal black men, whose faces could have been matched by a painter's pallet which contained the colors of soot or tar, mounted beautiful, elegant springy horses. The horses were black and spotted and white and roan and tawny and white-faced. They pranced and cantered and galloped far outside the camels. Some darted in close and burst back again to the outside. Some riders rode clockwise around the column, others counterclockwise. They cheered and shouted at each other, sometimes letting out long ululations, raising in the air rifles and long, wooden-hafted lances with iron tips. They brandished narrow, decorated shields, oblong in shape with fluted tops and bottoms. They sat on magnificent saddles of burnished leather and sometimes silver, the pommels in front rising up to the waists of the riders. The horses were richly caparisoned with ornate bridles, sometimes of leather, sometimes of silver, often elaborately inscribed and inset with jewels or beads. The reins wore clusters of scythe-like hangings of bright colors and striking designs.

The riders themselves were dressed to dazzle the eye. Some were dressed entirely in white from their turbans through their long, flowing robes. Others wore white turbans with bold, decorative robes, all elaborateley embroidered—green, or red and white stripes, a blue overlay, or a deep maroon velvet. The embroideries covered a wide array of styles—some starkly simple, some so detailed and complex as to seem beyond human contrivance. Many riders wore indigo turbans to top the magnificent coloring of their vestments. Some of those with indigo turbans wore chain-mail over their arms and chests.

Stephen knew as he looked that the caravan forming before his eyes was the one they were to have joined, readying itself to travel 1500 miles, returning home. It was going back to whatever majestic land had produced those dashing horsemen, those proud camel drivers, the cultured civilization which had adorned and nurtured them.

Stephen looked and could not fill himself enough with looking, because before that day—even with all he had learned since he had been in Africa—he would not have believed that there could be such a place as they must have come from.

Such a place. Where the people are so dark as to be black. Grandma Goodie had talked about how the Wenders men were always dark, always dark. Whatever they were mixed with the dark always came through. She had said about Stephen's great grandfather, the Seminole: *"He had a lot o' African in him, too. For one thing he was Black as midnight."*

Black as midnight.

Stephen gazed at the light-absorbing faces of the cavalrymen who rode before him at the foot of the High Atlas. Getting ready to go back home. To the land of our birth. Darkest Africa.

He reached inside his shirt and touched the piece of cloth which he had there.

The emotions which had seized him off the coast of Africa came roaring back. He was powerless against them. He did not want Wilderness to know so he kept his back to him, though he could not control the convulsions of his sobbing. He had no way of knowing that Wilderness was incapable of witnessing his collapse. Wilderness had slumped over the steering wheel, his heart breaking.

* * *

The Black Cross did not return the way it had come. The men forsook the route that would have taken them back through Casablanca and followed the high road that traversed the base of the High Atlas and ran along Oued Oum to Beni Mellal and Khenifra and from there across the lower reaches of the Middle Atlas to Fez. There it was they learned of "Avalanche," the main invasion of the Italian mainland through Salerno.

Until that time they had been so preoccupied with successful flight that they had not dwelt on the meaning of what had happened in that room of pillows in Marrakech. In Fez that meaning hit them with full force. Their dream of escape from North Africa, the Army, from regimented madness had been murdered, its throat slit from ear to ear.

There was no escape.

The men of the Black Cross collapsed. They fell apart. They went into the bars and they would not come out. They found the whores. They pursued complete dissipation.

For the first time Stephen looked into Wilderness' face and saw something he did not know those features could express. Defeat.

It took Stephen a week, working by himself because Wilderness, too, had gone beyond the pale, to pull his men out of the bars and brothels.

Wilderness, speaking for the men, told him at last that they were ready to go back to Oran and face the music.

Stephen said, a smile playing on his lips. "I just want t'know one thing—what about McCauley's Woman?"

"Oh—she comin' with us."

The Black Cross had pulled out in line and was ready to start the leg from Fez to Oujda when who should appear marching toward them down the street but the whole cadre of British officers with Private McCauley at their head.

"We taken the train," said McCauley when he reached Stephen.

The men of the platoon hung on their truck doors staring in disbelief.

"I figured by takin' the train we'd catch y'all before you got to Algiers, and if not I'd cooked up some cock and bull story about how the Englishmen with me as their interpreter got shanghaied by some Arabs. They went along with it." He pointed his head in the direction of the English ring-leader who nodded with a big smile all the way across his face.

"Well, sir," said Stephen talking to the Englishmen, "why don't you gentlemen fall out and fall into your respective trucks. We'll be leaving directly."

The Britishers complied immediately.

As Stephen watched them sort themselves out, he asked McCauley, "Are they still drunk?"

"They ain't had a sober minute since they left Algiers."

"We thought we'd lost you, McCauley," said Stephen.

"How could you? You got My Woman," McCauley smiled.

"To tell the truth, I almost didn't come back, after I found out we couldn't git on that caravan headin' out o' here. I sure as hell didn't want t'go back t'no army—and then back to whatever they was gon' open up next—course, they done done it now and we all know where it's at. So, anyway, I was determined I wasn't gon' be in Marrakech and not see them 'ho houses. Well, man, after I seen them, I knowed I wasn't comin' back. Heaven. Heaven right here on earth. I ain't never seen nothin' like it! I ain't lyin'. But uh after a few days I got t'thinkin' about My Woman and all that the Black Cross done been through together. Now, I ain't gon' tell you I wasn't still in Seventh Heaven in them 'ho houses, I was, but, you know, every now and then them thoughts would go through my head. So, I had run into them Englishmen a couple of times up in the houses, so I decided to see if they was still around, and they was. After a few mo' days they time was about up, so I talked them into gittin' on the train—it had started runnin' again. The MRS and engineers done repaired the bomb damage. They was game to tryin' t'catch up with y'all. We looked for you in Casablanca and Rabat and Port-Lyautey."

"We didn't go that way."

"Yeah, by the time we had left Port-Lyautey I'd done talked to enough Arabs to figure that out. So we didn't even get off t'look at Petitjean."

"We're glad to have you back," said Stephen, "and with those Englishmen in tow, we won't have to use the fabulous lies we've dreamed up. That takes a load off my mind."

"I'm glad I done what I did, though," said McCauley. "It helped me make up my mind about a few things. I cain't go back to the states when this is over. I cain't live the way I want to live there. I'm gon' go back t'Marrakech t'live. It's heaven on earth. I think I can make out alright. I got plenty o' contacts. And with my share o' the special treasury I'll be able to set myself up just fine. I'll, you know like they say, prosper. I can have my harem there—and whenever I get bored I can go to them houses, them paradise houses. I can travel. First thing, though, I'm gon' marry My Woman. She gon' be my first wife. Everything after her gon' be gravy—and let me tell you, I'm gon' be swimmin' in gravy! I hope this war hurry up and get over with so I can get back quick.

"I'll tell you somethin' else—maybe the real reason I come back. I figure they gon' send us to that new front they opened up—in Italy. And I ain't never had no Italian pussy. I want t'taste some o' that."

"We ready t'go," called Wilderness.

Stephen saluted McCauley off.

McCauley ran back to his truck. His Woman could not conceal her smile as she got back in the truck and slid across the seat away from the steering wheel.

Stephen walked back to Long Swamp shaking his head. He muttered, "That man, that man."

When they got back to Oran the whole of C Company had assembled there and was waiting for them. The Company had its orders. The Fifth Army had finally joined up with the Eighth Army, had broken out of its beachhead and would need logistical support to continue its offensive.

They were bound for Italy.

The last most desperate dreams of freedom had died.

A Way You'll Never Be

"They lay alone or in clumps in the high grass of the field and along the road, their pockets out, and over them were flies and around each body or group of bodies were the scattered papers."

"A Way You'll Never Be"

Ernest Hemingway

1

The Focke-Wulfs materialized out of a clear sky. No warning hum of engines, no deterrent ack-ack, no shouts of battle stations. The screaming whine of the planes in their bombing dives and their shadows across the sun were the first warnings anyone had that they were coming.

The ship was not hit, but the near misses caused some damage, a few casualties, and the men were terribly shaken.

As they approached the landing docks set up on Salerno's beaches, Stephen sensed the shrinking in his men.

"I don't blame 'em," said Wilderness. He could see wrecked hulls in the water and, closer in, parts of landing craft and other unidentifiable equipment. On shore he could see bomb and shell craters and piles of debris that had been shoved to the side.

"I'll tell you what," said Stephen, staring Wilderness in the eye. "I'm not going to let them disgrace themselves."

When the first ramp went down Stephen jumped into Long Swamp and drove her straight off onto the dock. The other men of the black Cross were not far behind. Especially in imminent danger they were not going to let their luck get away from them.

* * *

C Company pulled out of Salerno at exactly 1300

hours. They saw the cemeteries on the way out. Too many, far too many dead to count.

As they left Eboli and headed up into the hills, places the salvage teams had not had time to reach, the wreckage of war was everywhere.

It started raining. At first it dampened the dust. As it fell longer, it dampened and softened the unpaved roads making them more tractable, not as hard as concrete, but still firm. By the time C Company had made its dump and started back, the roads had become slippery. The road surfaces had not yet become mud, but the water pouring over them made them like soft ice. The tires would not grab. The trucks came sliding down the hills and around the hairpin curves as if they were on skis. Going up the hills became a painful matter of zigzagging and backing up, crossing the road until a spot could be found where for an instant all ten wheels would grab.

By the time C Company returned to Salerno the strain on everyone was obvious. The men nevertheless had to turn around and go right back out by platoons. When the army was advancing successfully, it used up a lot of ammunition and fuel and had to be rapidly resupplied.

The Black Cross was sent up route 88 through Avellino to supply the 3rd infantry. They got stuck five miles out of Avellino, where two trucks lost their axles in the mud.

Stephen and Wilderness walked back to Long Swamp after looking over the broken down trucks.

"Alright, do we fix these trucks or reload their stuff and continue on?" said Stephen.

He had ordered a rest stop, so there was no need to decide right away. The trucks were strung along a lengthy uphill grade.

"Why don't we look up the road a piece and see what's up there?" said Wilderness.

"Good idea."

Stephen left Bynam in command while he and Wilderness took M-1s and left the road to reconnoiter along a steep goat trail which kept the road in sight. The climb was almost vertical, but after a short time of maximum exertion, they had a surprising reward.

About a quarter mile straight up from where they left the road they came upon a broad sheep run about eight feet wide. Rocky, it ran along the ridge lines in the general direction of the road. They followed it for two miles, taking sightings from well-placed vantage points where even in the rain they could look across crests and through defiles to make out its further course. They returned to the platoon with the decision to fix the two axles. While part of the platoon worked on replacing the axles, the rest cut boughs and laid them on the angled, sharply ascending road up to the point where the sheep run crossed it. In that way they made a good cordouroy road. Once the axles were replaced, the whole platoon headed up and soon was following Long Swamp at a slow, steady pace, bouncing along the rocky ridge lines.

When they rumbled up to the dump-site, a sergeant emerged from a lean-to. Other men were in the lean-to and tethered near it was a string of pack-mules.

The sergeant's poncho did not seem efficient, as it was punctured in several places. Nevertheless, it was dutifully draped over his large frame. He walked up to the sentry who stood at the perimeter of the site. The sentry's overly-large poncho dragged along the ground.

Wilderness got down from Long Swamp and walked over to the sergeant and the sentry.

"Damn, boy, you messed up our rest period," said the sergeant. "I didn't expect nothin' t'get up here through that mud for another week."

"Well, boy," said Wilderness, "probably nobody else could get through that mud for another week, but you good ol' boys just popped lucky. You got us." He lifted up his poncho to show the Black Cross. Then he dropped it.

* * *

Much of the work was terribly slow and depressing. Miles and miles of trucks stood end-to-end, mired in the mud, unable to go forward or backward. From the crests of hills one could see the trucks topping each hill as far as one could see both forward and to the rear. Or one could look down the "camel backs" looping down the mountain and see trucks filling the whole stretch of S-turns. The brilliant ingenuity and cavalry-like dash of the Black Cross were negated by such conditions. They spent most of their time outside of their trucks pushing and hauling the fully loaded vehicles. Sometimes they had to unload, push, and then load again.

They never dried out, particularly their feet, and the mud became so much a part of them that they began to feel it was normal to carry around twenty or thirty extra pounds caked to their clothes. Sometimes the trucks were so deeply immersed in mud that the men poled through it, like boats. Unfortunately, that was impossible to do on uphill grades. There were many, many uphill grades. Sometimes it took the engineers to uncork a mud-jam. Sometimes the drivers were able to build enough of a cordouroy road to free themselves.

After a few hours in the rain and mud, and pushing against cold steel, hands became useless blocks of flesh. It was impossible for them to grip steering wheels or gear shift knobs. Sometimes they steered by wrapping their arms around the steering wheels and shifting with their elbows or knees.

When the Black Cross began its runs to support the Volturno front, it began to find ways around the mud-jams and to show up at dumps with supplies while the main convoys were still mud-logged fifteen or twenty miles away. The more such successes the men experienced, the more they wanted.

In fact, if it had not been for the improvisations of the Black Cross many units would not have had the supplies to mount or to continue their offensives at critical times and simply would have stopped and waited.

The supply officers and porters for the units the Black Cross supplied started calling them "the magicians." Often when supplies were delayed or were running very short, these supply officers would call headquarters and ask why they didn't assign the load to "them magicians." They knew they would find some way to get through.

2

The men of the Black Cross were greatly relieved when the allies reached the German Winter Line and the platoon was ordered to Naples for a rest.

McCauley, however, was not relieved, he was elated. He had heard in his comings and goings, and his Italian informants had confirmed it, that at least 40% of the women in Naples had to be selling their bodies.

"I'll go wild," he kept repeating to anybody who would listen, "I'll go wild!"

He was usually met by incredulous stares. No one could imagine him any wilder than he already was.

* * *

Acorn let Stephen have a day of rest, then he asked him to headquarters.

"Sit down, Wenders," said Acorn. "Excellent job. The reports we've had from the field have been nothing less than acclamations. Marvelous. Congratulations."

"Thank you, sir."

"I'm recommending you for promotion again."

"Thank you, sir."

"Your platoon has been nominated for a Meritorious Service Plaque again for its outstanding work in supporting the 3rd and 45th infantry divisions in their assault on the Volturno and beyond. This time I think you'll get it."

Stephen smiled. "I hope so. The men would like that."

"Wenders, I just want you to know: it's an honor to serve with you."

"Thank you, sir. I . . . well. You are . . . an officer and a gentleman."

Ahasuerus brought the first platoon screeching into Naples three days after the arrival of the Black Cross.

Stephen was glad to see his buddy and invited him out for a drink.

"I want to know one thing," said Ahasuerus after a long swallow of wine. "Hast thou sampled the Neapolitan cuisine?"

"Uh, a little bit," said Stephen, "I don't know much about Italian food and I'd sure make a bad judge of it because anything tastes extraordinary after a steady diet of K-rations and mud."

Ahasuerus leaned back, savoring the wine. "That's not the variety of cuisine I'm talking about," he said. "I'm talking about the type which one tastes with the long muscle."

"Oh . . . well . . . I . . . no, I haven't."

"The man is mad," said Ahasuerus, "saving it all for the little Evelyn I presume."

"Well—"

"Wenders, do you know how long you're likely to be over here? If you live?"

"Well, I just haven't . . . I haven't wanted to. I'm not trying to martyr myself or anything. I just haven't felt like it."

"Good. That's all the more for the rest of us. I hear there's a fellow in your platoon, though, who makes up for you and all the other teetotalers in the world. You've heard of him I presume."

"Yeah. McCauley."

"That's right. McCauley. The infamous Private Mc-

195

Cauley. I've heard he could find women in the dugout of the New York Yankees. Of course, in Naples there's no need to find them."

"No, it's more like he just gathers them up."

"How does he do it?"

"I don't know. We arrived in Naples three nights ago. He left for the pro-shop within ten minutes and no one has seen him since."

"Ripping, ripping, I say," said Ahasuerus.

"Who in the hell have you been hanging around with?" asked Stephen.

"We gave a ride to some Tommys on the way back to Naples," said Ahasuerus, "jolly good chaps they are."

"Ahasuerus, you're an intellectual chameleon."

"Nice turn of phrase that—eh, what?"

Stephen shook his head. "When have you seen Charles or Lang," he asked.

"I'm afraid Charles won't be with us for some time," said Ahasuerus. "They've got him running some kind of shuttle on this side of the Winter Line. As for poor old Lang, he's got battle fatigue. Of course, John Barley-corn won't admit it, but Acorn's doing everything he can to get him off the line."

"Have you seen him?"

Ahasuerus nodded. "Hysteria, pure hysteria. It did not help, to begin with, that Johnson and Dafney were in his platoon. Our first casualties—fatalities at that—were his men. He took it hard. But he seemed to be recovering when we were shipped over here. Unfortunately, Europe did nothing to improve his luck. His platoon had the misfortune several times of being in columns that were bombed and strafed by the Luftwaffe. Those attacks gave Lang a bad case—a very bad case of the jitters. In addition, outside of Cisterna the truck just ahead of his hit a mine that had been missed until then. It was carrying gasoline."

"God."

"Right. Then on top of that some idiot sent him with a load into Liberi before it was secure. The 88s took the cab off his number two truck."

"The men—"

"Dead. Bits and pieces. Lang keeps trying to get under the hood of his truck."

"The hood—"

"Yep. The hood. Don't ask me why. Runs around, throws it up, tries to climb in.

"When he's uh out with the platoon they have to keep him strapped in the shotgun seat. If they don't, as soon as they stop to unload or set up, he runs around and tries to climb under the hood."

"And Barley won't have him pulled out?"

"Right. Perhaps he thinks he's not eating right. Says, 'There's nothing wrong with Lieutenant Lang. He's got men to lead, men to lead, he'll not get out of serving his country as easy as that.' "

"That son-of-a-bitch."

"Right you are."

"Where is he now—Lang?"

"Supplying the troops on the Winter Line. He makes the whole run—rain or shine—Naples, across the Volturno, up highway 7, sometimes 85, as far as the forward dump sites."

"In those long, slow-motion lines?"

"Yes, Stephen, that's the way the rest of us do it, you know."

"Mmhmm. Yes, well . . . if they don't get him out, he'll be irrecoverable."

"Mad as a hatter," said Ahasuerus. He drained his glass and reached for the bottle.

Stephen picked his cigarette up out of the ashtray. "Lang's fit to lead his platoon and the sky is brown," he said.

"Good show, old chap," said Ahasuerus after swallowing another half glass of wine. "I dare say this stuff is going to my head."

Stephen looked over at his friend, watching the effects of the wine flush his face. He could see that Ahasuerus was finally starting to relax. Stephen smiled. He said, "You know what? It feels damn good to be warm and dry."

"Try this one," said Ahasuerus, his grin popping out, "warm and dry and horny."

* * *

Acorn was deliberate when he brought the recommendation to Captain Barley.

"How's the chow?" asked Captain Barley.

"Up to par," said Acorn, an irritated expression passing over his face.

Captain Barley caught the expression before it disappeared. "An army marches on its stomach, you know. In this instance," he said, making a joke, "it *drives* on its stomach. Heh, heh."

"Yessir."

Acorn placed the papers on Captain Barley's desk.

"What's this," said Captain Barley. He looked over the form. "Recommending third platoon's leader for first lieutenant again. My, my, Quartermaster command doesn't seem to hold our Lieutenant Wenders in the same high regard you do, do they?" Captain Barley laughed. The sound was malicious.

"Anything else, Acorn?"

"You will give this your direct attention, sir?"

"Of course, Acorn, of course."

And he did. He used it in the same way he had used the earlier recommendations, as toilet paper. As a result, he did not see the bottom where Acorn had noted that copies had gone to Quartermaster command and G-1.

3

When the Black Cross was sent north again, their assignment was to stock an offensive which was scheduled against the Mignano Gap in the Bernhard line. As Stephen approached the Gap on highway 6 he could not believe his eyes.

He saw a valley immediately ahead of him, but on the far side of the valley were mountains. To the left of the valley were mountains. To the right of the valley were mountains. Beyond, as far as he could see, stood lofty mountains which seemed to rise higher and higher, their tops white with snow.

"My geography lessons never told me a damn thing about all these mountains in Italy," said Stephen.

Wilderness bit his tongue. "Ain't no way in the world the U.S. army gon' fight its way through all them mountains," he said. "we gon' be here for the rest of my life!"

During one of the platoon's Naples duties Acorn called them in to headquarters. He instructed them to come in full dress uniform. They all had to rush around to the company supply sergeant to secure the proper attire. In a simple, dignified ceremony Colonel Evers presented them with the Meritorious Service Plaque, the highest unit award conferred upon a non-combat branch of the United States Armed Forces.

Captain Barley was beside himself with rage. He saw no reason why one platoon should be singled out of his company for such distinction. If anyone should get the award it should be the entire company. As commanding officer it should be presented to him. He knew he was far more entitled to wear the scarlet and gold ribbon than Wenders and his scraggly crew. That is why he had vetoed the award for them in North Africa when those infantry and amored commanders had nominated third platoon for it. What did those mud-heads know about who deserved glory? The company! The whole company, Captain Wilfred Everett Thomas Barley commanding officer, deserved the award. He was particularly irritated when after the presentation Colonel Evers asked to speak to him privately.

"Well, Wilfred," said Colonel Evers, "we've been waiting for your papers on this man." He knew that Barley preferred to be called Thomas, but the Colonel delighted in labeling his subordinate "Wilfred". He had so few opportunities to use such a thoroughly reprehensible name.

"What papers, what man?" asked Wilfred Barley.

"This man, Lieutenant Wenders. The one we just awarded the Meritorious Service Plaque."

"Yessir, and if I may—what papers?"

"Damnit, Wilfred, the papers recommending his promotion."

Captain Barley blinked. "Oh?"

"What's going on here, Barley? Don't you read your own internal correspondence? Acorn recommended his promotion weeks ago."

How in the hell did they find out? Wilfred Barley was livid.

"Uh, yessir. You haven't received them? Well, it's this . . . well, the quality of our clerical personnel is not all that could be desired. I'll look right into it."

"Good. You know, despite Wenders' fine record this promotion is problematical. It raises certain questions for us."

"Yessir." Barley waited. He wanted to catch the Colonel's drift so that he could latch onto it to his own advantage.

"If Wenders is promoted, he'll be the same rank as your exec and your two company officers."

"That's right, sir." Barley thought he could see where Colonel Evers was headed. He smiled.

"We don't have Negroes with the rank to replace your senior officers," said Evers.

Thank God for that, thought Barley.

Colonel Evers stared at the Captain.

"Yessir, I thought of that in my own assessment of Acorn's recommendation," said Captain Barley.

"Good. I just wanted you to know headquarters' thinking on this."

When Colonel Evers had gone, Barley called in Acorn.

"We've had a clerical mix-up," mumbled Barley.

"Sir?"

"Uh, those promotion papers you gave me on your precious Lieutenant Wenders. One of the clerks lost them. You'll have to resubmit."

"Yessir." Acorn's eyes lit up. He knew Barley would never have taken such action voluntarily. The wheels of justice grind slowly, he thought, but they grind exceedingly fine.

Within half an hour he had a new set of papers into Captain Barley.

Barley sat right down and for two and one-half hours constructed a detailed and carefully reasoned explanation of why he could not approve Lieutenant Acorn's recommendation. Lieutenant Wenders needed more time for seasoning, he said. Though Wenders had an adequate service record, his training record was abysmal. He needed more time to overcome those deficiencies. This condition was clearly represented in that Wenders' actions had resulted in the loss of five trucks and two men's lives in North Africa, and that while his record had improved somewhat in Italy, some of his trucks had been unnecessarily damaged by exploding shells. Finally, he argued, there was the delicate balance between junior and senior officers. This was a factor which had to be given primary importance in maintaining military discipline. Wenders' promotion would result in a serious imbalance of senior to junior officers and would create great confusion about the qualification required for a senior officer.

He waited as long as he dared, ten days, before sending the package off to headquarters.

The Black Cross worked through the rain and through the long difficult assault on the Bernhard line and its final collapse. They carried loads for the build up against the Gustav line.

During this extended duty, the French Expeditionary Corps had arrived and McCauley had discovered the French ambulance drivers. They were women. The reputation of French women was well-known and he meant to explore every facet of it. He wasted no time.

It was also sometime during this period that Lieutenant Lang finally got his wish. He climbed under the hood of his truck. During the battle for San Pietro Infine, his platoon had gone on a long ammunition run all the way from Naples to Mignano. He had worked diligently and craftily at his restraining bonds the whole time. There was a point on the road where a mud flow was streaming across the highway. The men pushed the trucks through the mud one by one. His driver had put the truck in neutral, roped the steering wheel in position, and dismounted to help push. The engine was running.

A surge of triumph had swept through Lang's body.

He wriggled free of his last bonds, hurled open his door, clambered over the running board and onto the fender, ripped the hood open, and plunged inside. The fan took off his right hand at the wrist. An effective tourniquet and a French ambulance driver who happened to be nearby saved his life. But the war was over for Lieutenant Lang, as was the possibility of his ever returning to sanity.

Stephen lay on the mud, his chill ground-cloth beneath him. He was unable to sleep. He remembered how the squad of soldiers had flown out of the woods that time on the side of Monte Santa Croce and swarmed over his trucks. They had clung on for dear life. They had not cared what anyone thought of them. They knew that his trucks were headed to the rear and that is where they wanted to be. They could not go forward anymore. They could not go into the guns anymore. They had had too much.

Sudden fear is like that, too, he thought. That's why men are so unreliable the first time they're under heavy fire. They're unprepared for the fear. After the first time they usually learn to handle it, at least a little. It's still there, but they know about it. They find ways to control some of it.

But when there's been too much . . . it can do what it did to Lang. It can rob you of yourself. If it goes on long enough it can destroy you.

Stephen's eyes had opened while he thought about fear. He closed them again.

Remember that fish that summer? My, was he huge. What was the name of that . . . Deep Cedar Lake. Yes. Oh, was he big! He was a monster. Stephen remembered how the fish had surged through the lily pads. He remembered as sleep bore him away.

* * *

Christmas was a sad affair. The Black Cross gathered in a stone barn with no roof where the men opened packages from home and cried. A few tried to sing Christmas carols, but the day was bleak and they were all tired. After awhile, though a few men sat talking with each other and reminiscing, most went off to be alone.

Stephen tried to think of what Evelyn was doing. He put on the socks and scarf she had knitted him and held her card and tried to think of what she was doing, but he could not.

He remembered last Christmas, his mother, and his sisters, and his nephew meeting him at the station and the ride home on the 'L'. Home. He remembered eating until he thought he was going to burst, and telling them about Evelyn, and the way they had reacted. He wondered if Wynfried were home for the holidays again.

Home for the holidays. The phrase itself reminded him of the Christmas songs at home, not like the tragic effort his men had made a little earlier. Tragic and sad. Christmas caroling had never been sad. Stephen remembered it as warm. Even in the cold, even in the cold of December nights.

He remembered the little group of them, school friends, walking from house to house in the dark. It was exciting and it was fun to be out together. The cold was keen, it made your nose tingle and when there was a wind it brought tears to your eyes. The sidewalks were crusty with the crunch of sow. Evanston's distinctive black streetlight poles, with their barred and pointed caps like the helmets of medieval men-at-arms, stood like glowing-faced sentinels along the traffic-free streets. Only occasionally a lone car rolled crunching up to a stop sign, its headlights full moons illuminating the snow on the roadway.

The children stopped in front of each house and sang

a carol. All the houses looked warm with their yellow lights gleaming through the windows. Usually there were creches and Santa Clauses in bay windows, often framing or accenting a beautiful Christmas tree resplendent with multi-colored bulbs bright against the dark of the evergreen. He remembered how those bulbs glowed against the deep green of the trees—the magical trees inside houses. Each light bulb created a kind of womb, a kind of nest of warmth and comfort in the depth of dark pine.

People almost always came to the windows to listen, or to the front door, opening it wide.

They clapped and laughed when the song was over, often asking for another, sometimes inviting the carolers in for a cup of hot chocolate and snacks of popcorn or Christmas cookies.

"Here we go awassailing," that is how Stephen thought of it. "We are not daily be-eggars who go from door to door, but we are neighbors' children whom you have seen before."

Many, many times the people in the houses joined in the carols. Everyone became a caroler, singing to each other.

It had always felt good coming home after caroling, so good inside, so warm inside, and the family all around.

He looked up through the missing roof at the vacant sky.

4

San Pietro Infine was a dead town. It perched like a stone dragon's lair on the steep slope of the mountain and everything in it had been destroyed.

People lived here not long ago, thought Stephen as they drove past. But there is no more life here. He wondered how many people were living here during the bombardment, were living and dying here?

He thought about the Italians he had seen aside from those who had worked with the platoon. Mostly women, of all ages, and children, and very old men. There were young men, but you had to know where to look for them if you needed them. You had to know what would bring them out.

There were always women and kids and old men on the roads. Fleeing. He did not know where they were going. As far as he could tell every place had been destroyed. Even on the platoon's inimitable side-trips he had never come across a village or a farm house or even a barn which was completely intact. Most places were wiped out. They were worse than that because they were laced with unexploded shells and mines that were just waiting for someone to bump into them so they could go off. The Italians fleeing across the hills were always getting blown up that way. He had come across bodies where it was obvious that people had taken a long time to die. They had crawled awhile with an arm or a leg blown off and eventually bled to death or died of shock.

In fact it was such an atrocity, someone blown apart by a mine, that had made him start wondering about heads. The woman had been beautiful—slim, but magically swelling and curved in all the right places as some women can be. She was neatly, simply dressed. The impact from the blast had deftly lifted away the bib of her dress and the front of her blouse. She lay on her back. Her full conical breasts lay unmarred and open to the sky. Pointing to the sky. Touchable. Her right foot had detonated the mine. The leg ended in a jagged gash a few inches above where her ankle had been. Other than that her body was unmarked.

Her head lay a few yards away. Driven by the force of the blast a thin sheet of metal had sliced her graceful neck in half. Clean. Without serration. More delicately than a surgeon's scalpel.

Her lips were barely parted and her dark eyes reflected the sun. Her full head of hair, long and silky, framed her face like a black corona. When Stephen first saw her, her beauty momentarily overcame the horror of her death. But then her beauty turned the trick and underlined the capricious brutality of such wanton murder. Murder at large.

The recurrent vision of her dark mane spread out over the dirt and stones, the sky reflected in her eyes, an abstracted visage independent of a body, led him to wonder abut heads. He had seen other people decapitated. Never so neatly, but decapitated, nonetheless Soldiers. Refugees. A pilot still in his airplane jammed into the side of a hill. He knew that a body could still live, twitch—nervous reflexes they called it—after its head had been severed. The heart could still pump for a few minutes. Could the head live, too? While it still had oxygen in the brain? Could it see, and remember, and think? Had those heads lopped off by the guillotine retained the capacity to see and think . . . for seconds, for milliseconds? Had there been an instant of consciousness when body and head were no longer united? What had been the last sight, the last thought of this ineffably beautiful young woman?

He was unable to stop wondering about heads. Did they still live? Was there any fraction of time when the head knew it was not joined to its body? God.

He gazed at the ruins which had once been teeming with life. They run from this, he thought, and sometimes get their heads blown off They come back to this and sometimes get their heads blown off.

The woman's beauty was unforgettable. Where had she been going?

He wondered where all the Italians were going. There was no place to go. He understood that they were getting away from a place which had been destroyed. But what sense did it make to run to a place which also had been destroyed? It was not as if they fled long distances—to a part of Italy which the war had not yet engulfed. Such flight was impossible.

Sometimes they fled into the mountains and hid until the fighting was past. Then they came back. As he looked at San Pietro he knew that no one would ever come back. There was nothing left. Even a dragon would not return.

The Black Cross escaped the guns that time. They were able to bring the trucks to the dump without benefit of a road because the way from San Pietro was downhill and there was no steep slope. They returned to the highway under cover of night.

209

5

Ahasuerus was the one who told them about the 99th. It had been used in support of the Anzio landings and in two consecutive days had engaged German planes over the Anzio beachhead and shot down twelve German aircraft while losing only one.

"I guess they proved they're human," said Stephen.

"Yes, by the white boy's standard they've got to have proved it," said Ahasuerus. "They can kill."

Stephen closed his eyes. He thought of the trail they were making up the Italian peninsula and wondered when it would end.

He knew that a lot of Italy still lay ahead of them—most of it—places where people were still living relatively normal lives. Some of them had been bombed, but most had not. None of them had been subjected to the catastrophic horror of unending artillery barrages. They had not experienced tank battles in their streets, they had not experienced soldiers dodging from house to house with grenades and bullets. They had not seen their bedrooms turned into machine-gun nests. They were living normal lives.

Stephen remembered how it had been cleaning the drugstore down the street from college. He remembered what it was like swinging the giant mop along the aisles and how it felt to be alone in the store at night. When he had finished he had enjoyed walking between the lanes of cosmetics and deodorants and greeting cards and cure-alls admiring how the floor gleamed from his labors.

Afterwards he had gone down into the basement and burned trash in the huge furnace. Alone, under the building, with the fire roaring in the massive iron belly, he had felt at peace with himself. And the next morning he would go to class.

There are people further north in Italy still living like that, he thought. Heaven help them.

He opened his eyes.

"So we are certified killers, too," he said.

"Our pilots are," said Ahasuerus, "the men you guys knew, the 99th.

"Not only can they kill," he continued, "that, of course is no news to the white boy. They've always known that niggers can kill, as niggers have been killing niggers from day one. But these Negroes have killed while piloting a scientific marvel, a flying machine. They have not only killed while controlling this apogee of modern creation but they have killed, not other Negroes, but white boys, who were not even ordinary white boys, but white boys who were also in miraculous flying machines trying to kill them—and did it at a ratio of twelve to one. Truly, they must be human."

* * *

Wilderness and Stephen sat in Long Swamp and watched the bombing of the Benedictine Monastery atop Monte Casino. They sighed with relief as the ancient, priceless citadel of European culture, tradition, and art slid down the mountainside under the impact of 600 tons of high explosives.

"Well, we won't have t'worry about the observation posts on that no more."

How surprised they were when the very next day the ruins were manned by German artillery.

They also learned through their grapevine that the Germans had launched a counter offensive to wipe out the American beachhead at Anzio.

211

"Shit," said Wilderness, "we ain't never gon' git t'Rome."

Stephen had to talk to Wilderness alone, several days later. "Say, spook, don't drop out on me now. I need you too badly."

"Man, I don't want t'be here," said Wilderness. "I ain't never wanted to be here, and now it look like I ain't never gon' get out."

"You'll get out, we'll all get out," said Stephen. "It's just going to take a while."

"You know the thing that gets me, Steve, is we's helpin' 'em. I mean we's really helpin' 'em fight this war. They didn't give us that damn service plaque cause they thinks we's pretty. We done performed some valuable service for these goddamned fays and that hurts me, that hurts me bad.

"We should be outa here—someplace helpin' t'take care of our own folks. And here we is—fetchin' and carryin'. Helpin' this asshole save his hide. Man, shit, we should be away from here, let him save his own ass. But we as bad as the slaves what worked for the South in the Civil War. 'Yassuh masta, how'm else can we-uns help y'all?'

"Man, I don't know if I can keep doin' this shit. It ain't no reason. It ain't no reason to it."

"There's one reason," said Stephen, "to get our men safely home. Even Marrakech, if that's where home is to be. And to get them home with something in their hands, something they can build on, so they won't have to start off behind the eightball again."

"Yeah," Wilderness looked up resignedly, "that's somethin'."

"I've been thinking," said Stephen, "the old saying is definitely true here in Italy. 'All roads lead to Rome.' I think we should set up our whole Italian center of operations in Rome. I want you to start planning that so when we get there we can put it immediately in gear."

Wilderness nodded. "Yeah. That'll give me somethin' t'do. Somethin' t'keep my mind numb."

6

The leaders of the United States government and their top military subordinates had been receiving a lot of pressure from Negro leaders about the army's almost standard policy of freezing Negro officers in ranks. Unfortunately for Captain Barley the heat from that pressure reached his superior officers in the Quartermaster Corps about the same time as his non-recommendation for promoting Stephen Wenders. The papers arrived just when the Quartermaster command was running around in flabbergasted circles desperately looking for evidence their superiors could use to prove they were not guilty of the blatant bigotry the meddling Negroes had so unfairly accused them of. This evidence would be particularly significant over the next several months because elections were to be held in the fall, elections which might be close. Many Northern Negroes were likely to vote.

The memorandum which accompanied the papers back to Captain Barley told him that in normal times his opinion as Company Commander would have been routinely accepted. It told him, however, that these were far from normal times. Admittedly, morale had never been high among Negro troops and, generally speaking, that posed no particular problem. Now, however, since it was clear that in the future Negro soldiers were going to have to play a critical role in the war effort, it was important to keep their morale from slipping any further. Wherever meritorious candidates could be found they should be given every consideration for promotion. In specific reference to second lieutenant Wenders, while it was true that his training record in the states was atrocious and while certain unfortunate experiences had occurred under his command in the MTO, there were other factors cited by first lieutenant Acorn which bore considerable weight. His ratings since his arrival in the MTO had been uniformly superior. His unit had been recommended for a citation by combat commanders in North Africa. Under the direct orders of Captain Barley himself Wenders' platoon had been designated as the lead platoon of all company operations. Clearly, the Captain had great faith in him, did he not—otherwise why such a critical and ongoing assignment? Finally, in Italy the unit had again been nominated for the Meritorious Service Plaque and this time had received it. These factors and the army's general need, the memo continued, prompted the return of the papers to Captain Barley for reconsideration.

Captain Barley stared at the papers dumbfounded. They had done a complete about-face on him. He had been betrayed! He took time to calm himself down then he called Colonel Evers to see if the memo really meant what it seemed to mean.

"Of course, it does, Wilfred," said Colonel Evers.

"It doesn't really mean, 'reconsideration', it means—"

"Promotion! Goddamn it, Wilfred, have you got rocks between your ears? Promotion! Promotion! Promote his ass and get this shit over with!"

"But, Colonel, you just told me—"

"Forget about that. There's been a change in priorities. Be flexible, Wilfred. Adjust."

"But, but, that makes my situation here untenable."

"What the hell do you mean?"

He reminded Colonel Evers about the situation of the ranks of his company officers by race.

"That does make a rather sticky wicket, doesn't it, Wilfred? I'm sure you'll think of something." He hung up.

Captain Barley stared at the telephone. He hated Wenders and now he was going to have to recommend him for promotion.

"Acorn! Acorn! Get you ass in here!"

Captain Barley vented his spleen on Acorn. Then he faced the very difficult task of what to do. He brooded on it for a week.

"Colonel Evers on the phone," said his clerk.

"Good afternoon, Colonel Evers," said Captain Barley.

"Hell if it is," said Colonel Evers. "Do you know what it's like to be responsible for supporting a whole army of men who do nothing but eat, shit, and complain?"

"No sir."

"You're damn right, you don't. How's your reconsideration of this lieutenant thing going?"

"Just fine, sir, just fine."

"Yes, well goddamnit it better be." The colonel hung up.

Barley fumed.

It's against my principles. It's against everything I believe in. He began wondering how he could get revenge on Acorn. It never would have come up if Acorn had not recommended him for a promotion in the first place—if somehow the sneaky bastard hadn't let headquarters know he'd recommended him for promotion. Yes, Acorn was going to have to pay the piper.

But not right away. The only stratagem Barley had been able to devise which he could square with his conscience resulted in an immediate boon for the traitorous Acorn.

He would have to recommend that all his first lieutenants be promoted to captain. Since it would be unconscionable for a captain to command three other captains, Barley himself would have to be promoted to major. It was not hard for him to make the case. All of his officers had been in the war zone for over a year, had seen much action, and deserved a goodly portion of the credit for all the honors being heaped on third platoon. If its commanding officer were to be promoted, surely they, too, deserved promotions. It was all in the diet anyway and he had personally made sure that his men were always well fed. It took him three full days to get the wording just right, and then a fourth and fifth to stomach writing his approval of Acorn's recommendation of Stephen's promotion. That night he wept. I've sold my soul, he mourned. I've sold my soul.

* * *

Ever since Lieutenant Lang had lost his hand and his mind inside his truck's hood, only three of the original C Company platoon leaders remained, Stephen, Ahasuerus, and Charles. They did not see each other often, as each platoon operated under separate orders.

On rare occasions they had a pass or a leave that overlapped. That was the only way they were able to stay in touch with each other.

"So close yet so far away," said Ahasuerus to Stephen and Charles one day as they met at a sidewalk café in Naples.

Charles, for quite some months, had been uncharacteristically silent.

"I don't know if I can make it till we get to Rome," he said.

The words rattled Stephen and Ahasuerus. They had

become accustomed to a perpetual stillness from Charles.

"My nerves are shot," he said.

Ahasuerus and Stephen both downed their glasses of wine and poured new ones.

"I have lost eight men wounded," he said. "There are no replacements. Every clear day the Luftwaffe flies. The artillery never stops. Mines are everywhere. No place is safe. No place is safe. Two of my wounded were hit by short-rounds from our own guns. I was in Naples that day when the Post Office exploded—the Germans had been gone for weeks—they left a delayed mine. They're everywhere. Every little town. No place is safe. I saw a little girl's face, six feet high, plastered against a tree-trunk. Just her face. That's all. My men think the war will be over when we get to Rome. I know better. But I don't think we'll ever get to Rome. I could never last that long."

He stopped talking again.

* * *

Stephen started having intolerable nightmares. Every night he had them. He was in Arkansas with Evelyn or sometimes they were in a boat together in Michigan, just drifting around, fishing and laughing. Sometimes he was with his family in Evanston or in the warm woods of North Florida, the trees festooned with Spanish moss and the songs of frogs in the air. Or he was sitting in Grandma Goodie's big room listening to crazy old Abraham while his sisters laughed and played outside in a big field flooded with warmth and light. Occasionally he dreamed he was in school, sitting in class, or talking with Joe Dawson. Sometimes he was in his room at the Y studying for a test. Sometimes he even dreampt he was sleeping—in many different places—but always in

218

a large, soft bed with many covers. He dreampt in great detail and he remembered the colors and the aromas and the sounds of people's laughter. He remembered the soft touch of Evelyn's face and the way you feel when a big bass hits your lure and the rod arches to the water. He heard Mama-Ruth say, "I'm not studdin' about you, boy," and he knew every inflection of her voice. He dreampt a long time and he was always warm and comfortable.

The nightmare started when he woke up.

The spring not only brought the blessed warmth that allowed men's fingers to straighten out and flex, it brought also balmy breezes and the kissing scents of flowers. It brought the sun and cheerier dispositions. It brought hard ground. Everyone knew what that would mean. Men could run without sinking to their knees. Tanks and big guns could roll. There would be an attack.

Stephen knew it for sure when he had to start bringing heavy loads of ammunition off the railhead.

The name of the allied spring offensive was Diadem and the key to its success on the Gustav line was fashioned by the Goums. The Goums had struck up a close relationship with the Black Cross largely because of McCauley and His Woman. The Goums fraternized a lot with the Black Cross and did business with them. They were known to make minature fetishes of Long Swamp and to touch her for luck. Many of them attributed at least a fraction of their success to the magical truck which led the illusive men of the Black Cross.

The Goums were fierce, Moroccan mountain warriors who served with the French Expeditionary Corps. The Germans who fought against them fought to the death rather than be subjected to the cruelty which awaited them in capture. But fight to the death though they might, they could not stop the ferocious advance of the Goums and Monte Majo fell, splitting the Gustav line wide open. The Germans had to try to stem the onslaught by rushing in troops from other parts of the line. That resulted in a general weakening across the whole front and a broadscale allied advance.

The Black Cross became engaged in transporting wounded and prisoners back from the front. Time after time they brought back no prisoners from the Goum sector—except for a few badly wounded men who trembled and screamed hideously.

Two weeks later contact was made between the Southern front and the Anzio beachhead. As the lines of communication and supply stretched all the way from Naples to Anzio, thirty-five miles south of Rome, the stage was set for the drive to the Tiber River and the seven hills, the legendary city of Romulus and Remus.

Since the men of the Black Cross were not involved in the fighting, they spent most of the time with ants in their britches. They wanted to get to Rome. The truck columns stretched, it seemed, endlessly along both routes six and seven. MPs directing traffic stood at the same spot all day long without a single break in the flow of trucks.

When the Black Cross stopped to sleep and eat, the men gathered together cursing and hopping around in their impatience for the combat units to break through to Rome. Stephen reminded them that the allies had spent all winter trying to move forward three or four miles, that the thirty-five miles to the Capitoline Hill and its environs were not as close as they seemed.

"Well, let's break the boredom, anyway," suggested Sergeant Bynam. So the first chance they got the Black Cross broke out of the interminable columns and raced off into the hills to engage in their guerilla tactics of delivering the mail.

7

Frazer begins The Golden Bough with a description of Lake Nemi:

> ... *Diana's Mirror, as it was called by the ancients. No one who has seen that calm water, lapped in a green hollow of the Alban hills can ever forget it. The two characteristic Italian villages which slumber on its banks, and the equally Italian palace whose terraced gardens descend steeply to the lake, hardly break the stillness and even the solitariness of the scene. Diana herself might still linger by this lonely shore, still haunt these woodlands wild.*

That scene appeared to the Black Cross as they tooled free of the trees onto a secondary road heading for the village of Nemi which perched on the cliffs above the lake. The delicate, fragile gem of antiquity lay before them, exempt from the ravages of time.

The platoon carried supplies for the Engineering regiment of the 36th division. The regiment had set up a headquarters in Nemi.

No other trucking outfit had come as far as soon, but the regiment was in need of the equipment and Quartermaster command knew of only one unit which could get it past the clogged roads in time. It was necessary for the engineers to perform their important jobs of restoring roads and bridges in order that more allied troops could move forward to kill, cripple, and capture as many Germans as possible before they escaped.

Stephen alone of all his men knew something of the tradition of Lake Nemi. But none of them were immune to its fateful beauty. He led the platoon slowly around the edges of the lake. The spring day was glorious. Simply breathing was a delight.

A flight of American P-40s popped over the hills to the South. The truckers, used to their own motors, were irritated by the sound of the airplanes, which to their ears clashed with the serenity of the idyllic scene.

Stephen glanced skyward in time to see the lead plane roll on its side and drop straight down towards the little column of trucks. The pilot ignored Long Swamp which rolled serenely ahead. It opened fire on the second truck making a strafing run at the whole rest of the line. The other four planes peeled off, one by one, gunning at the trucks in single file on the narrow road.

Stephen jammed Long Swamp to a halt, leaped out of the cab and raced back down the road, waving his helmet in the air. He raised his face to the sky.

"Look at me! Look at me," he screamed. "Look at me! Germans don't have Black faces! Look at me! Oh God!"

The fourth truck blew up. Round bursts of orange flames consumed it and it blew up.

Stephen fell to his knees.

By now soldiers were out all over the road waving their helmets and turning their Black faces to the deadly sky.

The lead plane dipped once more then flew off. The other planes followed.

Stephen got up and ran stumbling to the burning truck. He was one among many making the same dash.

It was corporal Brady's truck. The cab was obliterated.

Stephen called for fire extinguishers and stood staring as the men put out the fire in what had been the cab. He remembered Brady in Arkansas when they had been together reconnoitering the route between Camp Robinson and El Dorado.

When the fire was out the wreckage was still too hot to approach. Stephen waited. He would look for the dog-tags himself.

Stephen wrote Brady's parents that night. He knew he would have to do it right away or he would not be able to do it at all. The dog tags lay on the crate beside the paper as he wrote.

He reached under his shirt and touched what he kept close to his heart. What had the woman in Casablanca said about it—a talisman. A Talisman. He raised his eyes from the paper. Lake Nemi. In his senseless, senseless way the King of the Wood has killed again.

The men in the platoon were badly shaken. All the members of the Black Cross were close. They had believed themselves invulnerable, bound together in a protected circle of invincibility. Now one of their number had been taken from them. They felt almost as if he had betrayed them by dying.

Each man also worried about himself. Not since they had landed at Salerno had any one of them felt threatened. No one had been in jeopardy since before even that, since Long Swamp's arrival. The truck's reputation had become legendary. All the other platoons in the company had suffered many casualties, even deaths. They envied the Black Cross' audacious daring, racing off to accomplish missions no other truck unit would even consider, and with complete aplomb, confident of Long Swamp's capacity to return them home, free from all harm. Even the Goums from the mountains of North Africa revered the truck's protective aura. Now, though the magic umbrella had covered Long Swamp—the fighters had ignored her entirely—the following trucks had been subjected to merciless fire. The men felt that the security which had characterized the platoon's world had plunged into a chasm.

8

From Nemi the platoon had orders to return to Cisterna. In Cisterna they learned they were to supply the 45th division on the Tiber Southeast of Rome.

McCauley was upset. "Man, why cain't we go straight to Rome? I can see all them little honeys waitin' for me now. Everybody know armor's gon' be in Rome by tonight. We should be right on they ass."

"Don't worry about it," said Wilderness. "We gon' be there soon. Them chics 'll wait. They ain't goin' nowhere."

McCauley, like everyone else, wanted to put Brady's death out of his mind, wanted to drown out fears and melancholy in wild diversion. He drove with his right arm holding tightly around His Woman's shoulders and prayed that Brady's *Auto da Fe* was a terrible mistake made by the powers of the universe, a trespassing on Long Swamp's jurisdiction which would never, ever be repeated.

One thing most of the men liked about supplying the 45th was that the way Stephen and Wilderness had chosen did not go through any hills. They could make the effort on the run and might not be much delayed in reaching Rome.

Stephen read the map and Wilderness drove. Outside of Campoleone Stephen brought the platoon to a halt.

"See those fields to the left?" asked Stephen.

Wilderness nodded. Nothing seemed remarkable about them.

"We have to cut across there," said Stephen. "Trouble is, according to McCauley, some of our informants tell us that there are heavily mined fields in this area."

"Don't know exactly which ones, though, huh?" asked Wilderness.

"You're on the money," said Stephen.

"Well, we can go ahead and sweep a path across here," said Wilderness.

Stephen nodded. "Tell McCauley t'get over here so we can decide which of these fields to try to breach."

All of the men were getting out of their trucks, stretching, relieving themselves. Wilderness walked over to McCauley's truck. Wilderness had started back when McCauley pulled out of the line and swung off the road to get by the other trucks to Long Swamp.

"Not in your truck, you idiot!" screamed Stephen, though there was no one around to hear.

Stephen saw the ground erupt beneath the truck and light flash through it before he heard the explosion and felt the concussion. Then the hood and cab of the truck flew apart amidst a column of smoke. Glass rained out in a mass shower. Pieces of the truck shot straight into the air. Other pieces sailed out horizontally—wicked, slashing missiles.

Stephen hit the ground running. He held a fire extinguisher. "Stay clear of the truck!" he shouted. "Wilderness, get a sweep!"

There was very little fire. Stephen ignored it as he leaped from the road to the remains of the right fender. He gashed his hands as he held onto the ragged side of the cab, coughing and waving the smoke aside to look for McCauley and His Woman.

He saw them. He wished he had not. He could not get the sight out of his mind. He wanted to scream. He leaped into the air, flinging his bloody hands over his face. He fell to the ground. He smeared his bleeding hands over his open eyes, but it did not help. He had seen them.

* * *

The men developed a new theory about Long Swamp. They knew that Long Swamp had been magical and protected. Hadn't they traveled all over North Africa and escaped unscathed? They had done there what no other truckers had dreamed of doing—rolled in darkness under the very guns of the enemy, steered two and one-half ton trucks in column along ledges perilous for mules. They had come to no harm. Long Swamp's magic had shielded them.

In Italy they had covered the Southern Peninsula as no one had. "Magicians," they alone had enabled some of the most daring advances against entrenched German positions and had suffered no losses, not even a wound. Besides that, they had carried on their lucrative businesses under every manner of hardship without hazard.

But all power has limitations. No well is bottomless. In extending immunity to them in such aggravated circumstances and for so long, Long Swamp had diminished her very considerable powers. She was drained. Her magic was taxed beyond its capacity to deliver and for the future she would be able to provide less and less protection.

Every mission which required her to summon her *mojo* would leave less and less for her to draw on until she had nothing left, until she could furnish protection for no one, not even herself.

This theory sobered the men, but it did not cause them to lose faith. They believed that Long Swamp still had plenty of juice left. Aside from Long Swamp herself, those drivers who had risked the most throughout their campaigns were the ones who had fallen. She must have enough *juju* left to protect the rest of us, they thought. Besides, they did not expect the war to last long after the capture of Rome.

9

The promotions for C Company's senior officers arrived in Rome a week after C company. Captain Barley was promoted to Major. Lieutenant Acorn was promoted to Captain, and the two baby lieutenants were promoted to baby captains.

Stephen's promotion came a week later. Acorn presented it.

The evening that Stephen was promoted, Major Barley called Stephen into the Major's new quarters on the Via Vittorio Veneta.

A comely housekeeper had Stephen take a seat in the parlor.

One half-hour later Major Barley entered the room. He returned Stephen's salute and had him resume his seat.

Major Barley sat behind a large, baroque desk and stared at Stephen for a long time. At last he said, "You think you're somethin', don't you?"

"Sir?"

"Don't play the innocent with me. You think you're God's gift to the army, don't you, Wenders—a Negro first lieutenant. Whoever heard of such claptrap in life?

"You know why you got promoted? Not because you deserve it—I swear, not because you deserve it but because of the Negro meddlers in Washington, D.C. and Eleanor Roosevelt. Do you think you ought to accept a promotion under those conditions, Wenders? Answer me! Answer me, Lieutenant!"

I fucked yo mama on a railroad track, thought

Stephen.

"Sir, I am not one to second-guess the army," he said.

Made those tracks go clickety-clack.

"Oh, you're smart. You're smart, Wenders. At least you think you're smart—because of your AGCT scores and because you were first in your OCS class you think you're pretty damn smart, don't you? Well—Well?"

I know yo mama she's a sweet old soul.

"Sir, I think I'm capable of performing my duties."

Got a high-toned pussy and a rubber asshole.

"Oh! Here it is! Here it is! You do, do you? You think you're capable of performing your duties, do you? Maybe if you were a sergeant that would be true. A corporal perhaps. But the duties of even a second lieutenant—an officer and a gentleman! And here you are, Wenders—a first lieutenant! It's a travesty. It's a travesty of everything that's right in the world.

"Let me show you just how capable you are!" Major Barley reached with trembling fingers for a volume on his desk. He opened it to a marked place which alone in the whole volume was dog-eared and begrimed at the edges, the other pages appearing crisp and new.

"Come here, Wenders. Read this! Read This!"

Stephen rose from his chair and walked over to the desk. Major Barley's finger shook as he pointed to a passage differentiated from the others by smudged finger prints and a surrounding ring of bold, black ink.

"Because we had so much trouble with you people in the First World War, a committee of field grade officers was assigned to study you—a whole committee. And that's what they did. They studied you people for years— for years. This is what they found, and this is what has guided and must guide our policy towards you people in the United States Army. Read—Mister, arrogant, intelligent, cocky, *capable*—First Lieutenant."

Stephen focused his eyes on the page.

"As an individual the Negro is docile, tractable, lighthearted, carefree and good natured."

He saw the men of the 6666th Infantry Regiment lined row upon row, stone-faced, death in their eyes, penants on their company standards streaming in the wind.

"If unjustly treated he is likely to become surly and stubborn, though this is usually a temporary phase."

He saw the two and one half ton tumbling down the wadi, heard the screams he never heard.

"He is careless, shiftless, irresponsible and secretive."

He remembered the Black Cross rolling over the goat trails in the North African hills, coming and going in the dead of night where no other vehicular column dared.

"He resents censure and is best handled by praise and by ridicule. He is unmoral, untruthful and his sense of right doing is relatively inferior."

He closed his eyes against the insides of the cab where the human forms of McCauley and His Woman had once been.

He could read no further. There were other words—smeared, encircled words, but he could not force his eyes to look at them. His breath was short.

He remembered how the black letters had looked on the stark, white paper.

DEAR MR. AND MRS. BRADY:

Stephen raised his eyes.

DEAR MR. AND MRS. BRADY:

Major Barley was pleased with himself.

"If you think those characteristics are fit for an officer in this man's army, then you're the fool I take you to be," he said. "Every white officer in the army who has

Negro troops lives by those lines."

Stephen was glad he had not worn his pistol because if he had his commanding officer would be dead and Stephen would feel no remorse. He held himself together very carefully as he turned and headed towards the door. The room was very large and the walk took a long time. In order to keep from cracking Stephen had to walk quite deliberately.

"I didn't want this promotion to go to your head, Wenders. Don't turn your back on me! Don't turn your back on me, you black bastard! I didn't want you to suffer under the delusion that you deserved it, or any rank in this army. Do you hear me? Only fool politicians have caused us to deviate from out correct policy. Don't walk away from me while I'm talking to you! You can blame your promotion on political interference—nigger—not on sound judgment. How do you like them apples—nigger? I wanted—personally—to puncture your little swelled head balloon. I wanted you to know the facts. Now get out of here!"

Major Barley felt a deep, filling satisfaction after Stephen had gone. he sat back in his chair, closed his eyes and reviewed the little interview over and over again.

He had upset that nigger. Driven him out of the room. Yessir, driven him out of the room.

Yes, he thought. Now I must provide Acorn with his just desserts. None of this would have been necessary if it were not for him. It's misfits like him who give Wenders and other menials the inflated notion of their worth.

Stephen dreamed with his eyes wide open about the mole on Evelyn's shoulder. He did not want to let any other thought enter his head. He loved that mole. It was black, and not very big, but to Stephen's taste it was perfectly shaped. He fantasized about the mole and how

231

it appeared looking down on it from above and how it appeared from the back and from the front, from close-up and far away. Sometimes as he looked the mole filled his whole field of vision. He loved the mole and the taste of it was sweet to the tip of his tongue.

* * *

When he was off the line Stephen drank and smoked more than he had earlier. He often sat at cafes by himself for hours drinking and smoking, not saying a word to anyone, just raising a finger to the waiter when he wanted another bottle.

Stephen had many, many nightmares because he always woke up. He dreamed about going down into the basement in the house where his mother lived in Evanston. Aside from Uncle Fends' inventions, which were stored there, the main thing in the basement was the coal bin. Stephen went down into the basement with a big pail. He scooped coal out of the bin and filled up the pail. Then he carried his weighty load up the steep basement stairs and slammed the heavy, angled wooden doors after he was back on the ground. He had to carry the coal up the front steps into the house because the house had no back door and because there were no inside stairs from the basement. He put the bucket down next to the stove in the living room where it was accessible for feeding the fire as long as anyone was up, and for stoking it when the last person went to bed. In the dream he carried coal up from the basement and then went to school for the spelling bee, though that did not happen in real-life because he always carried the coal up in the evening or at night, but in the dream he went to school where he won his sixth grade spelling bee and Evelyn was sitting in the crowd. He had been so excited and so scared winning that spelling bee. Even now he got a twinge of excitement whenever he ran across the word, "meticulous." It had been so scary. Sally Leffler had missed it, and then Stephen had to spell it. He said it first, "meticulous," then he started to spell it, "m . . . e . . . t . . . i . . . c (Sally had said 'k' next so Stephen had left it out). When he had finished it and repeated the word again, "meticulous," the judges had indicated their approval. The tension in the room had increased markedly. Someone had coughed and had felt embarrassed. The next word was "afternoon" and with a great sigh of relief Stephen had raced through it. The room had erupted into cheers and laughter and jubilation. Wilderness and Evelyn ran up to congratulate him and the army band blasted out Duke Ellington's "A-Train."

Then he woke up.

* * *

As the Germans retreated into the mountains North of Rome and the 5th Army followed, the platoon came to recognize the severity of the battles by the number of mule carcasses which still littered the hills. The men moved the human bodies quickly enough, but there was just not enough time or energy to deal with most of the mules. If the wind were right the Black Cross could tell those battle-sites long before they reached them. The summer heat burst the bodies and sent the aromas forth like the scent of some great, disfigured, pestilent flowers opening their lurid petals to flaunt a pollen of squirming maggots fertilized by swarms of fat flies so heavy their wings could barely sustain them in flight.

10

The Black Cross transferred to Leghorn about the same time that the 370th Regimental Combat Team arrived there. The men of the Black Cross laughed with excitement as they spread the news in the bars.

Stephen and Wilderness sat in a bar discussing the arrival of the 370th when a soldier coming in the door attracted their attention.

The tall, broad-shouldered Black man stood in the doorway carefully surveying the room.

"Now, you knows it's somethin' wrong with that cat," said Wilderness.

"Why's that?" asked Stephen.

"Here it is, middle o' the summer, and he standin' up there with his winter-issue jacket on and got it all done up."

Stephen nodded. That was unusual.

"Jacket look kind o' lumpy, too," said Wilderness. "You don't 'spect he one o' them, do you?" he asked.

Stephen shook his head. "No. They're up near the front being broken in with combat units."

The lieutenant and the sergeant continued to stare at the new-comer in the door. Eventually, he caught their gazes. He grinned and walked over to them. He stuck out a huge hand.

"Emile Harry," he said.

Stephen and Wilderness introduced themselves.

Emile sat down.

"Wonderin' about my jacket, ain't you?" he said.

They confirmed his conjecture.

"I'll tell you 'bout it in a while," he said. He ordered a bottle of wine.

"What unit you with," asked Wilderness.

"387th Engineer Battalion."

Wilderness smiled. "Oh, we done heard about you. Y'all supposed to be some crazy cats."

Emile chuckled. "We holds our own."

"Ain't no need to ask about you. I seen your monickers." He nodded at the little black crosses.

"Yeah, that's us," said Wilderness.

"Yeah, we done business with you," said Emile. "Spook by the name o' Anderson."

Stephen nodded. "Good man."

"Yeah," said Emile. "We had real good dealin's with him, real good. We lookin' forward to some more."

"Listen here," said Wilderness, "you know anything about this 370th Regimental Combat Team?"

"Just that they's Negro infantry," he answered, "the first regiment of a whole Negro division they gon' send over here."

"My, my, my, they must be some soldiers," said Wilderness.

"How you figure that," said Emile.

"Well, they been tryin' t'keep us out o' fightin' units all the way through the war, and have, too—now they sendin' a regiment—then a whole division of Negro infantry—well—"

"Wilderness, why do you ignore your own ideas?" asked Stephen.

"What you mean?"

"You are the one who invented brown sky."

"Brown sky—what the fuck is that," asked Emile.

"That's like when your commanding officer tells you that your replacements have been highly trained in your specialty and were hand-picked to support your unit and you're looking at their papers saying they're porters and they came directly from the African disciplinary barracks and the East Coast Processing Center's AWOLs."

"Yeah," said Wilderness, "it's like he's tellin' you the sky is brown and you can look right up over your head and see it's blue."

"Oh, yeah, well I know about that," said Emile. "that's everyday. So, uh . . . Steve, are you sayin' this uh 92nd division—that's who the 370th is attached to—are you sayin' that thinkin' they's good fighters just cause they was sent over here is brown sky?"

"I'm saying it *could be* brown sky," said Stephen.

"Well, I'm gon' agree with you," said Emile. "Cause I know one thing about the 92nd. They came from Fort Huachuca, and that place wasn't nothin' but a hell-hole.

"They did more fightin' with each other on that base than they ever could against any enemy. I mean, it was a straight-out whole Jim-Crow base. Only thing white on the whole base was the officers—and they was southern bigots—from the commander right on down. I don't see how nobody could get no trainin' at a place like that."

Wilderness smiled. "Even if they could, wouldn't be no point in usin' it against the Germans," he said.

"Now you talkin'," said Emile. "I'll tell you what—talkin' about sendin' fightin' Negro units over here, the baddest fightin' outfit I ever seen—bar none."

"Wait a minute," said Wilderness. "When you says—bar none—you mean even like the Germans, the 1st Parachute Division, the 4th Parachute Division, the Herman Goering Division? You mean, like the Gurkhas and the Goums?"

"I'm gon' put it to you this way," said Emile. "I said the baddest outfit I even seen—and that means the 1st Parachute, 4th Parachute, Herman Goering, and the Gurkhas. Now, I ain't never seen them Goums, so I cain't talk about them, but I done heard about 'em. But I'm

236

even gon' include the Nisei—the 442nd Regiment and especially the 100th Battalion, and they is tougher than all them German divisions put together, and they ain't but a regiment."

Stephen laughed. "You're going to include the Nisei," he said, "and you're going to say that some outfit is better than they are?"

"Let me put it this way," said Emile, "I'll say just as bad—because the Nisei got more combat experience—but you talkin' about spirit, you talkin' about polish, you talkin' about discipline, I ain't seen nothin' could touch these cats and they was Negroes—the 6666th Infantry Regiment."

Wilderness and Stephen looked at each other and then stared at Emile. "The 6666th Infantry Regiment," they said in unison.

"We knew them," said Stephen, "at Fort Polk."

"You right, they was bad," said Wilderness.

"I didn't know you cats was stationed at Fort Polk," said Emile.

Stephen and Wilderness laughed. "We weren't," said Stephen, "but we, uh, got around."

"Oh. Like you do over here."

"You got the picture."

"Anyway," said Emile, "them cats was some soldier's soldiers, and didn't take no shit from nobody. The junior officers ran the outfit, and their white officers better not get out of line. I'll tell you, those men would follow those Negro officers through hell and back out again. They was rough, buddy, they was rough."

"Where'd they go?"

"Sent 'em to Alaska."

"What?"

"Yeah. Sent 'em to Alaska. Army couldn't handle 'em. Didn't know what t'do with 'em. Sent they ass to Alaska.

"See—cause I'm gon' tell you somethin'; if they had sent they ass over here and those jokers had teemed up with the Nisei, they'd be in Berlin right now. That's how bad they was. Do you think the U.S. could stand that—a nigger unit and a Jap unit marchin' into Berlin together after kickin' the superman's, the Aryan race's ass? No days! No days! They couldn't stand it, so they sent they ass to Alaska.

"So, when you talkin' about sendin' somebody over here cause they a good combat outfit, that ain't why they sends Negroes. I figure they needed some bodies and they had this Negro division down in Fort Huachuca and the Negro newspapers always gettin' 'on 'em about where's our combat forces, where's our infantry—so they just sent what they had.

"But—shit—if I was from Fort Huachuca, the only way they'd get me to the front line would be to take away my weapons, cuff my hands and feet, chain me to a tank, and drag my ass."

"I don't understand it," said Stephen, "for the most part we don't want to be drafted, we don't want to fight in this damn war. But they go ahead and draft us anyway. Then they treat us like dirt. And they don't want to put any of us in combat. If they don't want to use us up to our capabilities, why not just leave us alone, why not just leave us at home?"

Wilderness and Emile both laughed.

"You ain't figured that out yet, Steve," said Wilderness. "Sometimes I wonders what college do to our boys' brains. Look ahere. Look at it. They gives all kinds of brown sky about why the army needs us. Some of it is true. Who would load and unload ships, stack ammunition, haul supplies, wash laundry, bake bread, build bridges, repair roads, recover bodies, bury them, guard posts and bases and POWs; transport dead and wounded,

238

shift people from front to front? they couldn't fight the war without us. That's true. But look at the other part—see how it looks. If we stayed at home, there'd be all these big, black, strappin' bucks with all them timid, frail, white women—"

"Especially southern white women," threw in Emile.

"And no white men—except old ones, weak ones, sick ones, feeble-minded ones, crazy ones, and babies," said Wilderness. "A country full o' niggers, decrepit white men, and white women."

"You know they think a nigger is just a nigger. When they thinkin' about NIGGER they ain't thinkin' about our women. They forget all about we of different sexes. Just like the signs on the bathrooms, they don't say nothin' about colored men or colored womens they just says, 'colored.'

"So when they thinkin' about the country full of nothin' but weak, old white men; white women and niggers, they ain't thinkin' about colored women. Every nigger they sees is a man with a great, big, hard dick."

"The white boys over here couldn't fight," said Emile.

"They'd be too busy worryin' about what we was doin' to they womens," said Wilderness.

"And what they womens was doin' to us," said Emile. "If you looks at the record, when they was doin' all that talk about gettin 'colored in the service, and makin' sure that we was drafted, and makin' sure that we was definitely sent into the army, all that pressure was comin' from southern Congressmen."

"So you see, they has to draft us," said Wilderness. "They ain't got no choice. It's the only way they can save the country. But you better be damn tootin' they don't want t'put no gun in our hands."

"Uh uh," said Emile. "We might could get ideas."

239

"Speaking of which," said Stephen, "I don't have the slightest idea of why you wear that long jacket and fully fastened up in the middle of the summer."

Emile smiled. "Oh, I always wears it, I always wears it when I got a pass or a leave," he said. "But usually it ain't fastened. He started unbuttoning it. He finished and held the inside open. Stephen's and Wilderness' eyes widened. He had a string of grenades down each side of his chest. The inside of the jacket was lined with grenades. His belt was filled with ammo clips and he wore a 45 automatic piston on each hip.

"My first night in Naples a bunch of white soldiers caught me in a off-limits bar. I didn't know it was off limits. I was just in there talkin' to a pretty Signorina. They didn't like that. They didn't like it at all. They dragged me out o' there and kicked my ass, kicked my ass somethin' terrible. Matter of fact, I spent three weeks in the hospital." He laughed. "Yellow jaundice couldn't put me in the hospital like it done everybody else, but the crackers did. Plus, after they beat me and I was layin' in the street, they put a pistol to my head, held it, cocked it, then clicked it on the empty chamber before they walked away.

"Now I goes anywheres I wants. Ain't no place, no woman, no thing, off limits to me. You saw me checkin' the place when I come in. If I sees any white boys, I just opens my jacket and comes on in. They ain't fucked with me yet, and if they tries, they gon' find out real quick that I don't play. I ain't had a bit o' trouble since I started wearin' my dress uniform, but if it comes, I'm ready."

"Yeah," said Wilderness, "but if you goes into them white hangouts they already got the womens turned against you—think you a monkey or cannibal or somethin'."

Emile laughed. "That's right, but you know what? One time I run into this fine chic who really liked me, you know. It was just somethin' automatic between us. Crackers couldn't stand it. Sat around starin' at me and rollin' they eyes. I had my jacket wide open and not one of them made a move. I just grinned all up in they face. I wanted one of 'em to make a move. But she said she couldn't leave the place with me. She told me she knew that us *soldato negro*, as they called us, was cannibals. I couldn't keep it a secret from her. The white boys had done told her and she was convinced of it. Now, I got t'tell you this woman was one of the finest women I ever done seen—shaped just like a coca-cola bottle, beautiful face, long black hair to her knees. Man—and I could tell she wanted to go with me, but scared to death and talkin' about how I was a cannibal. Man—I wanted her, so I just asked her if that was all what was botherin' her. When she told me, 'yes,' I just said I was not a *soldato negro*, I had on camoflague for night fighting. And she swallowed it—hook, line, and sinker. I still sees her when I goes down to Naples. One o' the sweetest honey-pots I ever dipped into. She know the truth now, but, at first she was convinced if I was *soldato negro* I was gon' cook her and eat her."

Stephen and Wilderness both enjoyed Emile's company and the three of them became running buddies whenever they were in the same town at the same time.

Stephen dreamed he was someplace in North Africa. He could not tell exactly where, but it seemed like a combination of Casablanca, Marrakech, and Djebel Abiod. There was a tall minaret and the mussein was on top of it, singing out the call to worship. It echoed off the hills and mountains, off Monte Casino and St. Peter's Cathedral. It was beautiful and wailing and when the

241

mussein had finished, Stephen went into the Mosque and he was in Grandma Goodie's favorite fishing place. Grandma Goodie was sitting next to him and they had their cane poles stuck in the ground in front of them. Grandma Goodie was telling him about the Old People.

She did not call them slaves because she did not think of them as slaves. She thought of them by their names. Even those who had died before she was born or before her mother had been born; she thought of them by their names because that is how they had been passed down to her as Jebuel or as Cainry who had done "such and such." And when she thought of them collectively, she thought of them as the Old People.

She was talking to him about the Old People and how they found magic and medicine in the woods, and how they sang their healing songs. Stephen enjoyed listening to Grandma Goodie and the singing in her voice, and the soothingness of it. She had a power.

He loved leaning back on the grass and learning about the mystical Old People and watching something start to play with his bobber—popping it, just popping it lightly.

He laughed it felt so good.

Then he felt Wilderness' hand on his shoulder, shaking him. It was his turn to scramble into Long Swamp's cab and head back into the mountains.

Stephen worried about his men's theory. There was no denying that they had lost the three.

He had lost the three.

I lost the three.

If their theory were valid, time was running out for someone else. They still undertook missions no one else would touch.

My responsibility.

My men.

242

My deaths.

Jesus please have mercy on my soul.

He did not know what to do.

He did not know how to get out of the mountains.

Rome was far behind them and the war gave no sign of letting up.

How much more could they ask of Long Swamp?

11

The army continued to climb into the Appenines. The trucks followed them as far as they could; only when they had gone as far as possible on the worst secondary roads, did they turn their burdens over to pack mules. In early September both the British Eighth Army and the American-led Fifth Army broke through the vaunted Gothic Line. The Fifth Army did it in the heart of the Appenines by flanking the major Futa Pass and fighting over the less heavily defended Il Giogo Pass.

"Lord, there's no rest for the weary," Stephen said to Wilderness as he steered Long Swamp along the route taken by the Fifth Army.

"For the wicked either," added Wilderness.

"Yeah," Stephen glanced over at his friend, "that means that neither of us gets any rest cause I sure am weary."

"You know what I would o' said back in the days when we played the dozens," said Wilderness.

"Uh huh. I know alright, but we're way too old for the dozens."

Stephen geared down to take a curve. As he came out of it a range of a dozen peaks leaped in front of the windshield, covering the whole sky in front of him.

"Damn."

"You know what," said Stephen, "when I get out of here I never want to see another mountain as long as I live."

Wilderness shook his head. He remembered seeing the same kind of sight the year before. He felt what he had felt then—a recognition of the impossible—the feeling that he would live out his life before he could ever get out of these terrible mountains.

* * *

Four divisions were involved in continual mountain fighting for two solid months with no relief.

It was that condition in part which resulted in the extreme difficulties met by elements of the 85th division on the slopes of Monte Castelazzo just three miles from Route 9, the main German highway across the southern end of the Po valley.

They had been leap-frogging each other, fighting from hill to hill, point to point for several days, trying to capture the mountain. Two units had reached the most forward position when they were counterattacked. The third unit which had not reached the forward position went back for supplies but was kept back by the regimental officer as there were no supplies to carry forward.

The forward units knew what the trouble was and asked for help. They asked their commander to send the "magicians." If anybody could get through, they could. Mules would simply be too slow. No other trucking unit would even try.

The Black Cross was operating out of Firenzuola, which was about fifteen miles from the forward position as the crow flies, and about thirty-five miles along bad secondary roads to a point where a few soldiers could be sent down the hillside to haul ammunition—that was the first priority—up to the beleaguered defenders.

By the time the order reached the Black Cross it was 2300 hours. Only half the men were in Firenzuola, since it was the half-way point. They had just finished a day's run. They were exhausted. Most of them were asleep when the order came over the radio.

Stephen roused them. They got dressed, he briefed

them, they checked their trucks, loaded them, gassed up and took off. Because of allied air superiority they did not have to run without lights.

Though the road was winding, though it climbed up and down to cross a major ridge separating two river canyons, and though it was subject to all the ravages known to a war-torn mountain road, Long Swamp led the Black Cross in good time over the first thirty miles.

At that point, Long Swamp had to break away from the road because two miles further the road entered German controlled territory. A bulldozer trail led 200 yards to an American observation post.

At the observation post Stephen got in radio contact with the beseiged units' commanding officer. He could hear small arms fire and mortar fire in the background. The mortar fire bothered him. He knew he had to push. He had to reach the transfer position before daylight, when his men would be vulnerable to the mortars.

Down a slight, rocky ridge from the observation post ran a cart-track which would be the platoon's route to the forward position. The track was no more than six inches wider than the trucks' wheel bases. On the inside of the track was a steep wall. On the outside was a sheer cliff.

"Easy does it, baby," Stephen said to the truck as he eased her onto the track. "Easy does it." The mountain cold left him right away. He had to switch to cats' eyes lights after one mile because after that headlights would be visible to the German observation post.

Maintaining the six inch differential while climbing grades, rounding sharp curves and boring up a twisting track was torturous.

One point on the track had bothered Stephen from the first time he had seen it on the map. In the dark, with six inches to spare, it would test all the skill and resourcefulness of his magical men.

The track shot up so abruptly that the trucks would not be able to climb the grade. They would have to be winched up, one by one. At the crest of the grade the track dropped off on the other side leaving only a narrow knob onto which they could be winched, before they would have to be driven down and out of the way of the oncoming trucks—all this to be done in the dark with six inches between the outside tire and 800 feet of uninterrupted air.

Just before Stephen put Long Swamp into position to winch her, the forward commanding officer came on the radio.

"Magician. This is Eagle. We've got two rounds left each. Get here as quick as you can."

Stephen was shocked. He had not realized how critical the American position was. There was a lot of firing in the background. Since each American had only two rounds left, the firing obviously was not coming from their guns.

"I hear you," he said into the radio. "Magician is on the way."

He climbed over the back of the truck to get to his second driver. Two men would be necessary to winch each truck, but what he had heard from the assaulted commander decided him. As soon as three trucks were up, he was going to lead them along. Bynam could bring the second group. Every minute mattered.

On the way down from the knob Stephen heard the muffled roar of artillery. Not the big ones, he thought. Probably 20 mm. He wondered why it wasn't louder. They must be fairly close. He hadn't seen any flashes, though. He couldn't hear any small-arms at all.

Ahead of him the track seemed to narrow. How can that be, he thought. It can't get any tighter. he signalled a stop. Out he went over the hood to the rocky trail. He measured the track ahead for ten yards. Coated with sweat in the icy mountain wind he stared at the hard ground. Eight inches of his outside tire would be off the track, hanging over the precipice. He pushed his helmet back and wiped the perspiration from his forehead.

Can we do it?

"Magician." The radio spoke.

Stephen crawled back over the hood and into the cab.

"Magician here," Stephen answered.

"This is Eagle. Have you spotted us?"

"No."

"We're going to have to return some fire soon. I mean real soon."

"I don't know how far we are from your position," shouted Stephen.

"I appreciate that. I'm just trying t'tell you we need help bad. Real bad."

There's no choice, thought Stephen. There's no choice. We have to try. He crawled over the back of his truck to explain to his two drivers what lay immediately ahead of them.

A lot of stones went over the edge as the three trucks inched over the narrow place, one at a time. A lot of stones, but the trucks stuck to the track and then sailed on, relieved at the luxury of a six inch margin. They left a trail-mark for the men coming after them.

Oh, God. Something was across the track.

Stephen stopped Long Swamp and used his taillights to signal his number two truck to stop. He crawled out over the hood and dropped to the ground.

A log. A goddamn, big-ass log.

It was too big and heavy for the truck to push on the narrow cart-track. He and the two other drivers would have to handle it.

The crackling radio made Stephen jump.

"Magician. Eagle here. Hey, buddy, if we get some

ammo we can fight these krauts. We're naked up here."

"This is Magician," said Stephen. "We've got some trouble on the trail—a down tree. But we'll get there. Hold on."

"Sorry," said Eagle. "We forget you guys got troubles, too. Good luck."

They used a jack, a portable winch and two crow bars to drop the log off into space.

Stephen shifted gear. He still could not understand why the noises of the battle were not louder—why he saw no flashes in the sky. Maybe they had come too far.

He was used to maps being wrong, but he was pretty sure about this distance. He had talked with the men at the observation post and they had said that five miles was just about right.

At first Stephen thought it was his imagination, but after a few minutes he was sure that the darkness was less intense.

He saw the reflected glare from an exploding shell.

They were getting close.

Suddenly with the little lightening in the sky, with the reflected glare, with his eyes straining through the gloom, and the image of it all stamped on his brain, he knew. He knew what was wrong. He knew why the noises were so hushed, why the flashes were invisible. He was on a reverse slope. The Americans were on the other side of the ridge. Soon he would turn a corner and they would be dead ahead of him. He could be very, very near. All that really separated them was a little turn somewhere, not very far ahead.

"Eagle, this is Magician," he shouted into the radio. "I'm on your reverse slope. Hold on!"

"Alright!" The radio barked back at him. "I think we can make it. I'm going to authorize one round. Hooray for the Magician!"

The flashes from the explosions were much brighter.

The switchback can't be too far. Oh, yes. Stephen heard the mortars.

"Magician. This is Eagle. I'm sending down a squad to wait for you. The jerries are moving up. We're fixing bayonets."

Stephen stared at the radio.

He had heard somebody cry out.

"Magician, do you read?"

"Magician reads."

Ahead. One hundred yards ahead Stephen could see the switchback.

He started Long Swamp up to the loop that led to the reverse-slope.

He stopped her just before the turn. He crawled out over the hood and dropped to the ground. He scuttled up the trail and around the bend.

The world exploded. The noise was deafening. Death trap. He was hoping that where the squad came down to meet them would not be far from the turn. But he did not see any men and he did not see any trail they could use to come down to meet him.

He put his field glasses to his eyes. Nothing. About a half mile down, the trail made a slight switch-in. The descending trail had to meet the track somewhere on the other side of that.

Stephen sat and stared at the track. He could hear small arms now. Pistols, carbines, spandaus. The mortars and the big guns weren't firing any more. They did not want to hit their own men. They were closing. The jerries were closing. Men now. Not abstracted metal-jacketed missiles. But flesh and bone. Climbing up the hill. To kill.

Two heads appeared behind him around the bend in the track. He waved them back.

As he scuttled back, Chivvers said, "Radio in Long Swamp's goin' crazy, Lieutenant."

"All right," he said. "I'll take care of it."

He could hear the squawking.

"Where are you? O God we need help. Where are you?"

"Eagle this is Magician. I left the truck to find your squad. I can't see them. Did they make it?"

"Magician. You're on our slope? I don't know. Their radio went out. You're here? Just pack in some ammo. You don't have to bring the trucks any further. Just pack in some ammo. Enough to hold us until we can get some men down there alive to bring back some more. We can't beat these guys with our fingernails."

"Their assault group is between us and you, and their artillery has the whole approach at point-blank range," said Stephen.

"Somebody could get through! Somebody could get through! I've got a whole battalion up here! Goddamn it, enough could get through to save our men's lives. Some of 'em anyway. Send me somebody, Magician!"

The small arms fire coming in over the radio was loud and insistent.

"Oh God! Oh God! They've wiped out my interdicting platoons. Magician, please! Please! We need help. Oh they've killed them all. Those son-of-a-bitches, they've killed them all!"

Stephen stared at the radio.

He remembered what it had been like on the other side of the hill.

In his mirror he could see that the other trucks in his platoon were arriving. The Black Cross.

"Magician. I'm going to have to authorize the last round. For the love of God, please help us. I know you don't want to lose any men but at the risk of two or three lives you could save a battalion—a whole battalion. Magician. Don't make me give you a direct order."

Stephen heard somebody howling. It was not the commander. The sound was too far from the radio. It was not a human sound. It was primeaval and it did not stop. Whoever it was just kept howling and howling.

"Fall back."

The radio was still on. Stephen could hear what the major was saying to his men.

"Avery, Krittenbacher. Get Horski over there. We're gonna fall back behind that tree line. We stopped them, but they'll be back. Look—look—stuff something in Jackson's mouth—I can't stand it. Who's hit? You're hit. O.K. O.K. Get whatever weapons and ammo you can off their bodies. The tree line.

"Weber—you and Smith—Porskey. Go down the goat trail and see if you can find Magician."

Stephen looked at the Black Cross solidly in line behind him. He closed his eyes.

"Magician. I'm sending three men down. Oh, God, please give us a break. Meet us half-way. Meet us half-way, Magician. We sent for you. We knew you were the only ones who could get through.

"Oh God. Here they come."

When Stephen next heard the major's voice he knew he had been hit.

His voice was raspy, but strong. "They're all over us. But we can hold out. Magician. Just get us some ammo. We can't even defend ourselves!"

After awhile the radio went off. It did not come back on.

When darkness fell, Stephen, Bynam, and Chivvers crawled around the cart-track all the way to the goat trail. It was almost a mile from the switchback. They lay in the dark listening. The Germans had pulled back. The position was too exposed for them to try to hold. As long as the Americans kept trying to take it, they could keep pulverizing it. Once Stephen was sure that the Germans were all back across the ridge, he left Bynam at the juncture of the track and the trail, sent Chivvers back for the other men, and using a black-light, climbed the goat-trail.

He found the bodies of the men who had been sent to meet him scattered along the whole length of the path. At the position he found the whole battalion dead. The Germans had taken no prisoners. Every man was dead. In the end they had not been able to shoot back. They had fought back with their bayonets and knives and rifle stocks and hands and feet and teeth. But they had all been killed. Stephen sat next to the Major's body. Eagle.

His initial wound had been a stomach wound or a leg wound. Stephen did not know which. Neither had killed him. He had no face.

Uncle Solders. Uncle Solders. I have become as mad as you. Stephen sat in the swamp scow while his uncle polled them across the dark waters. The whole swamp seemed to be veiled, veiled with gloom, veiled with mists, veiled with roots rising from the waters and Spanish moss hanging from the trees.

Uncle Solders brought the craft to a halt beside a great cypress tree. Then he motioned with his pole for Stephen to look up.

Hanging out over the water, draped with moss and swamp mold, was a yellowed, corroded human skeleton. It hung by its neck. Its toe-bones dangled six or seven feet above the water.

Stephen wanted to scream, to fall into the blackwater and keep screaming, screaming until the water stopped his sound and stopped his life.

"Don't worry," said Uncle Solders. "That ain't yo Daddy. He's one o' our'n, one o' our people. What y'all calls a Negro. Really a African. He's one o' us. But he ain't yo Daddy. I never did find yo Daddy."

For a week Uncle Solders polled Stephen around the swamp, revealing the grissly fruit. Stephen could not get them out of his head. He woke seeing them. He went to sleep seeing them. They hung before his eyes, imposed on everything he saw.

Every tree. Every bird. Every cloud. Every moon had the yellowed, molded skull and the long string of bones in front of it, standing in the air.

One day Uncle Solders said, "I'm gon' show you somethin' I ain't never showed nobody else, so's you'll understand."

He took Stephen into a part of the swamp where he had never taken him.

He showed him another skeleton.

"But this one's different," he said. "This one's mines."

He spent another week taking Stephen through this nether-world portion of the swamp where all the skeletons were Uncle Solders'. They were white men he had killed. Some misadventure or wayward impulse had brought them into the swamp. Never to leave. Solders had risen like mist from the blackwater and slain them, hanged them in the old way of dying and killing.

Solders could not stay long away from the swamp because someone might stumble into it. If the wayfarer were Black, he led him safely out. If he were white he kept him and provided for him an eternal vigil.

Stephen had lived from the time that Uncle Solders had showed him the first skeleton that was 'his' until they left the swamp, in abject terror that a white man would enter that place of dark waters while he was there and that he would have to witness or participate in Uncle Solders' monstrous ritual.

"Now, I have joined you, Uncle Solders." He sat in the carnage on the side of the hill, among the bodies that not long ago had lived and he knew that they had died by his choice. It was not one he ever would have asked to make.

He sat among 'his' bodies and wept. I thought you were mad, Uncle Solders.

You were.

So am I.

12

The rains came. The snows came to the higher peaks. Mud and ice and cold came. At last the higher command realized that no one was going to take Monte Castelazzo. It was time to dig in. The Fifth Army had another winter to spend in the mountains.

Stephen and Wilderness decided to take a trip to Rome. They hoped they would run into Emile there.

They did not find Emile in Rome. Each man went his own way. Wilderness went to bars and brothels. He found crap games and cockfights with heavy gambling. When he sobered up he checked on the Black Cross Operations Center. Like clockwork. It ran like clockwork. When he was satisfied with his inspection, he resumed his debauch.

Stephen visited the sights; St. Peter's, the Capitoline Hill, the Coliseum, the Victor Emmanuel Monument. He marveled at the Baths of Diocletian and the Trevi Fountain. He went to the opera. He loved it. He got the impression that he was not supposed to be there, but taking a page from Emile's book he did not care and went anywhere he pleased. He did not walk around with his long, winter coat thrown open, nor did he line it with grenades. But inside the coat against his belt, with a slit in his outside pocket so he could reach it, he wore his 45-automatic with a full clip.

The white soldiers and MPs must have seen something in his face, or that something was absent in his face, because they left him alone. In developing a taste for the opera, he became particularly fond of the works of Puccini and Verdi and Bellini. He also acquired an enthusiasm for certain performers; among them were Maria Caniglia and Beniamo Gigli, both of whom he later learned had been great favorites of the Germans.

He ran one day across Ahasuerus who sat on the Aventine Hill at the site of the Circus Maximus taking notes.

Stephen did not say anything. He stood looking around.

"Bread and circuses, my dear boy. Give the people bread and circuses," said Ahasuerus.

"Better amusements than war," said Stephen.

"You have a point. One must nevertheless be careful about what kind of circuses he means. Feeding Christians to the lions and having gladiators maim and kill each other are not circuses likely to develop wholesome attitudes.

Stephen smiled. "Touché."

Ahasuerus studied his friend. "How is it," he said, looking away, "that the only way two black boys from Chicago could get to the banks of the Tiber is as impressed mercenaries in a campaign of pillage and fire?"

"I wish I knew," said Stephen. "I wish I knew."

Ahasuerus turned back to his notes.

"I have an aunt who is The Light of the World," said Stephen.

"What did you say?"

"Light of the World."

13

Major Barley never left Rome. Even when the company was transferred north to Leghorn, he stayed in Rome. He sent his Company exec to Leghorn to take care of company business. He did not know where the baby captains were nor did he care. He loved his Rome apartment and he had no intention of leaving it. He loved the sophistication and the cultivated life. He loved the idea that he, Major Barley, was part of it. Now that he had become a major he had begun to think about how delicious the title of "colonel" sounded. Even lieutenant colonels were addressed as "Colonel." Major Barley began to look forward eagerly to his next promotion. The longer the war lasted the better chance he had of getting it. The war could go on forever as far as he was concerned. He loved Rome. He had rejoiced when the 5th Army had not broken out of the mountains before the onset of winter. He appreciated the Germans. They were good soldiers. They would keep the allied armies in the mountains all winter; then, if in the spring the allies managed another break out, the Germans could retreat to the Alps, and there they could hold off all the armies of the world forever and ever. Who knew? By then maybe he'd be a brigadier.

He never stopped to think that in all the histories of all the armies in the world there had never been a brigadier whose only command was a truck company, but that was because Major Barley knew that in war anything was possible. He himself had promoted a nigger to first lieutenant. A Brigadier commanding a truck company was hardly less likely than that.

But what he wanted, what he wanted immediately, was his revenge on Acorn. He sat in his sitting room and drank fine wines and conversed with his lovely secretary and plotted what to do.

He decided to make him winter in the mountains. Though the company was based in Leghorn, each platoon's forward base was in the mountains. Major Barley decided to order Acorn to spend the whole winter reporting on the condition of the halfway bases. That would mean he had to spend the whole winter driving over the impassable mountain roads, going from base, to base, to base, then starting all over again. Major Barley was rapturous. He had rarely been so pleased with himself. He took his secretary out to a good dinner, they took in a performance at a nightclub, then they returned to his apartment to share champagne and caviar before retiring.

In order to put his plan into operation, he had to find his two baby captains and send them to Leghorn to be in charge of Company Headquarters. That took a month. The two baby captains had been intimidated by Rome and had gone back to Naples where they felt more secure.

They had both decided to become career officers. After having been in the army less than two years they had been promoted to captain—for doing absolutely nothing. They had decided that if they could remain incognito long enough they might get appointed Joint Chiefs of Staff. Their plan might have worked had it not been for Major Barley's obsession with punishing Acorn. After a month of searching by G-2, S-2, and MPs, a company clerk ran across them one day while he was on leave in Naples and notified the Major's clerk.

Overmayer and Havershram were hustled North to Leghorn. Acorn was sent out on the road. And, sure enough, the roads were as Barley knew they would be.

259

Where there was not mud there was snow and ice. Nothing could have stopped the jeep from going off the road and taking the fall that cost Acorn his right leg.

Captain Barley was delighted. His strategy had turned out even better than he had planned.

That ends the promotions for Wenders, he thought. Even if his dumb platoon is getting another Meritorious Service Plaque. Who cares? He'll stick right there, damn it. He'll stick right there like a spot.

Major Barley made the two baby captains his new double-exec.

14

In the long days that approached the Winter Solstice
the men of the Black Cross made friends with the troops
of the 92nd division. The 92nd acted kind of like a magnet for them because there were so many Black men together in it, a whole division. Most Negro units were
small service or support units, companies or battalions
attached to other commands. There were large congrega-
tions of Negroes in the Quartermaster functions and in
the port operations, but they were still members of separate, company and battalion sized units. But the 92nd
was twenty-seven battalions—later thirty-six, after the
addition of the 366th Regiment. Like a magnet they
drew the Black Cross in.

The 92nd did not have the world's greatest reputation. There were scoundrels and wastrels in the 92nd.
There were known malingerers who had been added to
the division just to get its AGCT score averages high
enough to ship it overseas. In fact, one group of such
high AGCT scorers was called the Casuals. Everyone
knew they did just as they pleased and would not accept
any orders, but they were sent into combat because of
their AGCT scores. They had received no training and
weren't interested in getting any, yet the High Command put other men's lives, Negro's lives, in their un-
trustworthy hands. The men of the Black Cross did not
like the Casuals or any one else upon whom one could
not rely absolutely, anyone in whose hands they could
not place their lives in absolute trust, but they had no
trouble distinguishing between the Casuals and the
overwhelming number of the 92nd, good men whom they

knew as Jones and Roberts and Thompson and Williams, individual soldiers who had been stationed in the same places the Black Cross had seen in the states, or whose relatives or friends lived near where members of the Cross had lived at home. They liked those soldiers and felt good with them. They shared a lifestyle with them and a turn of phrase, and men from both the Black Cross and the 92nd knew all the degredation of the jim-crow army. They were, each to the other, an oasis in a strange land.

The Black Cross was given Christmas off and they decided to celebrate it with the 92nd at their base in the Serchio River valley.

With a tin cup full of scotch in his hand Stephen sat across a small room from Wilderness. In a stone house they shared Christmas night in a room crowded with laughing, black and brown faces, warmed by the crackling glow of the fireplace in the hearth.

The room was small enough to talk across in a conversational tone and there were probably a dozen conversations going on simultaneously.

"Little different from last Christmas, huh," said Stephen.

Wilderness nodded. He remembered the sad little affair in the barn. It had been stone, too. No roof. He wondered if its family had returned to it for this Christmas. He wondered if they had lived. He remembered the pathetic attempts at Christmas carols.

Stephen took a deep swallow of scotch. It burned on the way down, but it burned good, like the heat from the fireplace.

"It's a little duller this year," he said.

Wilderness frowned in perplexity. He had found Christmas night lively. Dull was not the word for it— especially after the last Christmas.

Stephen noted his frown. "What I mean," he said, "is the pain is duller. I don't hurt so much this year. Some of my feelings are gone."

Wilderness cleared his brow. He understood. Ever since the flight from Marrakech he had felt that all his feelings were gone. No hurt. No happiness. It probably helped, too, that this was the second Christmas out of the states, away from home. The second Christmas in a stranger's land. It was getting to be routine.

Not for the 92nd, though. This was their first Christmas away. Wilderness hoped it would be their last. He wondered how many mountains there were in Italy. Half the mountains in the world, he thought. Half the mountains in the world must be in this one country.

Stephen finished off his scotch and filled up his cup again. Tis the season to be jolly, he thought. Fill the cup with good cheer.

"Too bad about Acorn," he said.

"Yeah," said Wilderness.

"He's a good man, a good man," said Stephen.

Wilderness nodded. "Asshole John Barley-corn did it," he said.

"I'd like to kill Barley," said Stephen. He remembered the major's drawing room off the Via Vittorio and the passage in the book. He felt hate. He closed his mind to thoughts of John Barley. It was not the season for hate.

Before dawn on the morning of the 26th the roof fell in on the little house. The shock of a near miss from an 88mm cannon had knocked it in. WINTERGEWITTER had burst upon the Serchio Valley. Units from the German 148th infantry division and the 4th Alpine Battalion had launched a surprise attack to destroy the combat effectiveness of the 92nd division.

Stephen's coughing roused him to consciousness. He

kept coughing, violently, uncontrollably. He was terrified because he did not know if he could breathe as he coughed. He was afraid that if he did not stop coughing he was going to choke, or suffocate, or tear something loose in his throat.

He had no control. His body wracked and heaved with each cough.

Help me. Jesus. Help me.

At last his fits subsided. The violent spasms had forced tears out of his eyes. He had to fight to open them, rubbing them to break them free. They were coated with a glutinous substance.

Stephen lay still, trying to get his breath back and to let the panic die down. As he lay on his stomach, sprawled along the buckled floor, he realized that dust and debris had been driven down his breathing passages. He had been coughing for his life.

After awhile he heard movement and voices. He heard explosions everywhere and the rat-tat-tat of small arms fire.

He tried to look around, but there was a beam across his shoulder which limited the mobility of his neck and head. All he could see were dust, stones, pieces of splintered wood, and the heel of a combat boot.

Wilderness!

Fear seized his chest.

He coughed again—this time voluntarily—trying to get his mouth free to speak.

He wondered then if he were wounded, if he were bleeding badly somewhere he did not realize, if the beam across his shoulders had broken anything or paralyzed anything.

A double panic hit him.

He closed his eyes, counting and letting it pass.

When he opened his eyes he called as loudly as he could.

"Wilderness!"

"Wilderness!"

Nothing.

He knew he had to test himself. He had to know.

He hesitated a moment, afraid of what he might learn.

Then he tried. He closed his eyes and hurled himself into the unknown. He tried.

He could move. He could move. God.

He was able to work his legs free of the wreckage which entrapped them. Bearing down with his arms and his legs, he pushed up with all his strength. The beam remained absolutely immobile.

The beam's pinned, he thought. That's why it didn't crush me. It can't move up or down. It's pinned.

The thought spurred him. He worked his hands free enough to give them some mobility. He began to pull and pry and dig. He could tell that he was tearing them up, but he did not feel it too badly. He just kept at it.

In a few minutes he was able to slide out from under the beam. He sat up to look around.

Ruin.

Right away he saw two dead men, men who had been laughing and talking near him when he fell asleep.

"Wilderness," he called.

Nothing.

Rubble had him enclosed. He could see no one except the two men, but he could hear voices. He could not tell what they were saying, but he knew they were voices.

He got to his knees. Again disregarding his ripped and bleeding hands he began to tear through the wreckage around him.

When he pushed aside a barrier of tottering stone, the first sound he heard—loudly and clearly—was Wilderness calling his name.

"Wilderness!"

Wilderness helped him to break through.

They stood in the rubble of what had been a cozy stone house the night before.

Exchanging mutual glances of reassurance, they began to help others get out. After over an hour of feverish work, fifteen whole men stood in the remains of the house. Eight men were lightly wounded, seven were severely wounded. Five were dead, and six were missing. Junior officers from the 92nd took over.

Stephen, Wilderness, and two other men from the Black Cross were the only truckers who had been in the house. All four of them were unhurt.

"Let's roll, we got to get our men together and get our trucks out of here," said Stephen.

They started scrambling for the street.

In half an hour they had rounded up the whole Black Cross. Miraculously, not one was severely injured, though several had minor wounds.

As they raced for their trucks they saw a large number of men from the 92nd round a corner and bolt towards them. Some threw their rifles aside and sprinted madly. Others dropped mortars and bazookas and fled. Some kept their arms and still rushed on headlong. A few, very few, kept looking over their shoulders. Most looked straight ahead, all reason wiped from their faces.

As Stephen and wilderness reached Long Swamp, Stephen looked back to see men who had been in the house with them the night before dash into still-standing houses, preparing for house-to-house combat.

"I'll drive, Charlie," said Stephen.

"Fuck you, Sam" said Wilderness as he climbed into the passenger's side.

The wonderful truck started right up. Wilderness checked to see that the whole line's motors were running.

"Let's roll 'em," he signaled to Stephen.

266

As Stephen swung the truck around to head out of town, his side mirror showed him the profile of a Mark IV tank about to turn the corner that the soldiers from the 92nd had rounded in panic. Darting, covering the flanks of the tank were German infantrymen. In all his years of war this was the first time Stephen had seen the Wermacht close-up, in attack.

Soldiers from the 92nd clung desperately all over the Black Cross' trucks as they wheeled and sped out of town.

Stephen never saw what tore through Long Swamp's hood. He only saw the streak of flame that leapt out of the engine compartment and through the shattered windshield.

When he turned to Wilderness, he saw his buddy sitting in his usual position; his uniform was begrimed and ripped up from their recent turmoil; other than that he was normal—except that his head was a fire.

Where his head should have been was a cone of fire.

Stephen jammed on the brakes, threw the truck out of gear, hurled himself over his friend's head and pulled him out of the driver's door.

They hit the ground rolling. They tumbled down a slight embankment. When they hit the bottom Long Swamp was enveloped in a single, gigantic swoosh of flame.

Stephen smelled then, overpoweringly, the odor of cooked meat.

He unwrapped Wilderness' head. At his first glimpse he opened his mouth to scream. No sound came out, but his mouth was wide open. He gagged. He could not stop himself. The convulsive contractions of his esophagus locked his mouth open. He felt the mass, slimy, working its way up his throat and there was nothing he could do to stop it. In rage and helplessness, tears poured down his face but they could not stop the remnants of his

Christmas dinner, reeking slightly of scotch, from pouring in spasmodic gushes out of his mouth and onto the remains of his friend's head.

His fouled mouth still hung agape when the men from the platoon reached him.

These is mines, said Uncle Solders, pointing to the hanging skeletons. These is mines, said Stephen pointing to the corpses littering the side of the hill. These is mines, said Wilderness who had changed himself into a pillar of fire and embraced the planet.

15

Stephen got a new truck, but it was just like every other truck. He did not give it a name. It broke down and had flat tires and failed to start. It stalled in the wrong places and sprang leaks in its radiator.

The men knew they were good drivers, that they worked well together as a unit, and that they could trust each other, but they did not any longer feel daring, willing to risk death. Stephen refused to accept any more special missions. He lined his men up in the long caravans and they abided by the traffic control MPs and diddled along in place, and stopped, and waited just like everyone else.

He went to Rome as often as he could. He went to the opera. He became even more knowledgeable about it. He read and listened to people talk. He bought books and played records. He learned that if he stayed absolutely drunk he could not tell whether he fell asleep. He went so long without sleep that when he did fall into a drunken stupor for an hour or two he did not dream. That was much better than waking up after having been with Mama-Ruth or Evelyn or somebody he loved, or being at ease floating on the St. Johns or on some shimmering lake when the mists were rising. Whenever he had a pass he got drunk right away and stayed drunk until his next duty. He decided he was going to write a book about how it was possible to live without sleep. That would save many people from night terrors and still others from the mornings.

He went to the opera every chance he got and also into every other place he was not supposed to be, but anyone who had ever looked into his eyes would not bother him, so he went unchallenged. They simply pretended he was not there.

* * *

The baby captains had turned Company Headquarters into bedlam. Just about the time the spring offensive started, Quartermaster command called Major Barley to Leghorn to answer for the condition of his command. There was no answer. Major Barley was relieved of his command, promoted to lieutenant colonel and shipped back to the states. The two baby captains were promoted to major and sent to the Pacific Theater. Stephen was summoned to Leghorn where he was named Company Commander with no change in rank.

Less than a month later, on May 2nd, 1945, the German commanders surrendered to the allies, Army Group C, all of their armies in Italy.

Soon afterwards, on a jubilant troop-transport, Stephen Wenders was on his way home.

With hundreds of thousands of men coming home, and hundreds of thousands more still in transit to and from the states, and more switching from the ETO to the Pacific front, connections were far too haphazard for Stephen to be able to wire anybody about when to expect him, and to meet him at the train. He decided just to drop in unannounced.

He was not worried about his future. He was not thinking about it, either. He was not thinking about too much of anything except remembering how to get home from the Union Station. It had taken him over a month to get to Chicago from Italy, time to reach the states while everyone was still ecstatic over the complete Euro-

270

pean victory, while he was still universally recognized as a conquering hero.

Stephen had no illusions on that score. He knew which of his countrymen were returning covered with glory and which were not. What men had done overseas—or had done to them—had little to do with what separated the wheat from the chaff, the heroes from the idlers. The difference between the two was plain. It was proclaimed by skin color, nose shape, hair texture—hero or goat. Stephen held no illusions. He had returned home on a segregated troop ship. Home. He had avoided military trains so that he would not have to ride in segregated coaches from New York to Chicago. He could have arranged passage on a military train more quickly. But there were some things, some things which Stephen had decided he would no longer abide. Not ever. Not ever in his life.

He had no illusions about coming home. Still Evanston and Chicago had never been like the deep south, and so much had happened. Things actually had happened during the war—and not just to me, he thought. Bynam. McCauley and His Woman. Wilderness.

Not just to me. The twisted and blackened metal shards of what had once been an ammunition truck still lay at the bottom of a wadi somewhere between Ouled Rahmoun and Tebessa. Though Johnson and Dafney were nowhere in evidence. Nowhere in evidence.

He remembered the mounted Black riders on the high North African plain and running through sinuous streets with McCauley and His Woman and Wilderness. Who were no more.

He remembered crouching in the cab of his truck perched precariously on a spindly rutt along a ridge in the Appenines. He remembered how hot he had felt and how confined, the sweat streaming down his face; he re-

271

membered not moving, holding onto the radio, hot, sweating and not moving, his head threatening to burst his helmet while perhaps a mile away, perhaps a mile away, Eagle and his whole battalion were slaughtered . . . slaughtered by the Germans. Without ammunition. Without succor. Without a chance.

Stephen had no illusions, but time had not stood still as he, at least, had changed. Maybe something else had, too. He did not believe it. He did not believe that the world had changed in any important way, but inside, somewhere inside, buried so deeply that it had hidden from him, lay a point of hope.

It was like rowing out onto Deep Cedar Lake each morning and knowing that the monster fish was there. Somewhere. He might never catch it, but it was there.

Stephen did not know he still hoped, and might never have learned he did. He experienced much of himself as dead, because he was immune to the world, oblivious of it. It was almost as if he had seen everything so that nothing he saw was new; it had all happened somewhere, sometime. Life held no surprises. For him the war had been over for quite a spell, since Christmas day. He had been coming home a long time.

The time had almost been enough to let him think some—not quite, but almost. It had been enough at least for him to accept that he was going to a country where he knew the language and where the plumbing worked and where the cities and towns had not been destroyed and where the babies had not been blown up and where women did not hang from the windows and run out into the streets to sell themselves.

He was not worried about his future because the Black Cross had seen to that. No man in the Black Cross or surviving family of a man who had died in the Black Cross had to worry about the future in the same way that they had all worried about it before the war.

With his share of the Black Cross' special treasury Stephen would be able to finish his college education at his leisure and to make some prudent investments. But that would wait until the fall. He had the summer before him to fill with his emptiness. He had Evelyn before him. Unlike so many others he had life before him. Life before him.

He was hungry. He decided to get a good old American hamburger before he found his way to the 'L'.

He was not surprised by what happened at the food-stop. He had not forgotten or glamorized Chicago in his memory. What he had not counted on was hope. That is what got him. Because he had not even discounted hope, he had forgotten about it. But it got him.

He looked dashing in his polished khakis, a gleaming spit shine on his shoes, his campaign hat cocked nattily on his head. His first lieutenant's bars glinted silver on the hat and on his shoulders. On his lapels shone his brass "U.S." insignia and below that the quartermaster logo, a key and sword crossed over an eagle perched on a wheel. Near the end of his right sleeve the three small, gold embroidered bars marked the time he had served in foreign campaigns. His army decorations were arrayed above the pocket on his left breast: the Army commendation Medal ribbon—green and white; the Bronze star, a silk ribbon of red with white and blue stripes. A kaleidescope ribbon of brown, green, white, red, blue, and black stripes represented his African, Middle Eastern campaign medal. It was adorned with three battle stars. The Meritorious Unit Commendations were marked by a scarlet ribbon trimmed in gold with two oak-leaf clusters. He wore also the Southern Cross. He carried his duffel over his left shoulder.

He stepped into the White Tower hamburger shop.

He looked around for the posted menu as the door closed behind him.

273

The waitress raised her unleavened eyes to his. "I'm sorry," she said. "We don't serve Negroes here."

* * *

Afterwards, when he and Charles and Ahasuerus sat around his mother's living room drinking whiskey and scotch by the case—alternating them—one case of whiskey then once case of scotch, he remembered her. They slept the days away into the late afternoons and stayed up all night every night in their officers' khakis drinking. While he was trying to formulate—with the assistance of alcohol—what to say to Evelyn on the phone or in a letter, he thought of the girl in the White Tower. He thought of her every bit as much as he thought of other things—of Lang, and the Arkansas pine woods, and a glorious rococo suite on the Via Venito. And he talked about her, too. She had entered his life.

Yes, he talked about her often, and though she was no surprise to him, and though he had heard those very words before the war, and though he had seen much worse things including the head of a beautiful Italian woman with her black hair arranged around her face like a dark aureola, he never forgot her.

Sometimes he wished he could. Sometimes he and Charles and Ahasuerus all wished by the time they got to the bottom of their next case of liquor they would have forgotten everything. But they never did.